Neither Present Time

Books by Caren J. Werlinger

Currently available:
Looking Through Windows
Miserere
In This Small Spot
Neither Present Time

Coming soon:
Year of the Monsoon
She Sings of Old, Unhappy, Far-off Things
Hear the Last Unicorn

Neither Present Time

By
Caren J. Werlinger

CORGYN
Publishing

Neither Present Time
Published by Corgyn Publishing, LLC.

eBook ISBN: 978-0-9886501-6-9
Print ISBN: 978-0-9886501-7-6

Permission to reprint lines from *Take Three Tenses: A Fugue in Time*, copyright 1945, by Rumer Godden is generously granted by Little, Brown Book Group, publisher, and by Curtis Brown Group, Ltd, on behalf of The Rumer Godden Literary Trust.

E-mail: cjwerlingerbooks@yahoo.com

Cover photo by Beth A. Skinner

Cover design by Patty G. Henderson
www.boulevardphotografica.yolasite.com

Book design by Maureen Cutajar
www.gopublished.com

Dedication

To Corinne and Helen, whoever you were.
I hope your story went something like this.

Acknowledgements

Although this book is a complete work of fiction, it is based on one fact. I really did find an old book with the inscription described, though I have changed the date. It didn't send me on the same type of quest that it does for Beryl in this book, but it did plant the seeds for this story.

I wish to thank Rumer Godden's publisher, Little, Brown Book Group, and The Rumer Godden Literary Trust, administered by Curtis Brown Group, Ltd for their willingness to work with me to include a quote from *Take Three Tenses: A Fugue in Time*. I have taken the liberty of moving up by one month the date of that book's publication in 1945 to fit my timeline.

I also want to thank Dr. Geoffrey D. Smith, the Head of The Ohio State University's Rare Books and Manuscripts Library and his colleague, Dr. Eric Johnson, for their invaluable assistance with my research into the world of rare book librarianship. Their enthusiasm for the world of rare books made me think that if I had my career to choose again, I might have chosen differently.

To Sylvia Goodstein, my research into what Washington D.C. was like in the 1940s would not have been complete without your assistance.

As always, this book would not have been what it is without the early reading and feedback of my partner, Beth, and my beta readers, Marty and Marge. To all of my readers, thank you.

Neither Present Time

The house, it seems, is more important than the characters. "In me you exist," says the house.

Rumer Godden, *Take Three Tenses: A Fugue in Time*

Chapter 1

With a silvery tinkle from its old-fashioned bell, the door swung shut behind her and she felt, as always, that she had entered a sanctuary where the noise and congestion and rudeness of the world outside couldn't follow, where time itself hardly seemed to exist. She breathed deeply, taking in the unmistakable smell of old books.

"Miss Gray! How are you, my dear?" the elderly gentleman behind the counter greeted her graciously.

"Hello, Mr. Herrmann," she smiled. "I'm well, thank you." The unchanging nature of Mr. Herrmann's appearance was part of the charm of coming to this shop. His crisp white shirt and bowtie, his tweed jacket and neatly trimmed silver goatee all contributed to her feeling that this establishment could have existed any time in the past century.

"Stuffy old fart," Claire would usually mutter on the rare occasions when she tagged along.

"No, my dear," Mr. Herrmann would have said had he overheard her. "These are manners, something most young people today sadly know little of. My grandfather insisted we maintain the same standards of courtesy here in America as he was accustomed to do when he ran his bookshop in Budapest."

A younger man, fortyish with red, curly hair emerged from the labyrinthine depths of the store, carrying a heavy stack of books.

"Hey, Beryl," he grinned, his wire-rimmed glasses giving him a decidedly bookish air. He grunted a little as he folded his tall, lanky frame to set the stack on the floor.

"Hi, George," she said. "How was the auction? Did you get anything worthwhile?"

"Oh, yes," said Mr. Herrmann enthusiastically. "Three boxes. I think some may be very fine, but I haven't had time to research them." His eyes twinkled in a knowing smile over his half-glasses. "Would you be interested in doing some appraisals?"

"We've been too busy with all the drop-offs," George said.

"Yes, please," Beryl said excitedly. She followed George through the maze of towering shelves reaching nearly to the embossed tin ceiling – shelves containing hundreds and hundreds of books, mostly old, some very rare: history, religion, philosophy, biography, politics – but Beryl's favorite section was fiction and literature. She could – and frequently did, she would have admitted – get lost for hours here.

Today, though, she did not tarry as she followed George to the back room in which there was barely room to move. Here, there were more shelves packed with books, and yet more stacks of books stood tottering on the floor, books brought in by people needing to clear space on their own shelves, or perhaps emptying out the house of a deceased relative. Squeezing between piles, George led her to three large cardboard boxes, each marked with a lot number from the auction.

"Have fun," George said, filling his arms with another stack of books to be shelved.

Beryl lowered her backpack to the floor, fanning her damp shirt to unstick it from her back. She'd lived in D.C. her entire life, but the heat and humidity, even now in mid-June, seemed to bother her more the older she got. Her glasses were sliding down her sweaty nose. She took them off, wiped her face with her sleeve and then replaced the glasses. "If I'm this bad at thirty-six, what am I going to be like when hot flashes start?" she muttered to herself. She found a wooden folding chair leaning against the wall, and set it up next to the first box. Pulling a notebook from her backpack, she began making notes on the books in the box – date published, edition, general condition. There was a wide variety – Hawthorne, Twain, Cather, Hugo, Bacon as well as some histories. Looking them over, a puzzled frown creased her brow. Almost every single one was a first edition and they were in pristine condition. She set aside a couple that she was interested in purchasing, and then tugged the second box near, repeating the process. Again, most of the books were first editions in wonderful condition. She began to look more carefully inside the front covers and noticed several inscribed with names: Mary Bishop, Eugene Bishop, and other Bishops dating back to the 1840s, though some of the books were considerably older.

Eagerly, she dove into the third box, continuing to make notes as she pulled books out. Tucked along one side of the box, standing upright so that it was nearly undetectable, was a tiny volume. As she tugged it free, her cell phone rang, startling her. She flinched when she saw who was calling.

"Where are you?" came Claire's irritated voice.

"I'm at The Scriptorium," Beryl admitted guiltily, glancing at her watch and startled to see that she'd been there for nearly two hours.

"You were supposed to be home thirty minutes ago," Claire reminded her unnecessarily.

"I'm sorry," Beryl said. "I'm on my way."

"Don't bother," Claire said. "Just go straight to the restaurant."

"All right."

"Oh, and Leslie's coming," Claire added.

Beryl closed her eyes, pressing her fingers to her forehead.

"She and Bob had another argument last night," Claire continued, ignoring Beryl's silence. "She just needs to talk. Get there as soon as you can."

"Bye."

Beryl sighed and quickly closed up the third box. She picked up the handful of books she had set aside for herself and took them up to Mr. Herrmann.

"Oh ho," he smiled. "It paid off, getting – how do Americans say – first dibs? Yes?"

Beryl smiled. "Yes." Mr. Herrmann's grandfather, as she had heard more times than she could count, had immigrated to the United States after the first World War, deciding to open his bookstore in his new country's capital. Though the family had spoken Hungarian at home and Mr. Herrmann's English still had a slight accent, he was as American as she was, but he liked to pretend he was more European than American and Beryl always played along.

"I'll get back to you as soon as I can about the other books," she said. "I think you'll be pleasantly surprised at their value." She placed her chosen books on the counter. "How much for these?"

He looked them over. "How about an even trade on your time?" he suggested.

"How are you going to stay in business if you keep doing that?" she asked, tucking the books into her backpack.

"You help me stay in business," he reminded her.

"I'll see you soon, Mr. Herrmann," she smiled as two teen-aged girls entered the shop. "Bye, George," she called.

"Bye," came his voice from somewhere in the maze of shelves.

Beryl hurried toward the door as Mr. Herrmann's voice rose indignantly, replying to the girls that he most certainly did not sell e-readers.

*   *   *

"How could you be so rude?" Claire asked a couple of hours later as she unlocked the door of their Adams Morgan rowhouse.

"It wasn't rude," Beryl protested, trailing behind her up to the second floor living room.

Claire placed her purse and briefcase in one of the stacked wooden cubbies against the wall. "I invited her to stay with us tonight, and you told her she should go home. You don't think that's rude?"

Beryl turned her back to Claire as she pulled out a dining chair and deposited her backpack on it. "All I said," she said, bending down to pick up a brindle-striped cat winding himself around her ankles, "was that she and her husband need to talk and that maybe she should go home so they could." She kept her head tilted toward the cat so that her hair swung forward, curtaining her face.

"Or don't you want them to work things out?" she added as Claire went into the kitchen to get a diet soda from the refrigerator.

"Oh, here we go again," Claire said with a roll of her eyes as she let the refrigerator door shut a little more loudly than was necessary.

"It's just that she's been hanging around here a lot," Beryl pointed out, not for the first time.

Claire popped open her can of soda, saying, "I wish you'd stop being so..." But she didn't finish as she poured the soda into a glass and rinsed the can before placing it in the recycling bin.

"Stupid?" Beryl finished for her, setting the cat down.

"No, silly." Claire's tone had changed instantly. She came to Beryl and kissed her on the cheek. "I was going to say jealous," she said placatingly. "Leslie is just really lonely. I wish you would try and like her more. She would love to have what we have."

"That's my point!" but Beryl didn't say that.

"I'm going up," Claire said, heading toward the stairs. "Beryl?"

"Yes?"

"The chair."

"Oh, sorry," Beryl said, taking her backpack off the dining chair which she slid back into position under the table. She went into the kitchen and opened a fresh can of cat food.

"Here you go, Winston."

She snapped a lid on the unused portion and put it in the frig. As the door closed, her eye was caught by the collage of photos covering the front of the refrigerator.

Claire and her shadow.

It had started as a joke between them, but it was true. From the moment Claire had come to the library asking for help with a reference for her master's thesis, Beryl had been smitten. Claire wasn't enrolled at Georgetown, but she began coming to the Lauinger Library for her research, flirtatiously chatting as she stopped by the research desk, enjoying Beryl's worshipful attention. Claire, with her luxurious dark wavy hair and beguiling dark eyes, was beautiful, Beryl thought, whereas her own appearance was nondescript – hair neither brown nor blond, eyes a boring hazel behind her old-fashioned round eyeglasses. Everybody noticed Claire; nobody noticed Beryl. Beryl used to take pride in that, pride that she was the one who got to be with Claire. She was content to be in the background, the shadow. Only lately... lately, it was hard not to wonder if Claire really still loved her, or just tolerated her because she was always there....

After eight years together, Beryl had thought that they had moved past the point of Claire needing to be worshipped to just being loved. But recently, with Leslie's rapt attention when Claire told stories, Leslie's laughter at Claire's witty comments, Beryl could see the light in Claire's eyes – the light that used to be there when it was Beryl doing the listening and the laughing.

That would make anyone feel good, Beryl thought now. Winston was done eating and was loudly demanding attention. *She's right. I'm just being stupid,* she told herself as she carried the cat to the sofa and turned on the television.

Chapter 2

How Cory loved this room with its immensely tall ceiling laced with delicate vines and flowers worked into the plaster, and its windows, nearly as tall, filling the east and south walls. She closed her eyes, feeling the cool morning air on her face, the sunshine dancing through her closed eyelids as it filtered through the leafy branches of the oak on the east side of the house. Soon, the sun would be too high, and the leaves too dense, "and they'll make me close the windows," she whispered. "They always close the windows." But now, with no one else about and her eyes closed, she could remember this room, this house, as it was.

Over against one of the windows had been her mother's desk where she sat every morning after breakfast to write her letters. The room had been filled then with sofas and chairs and chaises gathered in small groupings, not too large, not trying to pull the entire room together. The arrangement invited intimate conversations and confidences and reading and contemplation. The two walls not occupied by windows held floor to ceiling bookshelves, as did most of the rooms in the house, with rolling ladders attached to tracks to allow access to the highest shelves. *Remember it as it was,* she thought. *Remember it filled with people and furniture and books and laughter and talk.*

Some things remained – the elegant mouldings crowning the walls as an accent to the ornate plaster ceiling, the layered wooden trim

9

around the windows and doors and fireplace mantel, all painted white to give the room a light and airy feel next to the pale spring green color of the walls, faded and worn now.

As a child, she had delighted in climbing in and out of the open windows to the veranda beyond. Her mother would smile indulgently, though the maids scolded her for not using the door like a lady.

She heard the kitchen door open and close. She frowned. She heard the noises of someone rattling about, making coffee and then footsteps.

"Miss Cory!" said a plump middle-aged woman as she bustled into the room.

Why do young people rush about so? wondered Cory.

"You're going to catch your death," said the woman, closing the windows and flipping the sash locks.

"Veronica, I'm ninety-three. I'm going to catch my death of something soon," said Cory.

Veronica placed her hands on her ample hips and said, "Well, not today. And not on my watch." She came over to the wing chair which, along with its mate and a side table that held a lamp, were the only pieces of furniture remaining in the room now. "Let me help you up, and we'll get some breakfast going."

Knowing it would do no good to argue, Cory allowed herself to be helped out of her chair, though she was perfectly capable of getting up herself. "After all, I got in here by myself, didn't I?" but she didn't say it. Veronica was paid to come each morning and see that she got bathed and dressed and fed – a concession to "the others" as Cory called them. And she didn't want Veronica to feel she wasn't needed or appreciated.

She sat at the kitchen table with a cup of coffee while Veronica made them both scrambled eggs and hash browns.

"Veronica, you can cook for me every day," Cory said, as she said most every day.

"Miss Cory, I do cook for you every day," Veronica replied, but she smiled, as she did most every day.

"What would you like to do this fine morning?" she asked as she cleared the dishes when they were done eating.

"I'd like to work in my flower garden."

"You can't be getting all sweaty and dirty," Veronica said. "You've got a doctor's appointment after lunch. You're seeing the heart specialist at Ohio State today, remember?"

Cory waved her hand as if shooing away a gnat. "What's the doctor going to say except I'm old," she grumbled. "I don't need a specialist to tell me that. My heart's as old as I am. It's not as if he can do anything about it."

Veronica chuckled and said, "Maybe. But it's bad manners to cancel at the last minute." She'd learned quickly that the easiest way to convince Miss Cory to do something was to point out that it was bad manners not to do it.

"Young people don't have any manners nowadays," Cory frequently complained. "I was never so disrespectful when I was their age."

"All right," she conceded grudgingly now. "I'll work in the garden tomorrow."

"That sounds reasonable," Veronica said soothingly. "How about you sit and enjoy that garden some before it gets too hot?"

She prepared a pitcher of lemonade and carried a tray outside where a cushioned bench sat in deep shade.

"Oh, it smells heavenly out here today, Miss Cory," Veronica said.

Cory settled comfortably on her bench and Veronica poured her a glass of lemonade, capping the pitcher to keep insects out.

It did smell wonderful in her garden – lilacs and roses and hydrangea. The blend of flowery scents smelled like Helen. She closed her eyes and breathed deeply.

*   *   *

The room Corinne works in has tall windows, like her mother's study at home, but these windows surround all four walls to let in plenty of light for the pool of typists sitting row upon row at the

11

desks filling the cavernous room. Unlike her mother's study, this room is almost uniformly grey: grey steel desks and chairs, grey linoleum floor, even the walls are grey. "They must have had leftover paint from a submarine," the girls often joke. From their east-facing windows, they can see the dome of the Capitol in the distance.

Today, it is raining – not a soft rain, but a heavy downpour punctuated by flashes of lightning and cracks of thunder. Their overhead pendant lights have flickered on and off all morning.

Corinne's desk is one of the ones nearest the stairwell, and so it is she who is deluged with droplets of water from a flapping umbrella. She flinches at the unexpected shower and then sees that the paper in her typewriter has been splattered as well, the ink running, the entire page ruined.

"Look what you've done –" she sputters angrily, but stops midsentence as she glances up.

The wet umbrella folds to reveal a darkly handsome woman, though she is wet and bedraggled. Her entire lower half – the part not sheltered by the umbrella – is thoroughly soaked and now dripping on the grey linoleum floor.

The woman, totally unaware of the havoc she has wreaked, glances down at Corinne and then around the room where everyone is now watching her. "I was told to report to a Miss Chalmers," she says to no one in particular.

"Over here," says Miss Chalmers, rising from her seat and inviting the newcomer to the chair adjacent to her desk.

Corinne pulls the ruined form out of her typewriter and begins to roll a fresh paper into the carriage. She has to realign it three times as she is distracted by the new woman. Everything about her, from her trench coat to her wide-legged trousers and mannish wingtip shoes, exudes an air of eccentric confidence. And money. As the others return to their typing, the sounds of the machines obscure some of Miss Chalmers' conversation with the woman, but Corinne is able to hear some of what they say.

"You've been assigned to us," Miss Chalmers is saying.

"Where will I be staying?" the woman asks.

Miss Chalmers is temporarily speechless as she gawks at the woman through her thick glasses. A smile flits across her face as if she has decided the woman is joking. "We do not provide quarters for census workers," she says. "You were to have arranged accommodations before you arrived. Surely your employment packet mentioned that."

The woman gives a vague wave of her hand as if she cannot be bothered with such minutiae. "I'll find something," she says.

Corinne hides a smile. This woman obviously has no idea how scarce rooms are in Washington. Not only are there hundreds of workers compiling the 1940 census, but she has noticed a definite increase in personnel related to the military and war offices. The United States isn't at war – yet – but the signs are pointing in that direction if you believe the papers.

Corinne begins re-typing her census form as Miss Chalmers leads the woman to a desk three rows over. Covertly, she watches as the woman takes off her wet trench coat and drapes it over the back of her chair. Miss Chalmers gives her a stack of hand-marked census forms to be transferred to the typed sheets. The woman picks up a blank form, pursing her lips as she tries to figure out how to roll the paper into the typewriter. Bemused, Corinne watches the woman glance sideways at her neighbor, trying to see how the machine operates. She mangles one form badly and pulls it out. Corinne looks for Miss Chalmers, but she has stepped out. Rising, she hurries over to the woman's desk.

"Let me show you," she says in a low voice, taking a new form and threading it onto the roller for her. "You have to line it up like this," she says, "or nothing will be in the right place." As she leans near the woman, she catches a scent, light and flowery, intensified by her damp clothing.

"Thank you," the woman says, her voice deep and musical. Up close, her eyes as she raises them to Corinne aren't brown at all, Corinne realizes. They are a hazel – now blue-grey, now grey-brown. Corinne blinks and straightens up.

"You're welcome," she says, feeling a hot flush rise to her cheeks.

*   *   *

13

"Miss Cory! It's time for lunch," Veronica called from the house.

Cory opened her eyes and sighed.

"I have to leave after we get back from the doctor," Veronica said as she came out to collect the drink tray. "Aggie will be by later, after she gets off work."

*   *   *

"Miss Bishop, can you help me with my story?"

Aggie glanced up from the papers she was grading. "I'm sorry, Becka. I can't today." She glanced at her calendar. "How about tomorrow?"

"Okay," Becka said somewhat glumly, picking at a pimple on her cheek.

Aggie hurried to finish the stack of papers before her and then gathered up her messenger bag containing another set of papers to be graded tonight. Gasping at the stifling hot air out in the asphalt parking lot, she lowered all the windows of her car, hoping moving air would feel cooler. It did not. By the time she drove from the school to her nearby apartment in Whitehall, she was drenched in sweat. She picked up Percival, her scruffy Jack Russell mix, who jumped eagerly into the front passenger seat, his head out the window with his paws propped on the arm rest.

"Our next car is going to have AC, I don't care what you say," she muttered as she drove to Bexley. Of course, as her Accord was going on fifteen years old and still running fine, she could never bring herself to think seriously about buying another car. She pulled into a long, tree-lined drive leading back to a mansion that must once have been stately, but now was in varying degrees of disrepair. The wood trim and soffits badly needed painting, the copper gutters were hanging loose in a few places, looking as if they might impale the unfortunate soul happening to be walking beneath when they finally speared to the ground, and there were a few broken slate roof tiles patched with cheap asphalt shingles. The yew and boxwood hedges lining the walks were so overgrown that they nearly choked the walks off completely. It looked sad and lonely, Aggie often thought. She drove around back and parked in the old carriage house that had been converted to a garage back when automobiles replaced the family carriages. It was so much cooler here in the deep shade of the trees. Percival ran around peeing on his usual bushes as Aggie retrieved her bag from the back seat. She peeled her damp shirt from her sweaty back and unlocked the kitchen door.

"Aunt Cory," she called, but received no response. With Percival leading the way, she found Cory in her chair in the study, a book lying open on her lap, her silver-haired head resting against the side of her wing chair as she napped. The windows had all been thrown open, and the breeze that came in was warm, but tolerable. Without waking her aunt – her great-aunt actually – Aggie took the other chair and quietly began grading her papers as Percival curled up under Cory's chair.

Within half an hour, Cory stirred. "How long have you been here?" she asked, rubbing her eyes.

"Hours and hours," Aggie teased.

"You're a bad liar, Agatha," Cory said. She eyed her great-niece more closely, taking in her polo shirt, crop pants and sandals. "Is that what you wore to work?" she asked disapprovingly.

Aggie smiled. "It's summer school, Aunt Cory. They relax the dress code to make it easier for all of us to be there."

She stuffed her papers back into her bag. "What would you like for dinner?"

Cory thought for a moment. "Deep-dish pizza."

Aggie laughed. "Deep-dish pizza it is. You and Percival set the table, and I'll go pick it up."

Cory looked at Aggie as she got to her feet. "Don't you have something better to do with your evening than spend it with an old lady?"

Aggie grinned. "What could be better than spending time with you?" To herself, she added, "And sadly, no, I do not have anything better to do."

Chapter 3

"I can't be that out of shape," Beryl huffed the next morning as she walked to the library from the bus stop.

She entered the air-conditioned building, wiping the sweat from her face, feeling rivulets running down her back and chest. She shrugged off her backpack which felt much heavier than usual. Inside, she found the books she had taken with her from The Scriptorium. She pulled them out, along with her notes. Her shift wasn't scheduled to start for another hour, but she planned to begin researching the auction books.

She went into the back office where her colleague, David Morris, was pouring himself a cup of coffee.

"You're early," he said, glancing at the clock. He held up the coffee pot. "Want some?"

Beryl shook her head. "Have to cool down first. Need some internet time," she explained.

"Why don't you guys get internet at home?"

"Claire says we both have it at work, so we don't need to pay for it at home," Beryl said, opening her notes.

"More book appraisals?" he asked.

"Yup."

David came over to shuffle through the stack of books she had set on the desk. "Why are you doing regular library work?" he asked, lifting his glasses to squint more closely at the binding of one of her books. "You have a doctorate in Medieval European literature. You should be working with a rare book collection somewhere."

Beryl shrugged. "I like what I do."

"You mean Claire likes what you do," he said cryptically.

She frowned up at him. "What does that mean?"

David shook his head apologetically. "Nothing. I'll let you get to it," he said as he returned to the reference desk.

Book by book, Beryl went through her notes and began the process of trying to find similar editions either recently sold or currently for sale. It was tedious work, but she enjoyed it. Every now and then, something really rare and wonderful popped up, but mostly this type of work was fairly routine. This batch of books, because so many were first editions, turned out to be worth more than usual. *Mr. Herrmann will be pleased*, she thought.

She turned to the books she had chosen for herself and looked them over more closely. One was a beautiful embossed-leather edition of *Wuthering Heights*, one of her favorite novels. "You already have three copies," she could hear Claire saying. Tucked in the middle of the stack was the little book that had nearly disappeared against the side of the box. She hadn't even realized she'd put it in her stack. It was by Rumer Godden, *Take Three Tenses: A Fugue in Time*. Opening the front cover, her eye was caught by an inscription, dated 1945:

> *Loving Valentine Greetings to Corinne,*
> *In memory of a <u>very</u> wet afternoon!*
> *Helen*

Intrigued, Beryl flipped quickly through the volume, but didn't see any other notes or inscriptions. She turned back to the inscription in the front, smiling.

By late in the week, Beryl had come up with estimated values for most of the books on her list. She planned to go over to the bookshop after work to bring Mr. Herrmann her notes, but privately, she had another reason for going. The inscription in the Godden book had captured her imagination. Even now, the little tome resided in her backpack, but it was to keep it safe, private.

"Oh, God, listen to this," Beryl had heard as she fed Winston a couple of evenings ago. Beryl had been reading the book and had left it sitting on the couch when Claire and Leslie came in. She heard Claire read the inscription aloud to Leslie, who laughed along with her.

Angry and humiliated, Beryl had snatched the book from Claire's hands, which only made Claire laugh more. "Watch," Claire had said mockingly to Leslie, "before we know it, she'll have imagined some grand romance instead of an afternoon fuck."

Beryl took the book upstairs, away from their derisive laughter, chagrined that Claire had turned it into something tawdry, indecent. Though she couldn't have explained why, Beryl had become convinced that the inscription spoke of so much more – of passion and promise and..."

"Romance," Claire would have finished cynically if Beryl had tried to express herself.

"No relationship can stay romantic forever," Claire often scoffed, but "Some can! Some must!" Beryl cried silently.

So, she turned to her books – not modern romances where it seemed everything revolved around sex – but classic stories where the world could be changed by a look or a touch, where feelings ran deep and remained true.

That's the thing, she had thought upstairs, blinking back tears as she stared at her book. *Remaining true. Keeping love from fading, from sliding unnoticed into something that's only comfortable and safe – safer than the alternative... Stop!* she thought. *Don't go there.*

Beryl glanced up now at the library clock. Almost quitting time. "David," she said, "I'm going to the stacks to put these away."

She pushed a cart loaded with research journals that library users had pulled and stacked on the trolley, carefully putting them back in their proper places. When she was done, she gathered up her backpack, greeting the next librarian working the evening shift at the desk.

19

"You leaving?" she asked David.

"In a minute," he said, looking up from his computer.

"Well, don't let a minute turn into an hour," she said, shaking her head. He always worked over his scheduled hours. "See you tomorrow."

"See you, Beryl."

The heat and humidity hit her like a brick wall as she stepped outside. She walked the few blocks to the nearest bus stop and headed to DuPont Circle. Circumventing the junkies and homeless people panhandling near the ellipse, she made her way to The Scriptorium.

"Hello, Mr. Herrmann," she said as the silvery bell announced her arrival.

"How are you today, Miss Gray?" he smiled as he finished ringing up a sale for a customer.

She wandered through the shelves, waiting patiently as the customer inquired about another book he was interested in. Mr. Herrmann took down the information and promised to do a search later that day.

As the customer thanked him and left, Beryl returned to the counter. She pulled out her notes. "I have values for you," she said. "Some of these books are worth a good bit."

He smiled as he peered through his half-glasses at her notes. "This must have taken you quite a while," he said. "I think I owe you more for the time you spent."

"Well, I do have a favor to ask," she grinned. "I need to track down where these books came from."

"Why on earth would you need to do that?" he asked looking at her over the top of his glasses.

She had anticipated this question. "I found a letter in one of the books and thought the family might like to have it returned," she said, thinking this sounded innocently plausible.

"Let's see," said Mr. Herrmann, pulling out an old-fashioned ledger. "George may have all of our inventory on the computer, but if it – how do they say? – smashes, I always have this," he said often. He ran his finger down the entries. "Here we are. The auction house was Wharton's in Philadelphia." He jotted down the date of the sale and the lot numbers of the boxes of books.

"Do you still have the boxes in the back?" Beryl asked hopefully.

"Looking for more clues to solve your mystery?" he asked with a wink. "Yes, I believe the boxes are yet unpacked. You may go back if you wish."

"Thank you," she grinned.

She found the boxes where she had left them. Pulling the wooden chair near, she went back through each box, checking every book quickly. There were no other inscriptions from either Helen or Corinne. Though she hadn't really expected to find anything, she was disappointed.

She glanced at her watch. "Oh, crap." Hurrying to the front door, she said, "Thank you, Mr. Herrmann."

"Let me know how you make out, my dear," he said with a wave.

She hurried to 19th street and waited for the next bus that would take her back to Georgetown. Thirty minutes later, she nearly ran up the paved walk of her parents' brick Federal house.

"Hi," she called out as she unlocked the last of the three deadbolts securing the front door. She deposited her backpack in an overstuffed armchair in the living room and headed toward the kitchen.

"You're late. Again," Edith Gray said to her daughter reprovingly.

"I know," Beryl said, giving her mother a quick kiss on the cheek. "Sorry. Big crowds on the bus today. Ummm, smells good."

Her mother's frown gave way to a grudging smile. "I hope it's not ruined."

Beryl grinned and pulled down dinner plates, bread plates, salad bowls to set the dining table. "Your family eats this formally every night?" Claire had asked in disbelief when she first met Beryl's family.

"Gerald, dinner," Edith announced, and Beryl's father emerged from his den, taking his place at the head of the table. Beryl gave him a quick kiss also on her way to her place.

"How's work, Beryl?" her father asked as he passed the platter of pork chops.

"It's fine," she answered automatically. "How's yours?"

Her father, now in his thirtieth year of civil service working for the Treasury Department, launched into a description of some of the recent office politics he was caught in.

"How can you have the same non-conversation week after week?" Claire had asked back when she used to accompany Beryl on these Thursday evening dinners.

"Better than your family who never talk at all except to snipe at one another," Beryl had wanted to say, but didn't. Now, she found even these boring conversations with her parents preferable to listening to Claire and Leslie go on about their work for Social Services where Claire, as Leslie's supervisor, was responsible for overseeing her case load.

Just last night, Claire had brought Leslie home for dinner – "again," Beryl had very nearly said – and Beryl had sat with nothing to contribute as they discussed a domestic violence case they'd been called in on. At one point, in an attempt to be polite, Leslie had asked Beryl how her day was.

"She's a librarian!" Claire had laughed. "How exciting can it be?"

"Beryl? You haven't heard a word I've said," came her mother's voice.

Beryl blinked and looked up.

"I was saying we've moved your brother's birthday dinner to a week from Saturday."

"Why?"

"Your sister had something she had to do this weekend," Edith said.

Beryl frowned a little. "Couldn't you have asked me first? What if I had plans for that next weekend?"

"You never go anywhere," Edith said in surprise. "It never occurred to me to ask. Do you have plans?"

"No, but –"

"Well, then, why on earth are you making such a fuss?" Edith asked as she stood, sweeping Gerald's plate out from in front of him. "Help me clear the table."

Chapter 4

Cory slipped out of bed, her thin summer night gown flapping about her ankles and slippered feet. In her hand was a small bouquet of lilacs – its fragrance wafting powerfully in her wake. Thin strips of moonlight coming through the slats of the shades lit up what had been her father's den. After the sale, she had agreed to have her bedroom furniture moved to the main floor of the house as a concession to Aggie and Veronica to keep them from worrying about her being upstairs by herself.

She walked out to the foyer, where the wide oak boards gave way to slate laid in an intricate sunburst pattern sited under the dramatic oval staircase so that when one looked down from the upper floors the sunburst was perfectly framed within the oval. Moonlight lit her way, but she did not need light. She knew every inch of this house. She turned to the wide, sweeping staircase, its oak treads clad in a handknotted Persian runner, "from when it really was Persia," she would have said. The oak banister, worn smooth by generations of the family's hands running up and down it, felt familiar to her gnarled fingers with their knobbly joints. She knew Aggie didn't want her to go upstairs – "you'll fall and break something and no one will find you for hours," she'd said – but upstairs, at night, was one of her favorite places to be. A medical alert pendant bumped against her chest – another concession to Aggie's worry.

Upstairs were six bedrooms and four bathrooms – an extravagant expense when the house was built in the eighteen sixties, but brilliant foresight. On the third floor were the servants' rooms, with three more bathrooms for their use. As she wandered the halls, visiting each room, Cory visited with the occupants – the occupants as she remembered them. Her mother and father's room, a room they had always shared – contrary to the custom of having separate, adjoining rooms – was a room where she had been welcomed as a child. Younger than her brother and sister by nearly ten years, Cory had grown up almost an only child. She would happily climb into her parents' enormous bed in the mornings, and lie snuggled between them, loved and protected.

Farther down the hall was her brother's room. Terrence, too, had indulged his baby sister, inviting her in and letting her watch as he made detailed models of airplanes and ships. He had left for college before she was eight, but, oh, how she had adored him.

Opposite was her sister's room. Candace had not shared the rest of the family's adoration of little Corinne. She strove, always, to force Corinne to follow the same rules she'd grown up with, but Candace never seemed to grasp or accept the fact that the rules she lived by were of her own making and Corinne could no sooner have followed them than change the color of her eyes. "She looks like a china doll," Candace often said spitefully, trying to make it an insult, but unable to hide the jealousy she felt at Corinne's naturally curly blond hair and large light blue eyes that did, after all, make her look like a doll while Candace was woefully plain with her straight, dark hair and little eyes hidden behind thick spectacles. *Poor Candace,* Cory thought with a smile.

The room at the end of the hall had a wonderful bay window with a deep window seat. This had been Cory's room. A rocker near the bay was the only piece of furniture remaining on this entire floor.

Those auction people had nearly wet their pants when they were shown the house's furnishings: beds, dressers, highboys and tables made in Philadelphia and Boston; Chippendale and Queen Anne mostly, with Tiffany table lamps in nearly every room as well as Tiffany stained glass windows in many rooms. And the art. The house had an extensive collection of landscapes and portraits by mostly American artists. "This will all fetch a very good price," the auction people had said greedily.

"I'm sorry, Aunt Cory," Aggie had said, nearly in tears herself. "But if we don't find a way to pay the back taxes, the city will take the house."

The "others" – Cory refused to name them, the other relatives – had argued that she should be "sent somewhere" and the house should be sold after all the furniture and books were gone. After all, why should one old woman rattle about in such a huge house all by herself? They didn't care where she went, just as long as she was gone. Agatha had stood up to all of them, including her own father, Terrence's son. She had insisted that Cory should be allowed to stay as long as she could be safe in the house by herself. It had been then that Cory had reminded them all that, as trustee, only she could decide when and if the house ought to be sold, but even she couldn't come up with an alternative to the auction. Agatha was the one who saved the books, or most of them. A few boxes had been taken and auctioned before they realized what was happening. But Aggie had kept enough furniture for Cory to be comfortable, and the books to keep her company for as long as she wanted to stay in her home.

"The books can always be auctioned off separately later," Cory had overheard her arguing with the others. "You can't take everything from her."

Now, in the night, Cory settled creakily into the rocking chair. "Is it me or the rocker?" she wondered. She knew they all thought she was off her rocker – she chuckled at her own pun – but she didn't care. Reaching forward, she pulled open a panel under the window seat so cunningly hidden that it was undetectable unless one knew it was there. This had been her secret hiding place for all her treasures as a child, but now, it held something far more precious. Lovingly, she placed her lilacs.

*   *   *

"I'm Helen. Helen Abrams," the woman says, extending her hand.

"Corinne Bishop."

"Well, Corinne, I can't thank you enough," Helen says. "A week in that hotel and I've had absolutely no luck finding a room or a flat anywhere."

Corinne looks at her. *Who says "flat"?* she wonders. "Where are you from?" she asks.

"New York, most recently," Helen replies with a bored air. "But I was schooled in Switzerland, France and England."

"Well," Corinne says, a trifle uncertainly, "my place isn't big, and you'll have to sleep on the couch, but if that's all right with you, you're welcome to it. While you keep looking for a place of your own," she adds quickly. She does not want there to be any misunderstandings.

Helen leads the way down the stairs to the foyer of their building where she has managed to talk the doorman into letting her leave three enormous suitcases stacked inside the entrance. The doorman is usually surly and hostile to all of them, but Corinne suspects that no one says no to Helen Abrams.

Corinne tries to lift one of the bags and immediately sets it back down. "Uh, my apartment is six blocks from here," she says dubiously, "and I don't think –"

"I'll get a taxi," Helen volunteers. A taxi, for six blocks? Corinne almost laughs, but Helen steps outside, wearing grey slacks and a white shirt that make her look like Katharine Hepburn, Corinne thinks. She looks down at her own boring tweed skirt and hose, the left one marred with a run, but these are the only good hose she has left. A couple of minutes later, Helen returns, cab driver in tow. The three of them manage to get the suitcases loaded into the cab's voluminous trunk. A short drive later, the cab deposits them and the bags on the sidewalk.

"I'm afraid we're three floors up," Corinne says apologetically.

"Pas de problème," Helen says.

"Aprés vous," Corinne replies as Helen's handsome face breaks into a smile.

Together, they manage to haul the cases up three flights where they take up nearly all the available floor space of Corinne's tiny apartment.

"Well," Helen says, somewhat disdainfully, "we could always turn them into a table." She looks around and asks, "Couldn't you get a larger place?"

Stung, Corinne says, "This is all I could afford on my salary."

"Salary or not, I'd be cabling my parents to ask for more money," Helen says absently.

"Yes, I believe you would," Corinne says coolly, regretting her offer to let Helen stay. "But I came here despite my family's objections. I'm not going to ask them for money. They'd simply say to come home."

Helen appraises her more closely. Though Corinne looks sweet and pretty, there is steel under the surface. She smiles in grudging admiration.

Corinne tries to squeeze by, saying, "Let me show you the kitchen, such as it is." She loses her balance as her foot catches on one of the suitcases and she falls into Helen. "Sorry," she mumbles. Her hands, in a clumsy effort to catch her balance, have landed squarely on Helen's breasts.

"It's my fault," Helen assures her, catching her around the waist and helping her regain her balance.

Helen is only an inch or two taller, but to Corinne, as she raises her eyes to find Helen smiling down at her, she seems immensely tall. She finds herself mesmerized by those changeable eyes and....

"You were going to show me the kitchen," Helen reminds her, and her deep voice sounds amused as they both realize that Corinne's hands are still resting on her chest.

Corinne blushes furiously. *What is the matter with you?* she asks herself. But as Helen follows her around for a very brief tour of the apartment, for in truth, nearly everything can be seen by simply pirouetting in place, she keeps catching whiffs of Helen's scent, a scent that reminds her of a summer garden, and makes her want to keep inhaling.

27

For some reason, Corinne blushes again and cannot meet Helen's eyes as she shows her the bedroom with its double bed.

*   *   *

Cory chuckled again as she rocked. The moon had shifted so that only a tiny sliver of light came angling in through the window. She closed the panel under the window seat and pushed to her feet, slowly making her way back down through the sleeping house.

Chapter 5

"It's like the steambath from hell out there," David complained, removing his glasses to mop his red, sweaty face with a napkin.

"I know," Beryl sympathized, looking up from her computer. "It wasn't bad when I got here this morning, but it'll be murder when I leave. The tourists will be keeling over by the dozens."

"They should have shot the first person to suggest putting the nation's capital in the middle of a swamp," David said as he dropped into his desk chair. His scant hair was plastered against his scalp with sweat, and his cotton shirt was soaked through, especially where his backpack had rested. Like Beryl, he took public transportation as driving and parking were such a hassle. Unfortunately, this left them at the mercy of the weather.

"Do you have any ibuprofen?" he asked. "I have a splitting headache."

"Sure," Beryl said, reaching for her own backpack and digging in one of the pockets. As she pulled out a small pill bottle, a folded piece of paper fell to the floor. She handed the pills to David and bent to pick up the paper. Unfolding it, she saw that it was the information about the book auction. She still hadn't called to follow up since Mr. Herrmann had given it to her last week. Every time she thought about it, she could hear Claire's voice telling her she was being stupid. But the book remained safely tucked in another pocket of her backpack.

"I'll be back in a minute," David said. "I'm going to get some water."

"Mmmm," Beryl responded, not really paying attention. She began an internet search for Wharton's Auctions in Philadelphia. She glanced up as he returned.

"Are you all right?" she asked. "You're awfully red in the face."

"I'm fine," he muttered, rubbing his knuckles against his forehead. "If my head would just stop pounding."

A student came to the desk requesting help with a search. "I'll take care of this," Beryl said as David started to get up.

The search turned out to be more difficult than usual, involving an obscure reference in a journal that was hard to locate. This was what she loved about her job. She knew it seemed boring to other people, but for her it was a combination of a treasure hunt and preserving something important. "Someone, somewhere put a lot of time and effort into this research, just like you will," she often reminded students. "Don't stop with the first few results when you do a search. Something really useful might be buried way down on your list of references."

She was occupied at another computer for several minutes before she became aware of commotion from the desk area. She hurried back there to see a crowd gathered at the reference desk. Pushing through the throng, she saw David lying on the floor, his face now an ashen grey. Someone had already called 911, and another quick-thinking individual had retrieved the automatic defibrillator from the wall. The pads were jolting him, but there was no response. She could only stand there helplessly as the paramedics rushed in, pushing a gurney loaded with equipment. They asked for space as they took over working on him and attempting, unsuccessfully it seemed, to revive him.

She gently shooed curious bystanders away from the scene, aware of how strange it was that her heart was beating a million times a minute while her friend's heart had stopped beating at all.

*   *   *

Beryl heard muffled noises and laughter as the front door was opened.

"What are you doing home?" Claire asked in surprise a couple of minutes later as she came up the stairs to find Beryl sitting in an armchair with Winston curled up on her lap. "I thought you were working late today."

"I was," Beryl said quietly. "David died of a heart attack at work today."

"David who?" Claire asked blankly.

"David Morris. The man I've worked with for the past five years. David, whose daughter just graduated from Edison." She suddenly realized Claire was still standing on the stairs, wearing sweaty tennis clothes, her bag over her shoulder.

"What –?"

Beryl got to her feet, dumping Winston to the floor with a grunt. She came to the stairwell where Leslie was standing on the landing, also in tennis clothes.

As Beryl stared silently down at her, Leslie cleared her throat and said awkwardly, "I should go."

Claire set her bag down and said, "I'll walk you back down."

When she returned a few minutes later, she found Beryl curled up in her chair again, Winston sitting with his back to her with an unmistakable air of indignation.

Ignoring Beryl's frosty expression, Claire went to the kitchen and got a soda.

"Did I ruin your plans by coming home early?" Beryl asked.

"I didn't have any plans," Claire said calmly, sitting on the floor and placing a towel behind her sweaty back so she wouldn't get the couch damp. "We played tennis after work and were just going to get something cold to drink."

"Is this what you do on the nights I work late?" Beryl asked coldly.

Claire tilted her head in amusement. "It depends on what you mean by 'this'," she said. "If you mean, have friends? Have a life? Then, yes."

Beryl pressed her hand to her eyes. "I'm sorry," she murmured.

"It's okay," said Claire. "You're upset. Tell me what happened."

"It was terrible," Beryl said, her voice breaking as she began to cry. In halting phrases, she recounted what had happened. "If I'd just realized," she sobbed.

"You couldn't have known," Claire said soothingly, kneeling in front of Beryl's chair and holding her by the shoulders. "Let me shower and we'll get some dinner, okay?"

Beryl sniffed and nodded. Claire gave her a quick kiss as she got to her feet. "That's about the only part of me it's safe to touch right now," Claire joked with a crooked smile – the smile that had captured Beryl's heart the first time she saw it.

Beryl closed her eyes as Claire headed up the stairs. "You're wrong, you're wrong, you're wrong," she whispered to herself, trying to block the sounds she thought she'd heard on the stairs before Claire realized she was there.

*　　*　　*

Beryl stopped abruptly as she neared the reference desk. A stranger was sitting in David's place.

The past couple of weeks had been filled – consumed, Beryl would have said – with mourning David. She had kept his chair vacant, refusing to sit in it even when she needed to be at that computer station. The viewing and funeral had been especially hard. She still felt so incredibly guilty, and the ordeal of having to face his wife and daughter, thinking maybe she could have, should have, done something. If she had, then maybe... "Stop!" she said to herself for the hundredth time.

The evening of the viewing, she'd rushed home to change and grab something to eat before heading to the funeral home. Glancing at the clock nervously as she finished eating, she called Claire's cell phone.

"Where are you?" Beryl asked.

"I'm still at work," Claire said impatiently. "Where else would I be?"

"Let's see... you might be here getting ready to go to the funeral home with me like you said you would," but Beryl didn't say it. What she did say was, "David's viewing is tonight."

"Oh," Claire groaned. "I completely forgot. I'm sorry. I'm tied up doing budget reports that I've got to finish. I'll see you at home later tonight, okay?"

"You operate on a July fiscal year. You did your budget reports two months ago." But Beryl didn't say this, either. *She thinks I don't remember things*, Beryl thought as she headed out the door. *But I remember everything – I know the names of every person she works with; I remember the names of their spouses and kids. She can't remember the name of the one person I was close to. And now he's gone.*

And now he'd been replaced.

What she'd thought at first was someone sitting in David's chair she now realized was a man in a wheelchair. David's chair was pushed back against the wall.

Beryl found herself staring into a ruggedly handsome face that looked as if it belonged on the cover of a men's magazine – piercing blue eyes, short, carelessly scruffy hair and a couple days' worth of beard. He startled her by pushing himself up with his muscular arms to stand on his one remaining leg as he extended a hand to her. "You must be Beryl," he said with a smile. "I'm Ridley Wade."

"Hi, Ridley," she said, taking his hand.

He lowered himself back into his wheelchair and said, "I was really sorry to hear about David. I only met him a few times, but he seemed like a nice guy."

"He was," Beryl nodded, setting her backpack under the desk and sitting down. "Did you transfer from somewhere else on campus?" she asked curiously. Trying not to stare, she noted, now that he was sitting and his pants leg had hitched up, that Ridley's right foot was a prosthetic foot attached to a pylon.

"Yeah, I was over at Dahlgren," he replied, "but medical students are a pain in the ass. They don't know enough to know how much they don't know, but they already think they're ready to walk on water."

Beryl laughed and was startled at how strange it sounded.

"I really like the humanities, so when I heard David's position here at Lauinger had posted, I applied," he said with a shrug. "I don't mean to come charging in, taking his place," he added, as if he had read Beryl's thoughts upon first seeing him. "How long have you been here?"

"Twelve years," she said. "Since finishing my degree."

"Twelve years," he repeated, shaking his head. "That's longer than I've ever been anywhere."

They were interrupted by a student requiring assistance.

"I can take this," Ridley volunteered.

Beryl watched him propel himself with his hands and right foot. Over at the shelves, he stood, balancing himself by bracing what remained of his left thigh on a shelf so he could reach up and pull the requested books down off the top shelf.

She hastily busied herself at her computer as he wheeled himself back to the reference desk.

"So where did you get your library degree?" she asked casually.

Ridley's face took on an expression of resignation. "University of Maryland," he replied. "After I got back from Afghanistan." He spun his chair around to face her. "Marine. Road-side bomb." He tapped something hard below his right knee. "Prosthesis. I have one for the left side, but it's too heavy to wear except when I need to. I have crutches, but then my hands are tied up. So," he spread his hands, glancing down at his chair, "the government generously provides me with a speedy set of wheels. Lets me get around and still have the use of my hands. In case you were wondering," he finished with just a hint of sarcasm and hostility.

Beryl blinked, taken aback at such an unexpected disclosure. "Wow, I... I never -"

"What?" Ridley challenged, his eyes narrowing a bit, and she could see a hint of the warrior in him.

"A brainy Marine. Who'd have guessed?"

He stared at her for a long moment, and then threw his head back and laughed. "All right," he said, shaking his head and still laughing. "All right."

Chapter 6

Aggie glanced over at her desk as she heard the buzz of her cell phone vibrating. She looked up at the clock on the wall. Thirty minutes left before the bell. Her students were busy writing a short story for her. These were all kids who had failed English, a mix of freshmen and sophomores. She tried to structure the summer sessions so they got their work done while they were at school – bad enough having to be in summer school without spending evenings and weekends doing homework. That had been the problem for most of them in the first place – not that they weren't intelligent enough to pass, but between work and sports and whatever else was going on at home, there was no way they were going to get their homework done at night. She also used the time to get as much of her own grading done as possible.

By the time the clock ticked toward the bell releasing them for the weekend, nearly every student was packed up, butts half-off their seats, ready to bolt.

"Pick up your papers on your way out," Aggie called, waving the stack. "Overall, a nice improvement."

Like sharks in a feeding frenzy, they scrabbled through the pile to find their work. She grinned as they each peeked at the last page to see her grade and comment.

"Julio, very nicely done."

He beamed. "Thanks, Ms. B."

"And Becka, nice improvement in your sentence flow."

Her pimply face broke into a rare smile. "Thanks, Miss Bishop."

As soon as the classroom had emptied, she pulled open her desk drawer and looked to see who had called. She pushed the recall button.

"Hey, Shannon, what's up?"

"Not much," said Aggie's closest friend. "I just wondered if you could spare some time in your non-summer to go out to dinner tonight? And I promise not to rub in how much I am enjoying having my summer off."

"It feels like a non-summer," Aggie admitted, "but I need the money."

"For your aunt, not for you," Shannon pointed out.

"Same thing," Aggie sighed. "She doesn't have anyone else."

"Yes, she does. At least, she should," Shannon said. "You've got brothers and a father who could be helping."

"Yeah, well..." Aggie grumbled. "They won't. You know what they're like. They just want to be rid of her and sell everything. I can't do that to her."

"What about dinner?" Shannon asked, getting back to the reason she'd called.

"Um..." Aggie stalled, knowing full well that she had backed out the last three times Shannon had called her. "I was going to bring something over to Aunt Cory's tonight. How about joining us?" Shannon was quiet, but Aggie pressed. "Come on. You're as pathetic as I am. No date on a Friday. We might as well have dinner with my ninety-three-year-old aunt. It's as exciting as anything else we'd do."

"Oh, all right," Shannon agreed.

"Great. I'll pick up dinner and swing by to get you at six."

"See you then."

*   *   *

Aggie pulled up to Shannon's house at the appointed time, while Percival hopped back and forth in the back seat between the driver and passenger side windows.

"Ummm, I smell fried chicken," Shannon said as she got in, sniffing.

"It's in the trunk," Aggie grinned. "I don't trust Percival quite that far."

"Smart," Shannon agreed, turning to rub Percival's scruffy head as he popped up on the armrest between the front seats at the mention of his name.

"I've always thought this was such a cool house," Shannon said as they entered the tree-lined drive and the house came into sight.

"Yeah, it is." Aggie opened the trunk and she and Shannon pulled out bags of food. "Aunt Cory?" she called as they entered the kitchen. Receiving no answer, she frowned. "I'll go check the garden. Be right back."

Percival led the way as Aggie headed out across the yard.

Shannon explored the main floor. It was the first time she'd been here since the auction. Where before, it had seemed just lonely, with only Aunt Cory wandering around, now it felt depressing, she thought. Most of the rooms were empty, only the books on the shelves and the odd chair or side table remained. The walls were pockmarked with smudges and lighter-colored squares and rectangles where paintings had hung for years. Now, there were only empty nails.

In the front parlour, propped on the mantel and bookcases, were a number of photos in ornate silver frames. She stepped closer.

"There you are," Aggie said a few minutes later. "Found her sitting outside. She's washing up."

"Is this your aunt when she was younger?" Shannon asked curiously, indicating one of the frames.

Aggie leaned closer. "Yeah."

"You look just like her," Shannon said, glancing from the photo to her friend. "Same blond hair and blue eyes. Who's that with her?"

"That's Aunt Helen."

"Aunt Helen?"

Aggie shrugged. "Well, she wasn't really an aunt. She and Aunt Cory were... companions."

Shannon turned to her in surprise. "As in...?"

Aggie shrugged again. "I honestly don't know. No one ever talked about it. But I heard she was devastated when Helen died. I think they lived together for, I don't know, something like thirty years."

"Does she know about you?"

"What's to know?" Aggie asked. "I haven't had a girlfriend in, what, three years? Percival is my only serious relationship and I like it that way."

"You really are pathetic," Shannon nodded wisely.

Aggie raised one eyebrow. "Better than a series of one-night stands."

Shannon held a hand up. "Don't even go there. That's all I want," she insisted. "After I finally got rid of that bastard husband of mine, I am not about to make the same mistakes again."

Cory called from the kitchen, wondering where they'd got to.

Aggie linked her arm through Shannon's, steering her toward the kitchen. "It's not safe, though," she said seriously. "I'm just afraid one of these guys is going to hurt you."

"Ha! No man will ever do that to me again," Shannon growled. "And if one tries, he's going to get kicked so hard in the balls, they'll end up as his Adam's apple." She was saying this last bit as they entered the kitchen where Cory was setting the table, a very attentive Percival following her back and forth.

"Well, that sounded like an interesting conversation," Cory said.

"It was," Aggie said, "and you're not old enough to participate."

Cory laughed as they passed around platters of fried chicken, potato salad and sliced tomatoes.

"Oh, thank goodness it's Friday," Aggie sighed as she took a bite of chicken.

"Don't wish your weeks away, wishing for Fridays," Cory said, sprinkling salt and pepper on her tomatoes. "Before you know it, the weeks have leapt by, and then the months and the years. And someday, you'll wish for more Mondays."

Aggie reached over and gave Cory's arm a squeeze.

"Aunt Cory, could you tell us about Helen?" Shannon asked innocently, pulling her shins out of reach of Aggie's kicks under the table.

Cory's pale blue eyes lit up, though. "She was my closest... my dearest..." She blinked rapidly, and said, "We met working in the 1940 census office in Washington."

"D.C.?" Aggie asked in disbelief. "I thought you'd lived your whole life here in Columbus."

Cory's eyes twinkled. "Not quite. I've seen a bit more of the world than Ohio."

"Tell us more," Shannon prompted, winking at Aggie.

Cory smiled to herself as she nibbled on a drumstick, her eyes focused on the past.

*   *   *

"How can you be twenty-one years old and not know how to type?" Corinne asks in bewilderment as she stares at the error-riddled paper in Helen's typewriter.

"My schools didn't focus on such mundane things," Helen says carelessly, bookmarking a volume of Wordsworth.

"You're going to get fired if you don't start doing better," Corinne says with a worried glance toward Miss Chalmers' empty chair. "And you're not getting paid to read poetry."

Helen laughs. "So I get fired. It's not like I'm doing this for the money."

Corinne frowns. "Me, either. But I still want to do a good job," she says, feeling as if Helen is belittling the work.

Helen realizes what she said and quickly adds, "I know this is important, but it's just not what I'm good at."

"What are you good at?" Corinne asks.

"I'm a whiz at languages," Helen says confidently.

Corinne rips the page out of Helen's typewriter and rolls a fresh sheet in. "Well, English is the only language they accept for the census, so you'd better focus." She crosses her arms and looks down at Helen sternly. "Miss Chalmers put me in charge of you. You'll make me look bad if you don't do better."

Helen looks up coyly. She has learned how to make Corinne blush. "For you, then," she says with a smile.

* * *

Cory shook her head. "She nearly got us both fired."

"Why haven't you ever talked about this before?" Aggie asked.

Cory smiled wickedly. "You never asked."

Chapter 7

Beryl came down the stairs, sealing the envelope of her brother's birthday card. "Why aren't you dressed?" she asked in surprise. "We have to be there in an hour."

Claire looked over from where she was lying on the couch watching a tennis tournament. "You won't be too disappointed if I don't go, will you?" she asked.

Beryl's shoulders tensed. "They're expecting us."

Claire's voice took on a slightly more petulant tone as she said, "I just want to enjoy a weekend with no obligations for a change."

"Like getting up at six this morning to play tennis with Leslie?" Beryl could have asked, but didn't. Instead, "You've backed out at the last minute for the last three get-togethers with my family. They're starting to ask questions."

"So?" Claire turned back to the television. "Stop making excuses and tell the truth for a change."

"What truth is that?" Beryl wanted to ask. "That we don't do anything together anymore? That our relationship is –" but she stopped those thoughts. Trying one more time, she said calmly, "They're polite enough to include you. You could be polite enough to come."

There was a subtle hardening of Claire's tone as she said, "I'm not coming," and Beryl knew further argument was pointless.

41

She gathered her backpack from its cubby near the stairs and turned to go.

"Beryl?"

Beryl turned, a hopeful expression on her face.

"Aren't you going to kiss me good-bye?"

Beryl walked stiffly over to the couch, leaned down and gave Claire a quick kiss on the cheek. As she straightened, Claire grabbed her hand and said, "You can do better than that." She lifted her face, waiting until Beryl bent again and kissed her on the lips. Claire released her with a small smile as Beryl pulled away and left.

A few minutes later, Beryl was on a bus, heading to Georgetown. Almost automatically, she pulled the Godden book from her backpack. She knew the inscription by heart and had read the book three times now. The story, about a house's hold on the family that lived in it, had become entwined in her mind with Helen and Corinne. She found herself imagining their story, making up moments in their life together – a life that spanned decades in which their love never faded, never morphed into something that was slowly decaying.

Reluctantly, a part of her was realizing how toxic her relationship with Claire had become, but every time that part of her said, "You've got to start thinking about this. What are you going to do when –?", the other part of her that couldn't, wouldn't listen, would turn to Helen and Corinne's world. It was a happier place to be lately. Sometimes, she thought again of trying to track down more information about them, but she hadn't attempted it since the day David died. Somehow, the two things had become entangled in her mind.

*　　*　　*

When she arrived at her parents' house, she took a bracing breath before entering. "Hello, everyone," she called.

There was no response. She looked into the family room where her brother was playing a video game with his son while her brother-in-law and another niece and nephew watched.

"Happy birthday, Nick," she said.

He glanced up and said, "Thanks," before wincing as he narrowing avoided getting blown up by aliens.

She went through to the kitchen where her mother was busy cooking, helped by her sister-in-law, Julie, who was laying dinner rolls out on a baking sheet. Over at the kitchen table, Beryl's older sister, Marian, was scanning the newspaper and munching cashews from a bowl on the table.

"Where's Claire?" Edith asked as she stirred a pot on the stove.

"Oh, she had some work reports she had to have done by Monday," Beryl lied, remembering that she'd used a migraine as the excuse the two previous times Claire had begged off a family dinner. "She asked me to send her love," she added, imagining the expression on Claire's face if she'd heard.

"What can we do?" she asked with a pointed glance at her sister who didn't look up.

"Could you girls set the table?" Edith asked, opening the oven to check on the roast.

Beryl ferried stacks of plates and bowls to the dining room where the table had been stretched to its max with three leaves. Soon, she had all the place settings laid with silverware. Returning to the kitchen, she pulled down water glasses for everyone. She carried an armful out to the table and went back to find her sister with the last two glasses in her hands.

Edith glanced into the dining room as she bustled by. "Oh, Marian, thank you so much. The table looks lovely."

"No problem, Mom," said Marian. "Hi, Beryl," she added, as if she'd just realized her sister was there. She deposited the glasses on the table and went to the doorway of the family room.

"Hi, Marian," Beryl sighed. "Dad in the den?"

"I think so," Marian said vaguely, already absorbed in the ongoing video game.

Beryl let herself quietly into the den, where her father sat in his chair, listening to classical music as he read. Pulling a book off the shelf, Beryl sat in another chair.

"Dinner almost ready?" Gerald asked after a few minutes.

"I think so," Beryl said.

"Okay. Go tell your mother I'll be right out."

Sighing again, Beryl put her book back on the shelf and returned to the kitchen. A short while later, Edith summoned everyone to the table.

"Whoa, Beryl," Nick laughed as they gathered to sit. "You're turning into a barrel. Don't you get any exercise?"

"Nick!" Julie scolded, noting the dull flush creeping up Beryl's neck to her cheeks.

"What?" he snorted. "I'm just saying. Maybe she can borrow Marian's bike and get some exercise," he teased.

"Let her borrow yours," Marian laughed.

Beryl's shoulders tensed again and she kept her eyes glued to her plate, refusing to reply as the tired taunts began to fly.

"You don't need your own bicycle," Edith had said in exasperation when Beryl was seven. "Your brother and sister will share. You can ride theirs when they're not riding."

That, of course, had almost never happened as the bikes had been jealously guarded if Beryl so much as looked at them. This became the cornerstone of the constant teasing Beryl had endured at the hands of her siblings.

"Why don't you ever tell them off?" Claire used to ask, but "It only makes it worse," Beryl always said, speaking from years of experience. The only way to stop them was to ignore them.

You'd think, she thought now, keeping her face carefully neutral, *that after nearly thirty years, they'd have tired of this*, but it continued until, "That's enough," Gerald said quietly. He was the only one who ever seemed to notice. She shot him a quick smile of gratitude.

As soon as she was done picking at her food, self-conscious now about what she ate, Beryl rose from the table and began loading the dishwasher. She was uncomfortably aware of her abdomen pressing against the counter as she stood at the sink, and she was glad to be left alone in the kitchen. Waiting for the rest of the dinner dishes to be brought in, she began hand-washing the pans and baking dishes. Marian brought in her plate and opened the dishwasher as Edith came in to get the birthday cake.

"Thank you for cleaning up, girls," she said.

"It's the least we could do," Marian smiled, wrapping her arm around her mother's shoulders. "After all, you cooked."

Chapter 8

"**B**eryl!"
Ridley reached over and gave her chair a little nudge. "I've been talking to you for, like, five minutes."

"Sorry," she mumbled.

"What's wrong?" he asked, his blue eyes probing.

"Nothing," she said, waving her hand dismissively. "What did you need?"

"I'm doing a presentation at the new student orientation later today," he said, "and I wanted you to look this over if you have time, see if I've forgotten anything."

"Sure," she said, swiveling her chair so she could see his monitor. "Here," she pointed, "remind them that there is a charge if they want sources we don't subscribe to."

"Oh, right," Ridley said, typing in some additional notes. "Thanks."

He glanced over a few minutes later. Beryl was sitting, fingering the corner of a small book. He'd seen her with it frequently and had assumed it was a devotional. On a Jesuit campus, many students and staff attended Mass and prayer groups on a regular basis. She got up to put some books away. Ridley rolled his chair over, feeling a little guilty for being so nosy. Beryl returned to the desk to find him smiling at the inscription.

"What are you doing?" she demanded, her face scarlet.

Ignoring her indignation, he said, "Makes you wonder, doesn't it? If they stayed together? If their love lasted?"

To his confusion and dismay, Beryl burst into tears and ran to the bathroom. It was quite a while before she came out, red-eyed and sniffling. She found the small tome sitting on her chair.

"I've got to go give this presentation," he said, wheeling himself around the desk, "but we are going out for a drink after work."

"I can't –" Beryl started to protest.

"You owe me," he reminded her.

"For what?"

He raised one eyebrow. "My firedance."

"Oh. That."

Just the day before, Ridley had lost his balance while standing. In an effort not to fall, he had hopped about madly – a difficult thing to do on a prosthesis – before he was able to stabilize himself.

Beryl, who was discussing something with one of the other librarians at the time, had dissolved into tears of laughter. "You look like someone is lighting a fire under your foot," she gasped, wiping tears from her cheeks as the other woman looked scandalized. "Not that you'd feel it," she added and the other librarian actually clapped a hand to her mouth in horror.

"Oh, very funny," he nodded, laughing with her at first, and then his grin faded. "But you shouldn't be laughing at a handicapped person."

The other librarian looked as if she wanted to crawl under the desk.

Beryl tried to compose her face into a suitably contrite expression, but unexpectedly snorted with laughter again. "I'm sorry, but you just looked so... so..."

"Ridiculous?" he finished for her.

All she could do was nod as tears were once again rolling down her cheeks while she laughed uncontrollably. The other librarian excused herself and left quickly.

"Okay," he conceded, grinning again. "But you owe me a beer. For being so insensitive."

"Oh, God," Beryl said, wiping her eyes, "we'll be alcoholics if I have to buy you a beer every time I'm insensitive."

"You're paying up," he told her now as he wheeled to the elevator. "No excuses."

*   *   *

A few hours later, they were seated at a tavern not far from campus. Ridley had rigged an ingenious system for fastening his crutches to his chair like ski poles. When they got to the tavern, he asked the hostess to store his collapsed wheelchair in a corner while he swung on his crutches through the closely arranged tables and chairs back to their booth, the last one, where he sat with his back to the wall.

"This would be a real pain in my chair," he muttered as he lowered himself to the booth's bench.

"So," he began after their server had brought the first round - a Stella Artois for Beryl, a Guinness for him - "what was going on today? And I know," he added as Beryl opened her mouth, "that it wasn't just today." He took a long swig of his beer. "What is it?"

Beryl looked at him. She wasn't normally someone who talked about deeply personal matters. Frowning, it hit her that she had no friends of her own, no one outside the small circle she shared with Claire in whom she could confide. She couldn't say she knew Ridley well, but "I trust him," she realized.

"Problems at home?" he prompted.

Beryl nodded and it all began to come out - "gush would have been a better description," she could have said - the frustrations of Claire and Leslie, how lonely she was, her continued sadness at David's death, her family's apathy toward her. "And I'm fat," she concluded, snuffling a little.

"Well, damn," Ridley said, sitting back. "I think we better order dinner. You're in worse shape than I thought."

Beryl smiled despite her misery. "Told you. I'm more handicapped than you are."

"Between the ears, I agree," he grinned.

49

She laughed. He signaled their server and they ordered food and another round. She pulled her cell phone out.

"I'd better let Claire know –"

Ridley covered her hand with his. "It might do Claire some good to wonder where you are. She can call you if she's that worried," he said gently. "Let's just have fun tonight."

By the time Ridley dropped Beryl off at home – "I am not letting you ride a bus this time of night," he insisted – she couldn't remember the last time she'd had such a good evening.

When she got up to the main floor of the rowhouse, she half-expected to see frost on the windows, the chill emanating from Claire's general direction was so intense. Fighting her normal impulse of trying to wheedle a few words from Claire as she stared resolutely at the television, Beryl embraced the silence and went into the kitchen where she fed a yowling Winston and then began to empty her lunch bag and wash her dishes.

"I think you owe me an explanation," Claire said, breaking the silence at last.

Beryl hid a small smile. Bracing herself, she said, "I went out with a co-worker."

"And you couldn't call?" Claire asked testily.

"What makes you think I didn't?"

Beryl swallowed a yell of triumph as Claire's eyes flicked to the telephone, trying to check the caller I.D. Beryl stepped out of the kitchen.

"You're never home anyway," she said bravely.

There was a curious glint in Claire's eyes and her tone changed, warmed as she said, "I was just worried, that's all."

This more conciliatory tone took all the wind from Beryl's sails as she stood braced for a storm. "I'm... I'm going to bed."

"Beryl?"

She turned.

"The kitchen."

Beryl went back to the kitchen where she dried and put away her lunch dishes, wiped down the sink and dried it before turning out the light. As she headed toward the stairs, Claire called, "Good night."

Beryl clenched the handrail as the words hung in the air for three... four... five seconds. "Don't do it," she could hear Ridley whisper, but, "Good night," she said.

Chapter 9

Aggie wasn't sure who was more excited about the end of summer school – her or the kids. Friday of that week was worthless as far as getting anything done, so she spent the day letting each of her ten students read something they had written at the beginning of the summer and something more recent so they could show off their improvement. Most of them had nowhere else to show off – either because no one was at home because everyone was working, or because they knew they'd be teased about showing off anything as lame as school work.

"You don't realize how far you've come," she told them proudly. "You could have the most brilliant ideas in the world, but if you can't express them, if you can't communicate with other people, no one will ever know how brilliant you really are."

At last the bell rang. Rather than bolting as they normally did, the kids dawdled, talking to her, seeming reluctant to go.

"Thanks... for everything, Ms. B," said Julio.

"You're welcome," Aggie smiled. "And you be sure and read that last story to your grandmother. She'll be so proud of you."

He beamed and left with a swagger as Becka approached.

"I signed up for your British Lit class in the fall, Miss Bishop," Becka said, sliding into one of the desks at the front of the room and showing every inclination of wanting to settle down for a long chat.

Aggie tried to look happy about this. Becka was a lonely girl with no friends that Aggie knew of, and it made her clingy. "You're going to have to set boundaries with that one," Shannon had warned her.

"Well, I'll see you in September, then," she said, gathering her bag and locking her desk. "You might want to get a head start on *Romeo and Juliet*. We'll be reading it in class. Goodbye, Becka."

Becka got up and left reluctantly.

Aggie said goodbye to the office staff on her way out. Walking to her car, she checked her phone. There was a voicemail from a woman at Aunt Cory's bank asking her to call or come by.

Groaning a little, she decided to stop by in person. She went to her apartment first to collect Percival, wondering why she bothered keeping an apartment at all. Except for sleeping and showering, she was hardly ever there.

"We could move in with Aunt Cory and save some money," she muttered to Percival as she flipped through her mail, pulling out bills for water, electric and cable. Grinding her teeth in frustration, she tossed the rest of the junk mail into the recycling bin.

"Ready?"

Percival barked and ran to the door.

When she got to the bank, she leashed Percival and took him in with her. She knew all the bank staff by name as this had been Aunt Cory's bank for longer than Aggie had been alive.

"Hi, Aggie," came a chorus of greetings, and Percival received dog cookies from three different people. He loved the bank.

"Hi, Tammy," said Aggie to one of the branch managers. "I got your message. What's the matter?"

Tammy gestured to one of the empty chairs near her desk and closed her office door. "Miss Cory came by this morning. She wanted to make a withdrawal," she said apologetically.

"Oh, dear," Aggie said, frowning. "How did she get down here?"

"I guess she walked," Tammy said.

"Oh, my gosh," Aggie said, putting a hand over her eyes for a moment. "How much did she want?"

"Only two hundred dollars, but..." Tammy paused, embarrassed. "Without your co-signature..."

"No, you did the right thing," Aggie assured her. "Did she say why she wanted the money?"

"No," Tammy said. "I'm afraid she was a little upset with us."

Aggie gave a wry smile. "Probably more than a little, if I know my aunt. I'll take care of it. Thank you for letting me know." She stood. "Come on, Percival."

Percival lolled, walking as slowly as he could while looking about, hoping for one more cookie. It worked. As soon as he had politely accepted the treat, he trotted ahead of Aggie out the door.

Aggie clocked the distance from the bank to the house, getting angrier by the second at the thought of Aunt Cory walking nearly a mile each way. When she got to the house, she went straight to the garden. She'd guessed correctly and found Cory reading on her bench.

Cory kept her eyes glued to her book as Aggie paced back and forth, fuming.

"They called you?" Cory guessed shrewdly, breaking the silence at last.

"Of course they called me," Aggie said angrily. "What were you thinking? Walking that far? Where was Veronica? And what on earth did you need two hundred dollars for?"

Didn't Cory remember that the others had very nearly initiated a competency hearing to force her to relinquish the house? Didn't she understand that only Aggie's resistance had stopped them? That they had only relented when Aggie had agreed to be the co-signer on the bank account and had arranged for someone to look after her each day?

"I'm not a child, Agatha," Cory said quietly. "And I ran that bank for nearly forty years before it was sold."

Aggie stopped mid-stride, her mouth open in preparation for more scolding. Chastised, she sat heavily beside her aunt.

"I'm sorry," she said guiltily. "I just worry about you."

Cory closed her book and reached for Aggie's hand. "I know you do," she said, "but you need to remember that living so cautiously that nothing could happen to you isn't really living."

Aggie felt as if cold water had been thrown in her face. Was Cory talking about her own life, or Aggie's?

Ever since Rachel had left for a new love - "my soulmate," she'd said, leaving Aggie's heart shattered - Aggie had lived in a safe space consisting of work, straight friends, Percival and a ninety-something great-aunt.

"Do you have any idea what it feels like to have no spending money?" Cory asked, still holding Aggie's hand. "To have to ask permission to do anything? Go anywhere? It's been months since I've been anywhere but the drugstore or some doctor or other."

Aggie opened her mouth to respond, but Cory cut her off. "I know you agreed to be my keeper to keep the others at bay." She glanced sideways at her great-niece. "And I know you're paying Veronica out of your own pocket. You must be having a hard time making ends meet."

Aggie sat, her silence acknowledging the truth of everything Cory had said. "What did you want the money for?" she asked, abashed.

"I wanted to take you out for your birthday," Cory said. "They're doing *West Side Story* at the Ohio Theatre this October."

Aggie's eyes filled with tears. "I love *West Side Story*," she said softly.

"Surprise."

Aggie chuckled, wiping her eyes. "I'm sorry."

Percival trotted over, snuffling in concern as he placed his front paws on Aggie's knee. "I'm fine," she murmured. Reassured, he went back to chasing squirrels.

"What would you think," Aggie said hesitantly, avoiding Cory's gaze, "if I were to give up my apartment and move in here with you?"

Cory was quiet for so long that Aggie thought she must be angry or upset with the suggestion.

"You... you would do that?" Cory asked.

Aggie shrugged. "I pay rent for an apartment I'm hardly ever at. I could use that money to take care of some repairs around here. And if you needed to go somewhere - like the bank," she said pointedly, "I could drive you."

Cory laughed and then became quiet, pensive. "I wouldn't want you to feel trapped," she said at last.

"And I wouldn't want you to feel like I was invading your space," Aggie said.

*   *   *

Corinne walks into her bathroom and nearly breaks her neck when she slips on a towel left lying on the floor. Shaking her head, she hangs it on a towel rack. Glancing back out into the sitting room, she hardly recognizes her own apartment.

Cast-off clothing covers nearly every surface. Helen's suitcases lie open on the floor so that Corinne has to pick her way carefully to get to the kitchen without tripping. The kitchen itself is a disaster, with nearly every cup, plate and piece of silverware she owns littering the tiny counters and sink.

"Haven't you ever cleaned or picked up after yourself?" she'd asked Helen in exasperation about two weeks after she'd moved in.

"No," said Helen, sounding as if that were the most preposterous thing she had ever heard. "I've always had staff to do that."

"Well, I am not your staff," Corinne had said, picking up an armful of clothing and handing it to Helen to be put away.

Not that it does any good, she thinks now, shaking her head again.

With a quick glance at the clock, Corinne realizes she'll be late to work if she doesn't hurry. For Helen, getting to her new job on time seems to be the only thing she is capable of. She loves her exciting position working with one of the war offices, translating sensitive documents. "I can't tell you what they are," she'd said apologetically after her first week.

"I didn't ask," said Corinne stiffly, feeling a little put off that Helen found her new work so much more interesting and important than working in the census office.

Helen seemed to have realized what she'd done. She took Corinne by the shoulders and said, "I'll take you out to dinner with my first paycheck."

57

Corinne's face broke into a reluctant smile and she'd looked brazenly up into Helen's eyes, enjoying this game of flirting that they'd adopted. "Deal."

Standing in the shower now, she shivers in anticipation of their dinner tonight. The last couple of months since Helen moved in have awakened feelings Corinne has never experienced before. In such a small apartment, it has been impossible not to see things: Helen naked and damp as she steps out of the bathroom to dress in the sitting room; Helen peering into the bedroom and staring at Corinne as she lies there, pretending to be asleep. Corinne runs the bar of soap over her breasts and down between her thighs, and she feels again that tingle in her belly, and she knows that she wants to feel Helen's hands touching her in all those places.

Rushing about, she hurriedly picks up what she can so that there is a clear path for them to negotiate when they return to the apartment that night. Looking back, she blushes and smiles to herself as she realizes the path leads to the bedroom.

*   *   *

Cory smiled fondly at Aggie. "One of the best things ever to happen to me came when someone invaded my space. I'd love to have you live here."

Chapter 10

"Come on, you wimp," Ridley taunted. "Ten more."

Beryl grunted as she forced out ten more sit-ups before dropping back to the mat, wrapping her arms around her middle. "Oh, I'm going to die," she moaned.

"No, you won't. You're not that lucky," he said unsympathetically.

In response to her complaint about being fat, he'd said, "That we can do something about." He was training her, "Marine-style," he said. "No wussy machines. Push-ups, pull-ups, lunges, squats." Her body was screaming, but already she could feel a difference in the way her clothes were fitting.

Ridley was, literally, awe-inspiring. He cranked out twenty-five and thirty pull-ups, did push-ups balancing on his right foot and did a variety of abdominal exercises that Beryl could only dream of someday doing.

Sometimes, when he was exercising, she could see the glint of something in his eyes as he tried to work his body hard enough, make it hurt badly enough to drive out the things that haunted him. He'd shared only a few with Beryl: the twelve-year-old boy his patrol had watched drop to the ground in front of them, shot in the head by a sniper because he'd become friendly with the Americans; his buddy who'd been blown up by a female suicide-bomber pretending to be pregnant. "We found a few bits of him to send home to be buried at Arlington," he said.

But, most of the time, he was gentle and soft-spoken, more a librarian than a Marine.

"Let's call that auction house," he had suggested the day after their dinner.

Beryl dug around in her backpack and found the information Mr. Herrmann had given her. Ridley found the auction house listed on the internet.

"Here's the phone number," he pointed. "Call them."

Nervously, Beryl dialed the number from her cell phone. "Hello," she said when someone answered. "I don't know if you can help me, but I need to try and track down the origins of some items you auctioned back on..." she checked Mr. Herrmann's notes, "June 13th."

The person on the other end must have requested the lot numbers, because Beryl read them off, then there was silence for awhile.

"Oh, thank you," she said, and gave her name and cell number. She turned to Ridley. "They're going to have to research it and get back to me."

Ridley seemed as intrigued as she was by who Helen and Corinne might have been. When they had quiet moments behind the reference desk, which wasn't often, he enjoyed speculating about their story.

"Claire thinks I'm being foolish," she offered, "just making up a romance."

Ridley snorted derisively. "There's nothing wrong with romance," he said.

He didn't like Claire, but "he doesn't know her," Beryl kept reminding herself. "He only knows what I've told him." And she felt guilty about that. "What kind of person talks about the one they love?" she asked herself. "But do you?" asked that other insistent voice, the one Beryl wouldn't listen to.

The auction house didn't call back for three days. "It looks like those boxes as well as several other things were purchased by our buyer at an estate sale run by... Mattingly Auctions in... Columbus, Ohio," read the woman who called. "On March 20th."

Beryl jotted as the woman spoke. "Thank you so much," she said as the woman finished.

"So, another search," Ridley said, reading over her shoulder. "The mystery deepens," he said dramatically. "Let's call them."

"Later," she said, folding the paper.

"Why later?" he asked, puzzled. "Don't you want to find them?"

Beryl frowned down at the folded paper. "Yes, but..." How to explain that Corinne and Helen had become her lifeline, that she'd come to think of them as friends? What if Claire was right? What if the inscription hadn't really meant anything, and it was just a fling? Beryl wanted – needed – to believe it had been more, and part of her didn't want to know the truth if it hadn't.

Somehow, Ridley seemed to understand these things without being told. "How about you take me to The Scriptorium after our workout today?"

Beryl raised her eyes hopefully. "We could go instead of our workout."

He gave a bark of laughter. "Good try, Gray. But no. After the workout." He wheeled back over to his computer. "Unless you had other plans for later."

"No," Beryl sighed glumly. "I'm supposed to meet Claire for dinner at seven. That probably means Leslie will be there, too."

Ridley was quiet for a minute. "Where are you meeting for dinner?"

"A Mexican place near DuPont Circle," she said.

"Mind if I invite myself along?" he asked nonchalantly.

She looked over at him, immediately suspicious. "Why would you want to do that?"

He grinned mischievously. "Just curious to meet the great and terrible Claire." At the dubious expression on her face, he held up his hand. "I promise to behave myself. Marine's honor."

"Uh, yeah," she said skeptically.

If Beryl had thought Ridley would ease up on the intensity of their workout now that they had plans, she was wrong. By the time they were done, her legs were trembling so that she wasn't sure they would support her, but she couldn't even complain when Ridley growled, "Just be glad you've got legs to exercise." Even he managed to do more with one partial leg than most people could do with two.

He insisted on driving them to DuPont Circle. "This makes it a whole lot easier," he said, tapping the handicapped tag dangling from his mirror. He rarely used handicapped spaces on campus. "Don't need to," he said when asked why. "But in D.C., all's fair," he claimed as he engaged his hand controls to back out of his space.

Having found a parking spot less than a block from the bookstore, he pulled his crutches out and slung his messenger bag over his chest. As she'd known he would, Ridley loved the bookstore. Mr. Herrmann and George were charmed by him. In fact, Beryl caught George watching him covertly through gaps in the book-shelves, and she found herself wondering if Ridley was gay. For some reason, it hadn't occurred to her before. He'd never talked about dating anyone, or about any relationships at all, but she wondered now if that's why he seemed to understand her so well.

Mr. Herrmann found her in the fiction section while Ridley looked through history.

"So, my dear," said Mr. Herrmann secretively, "is this young man someone special?"

Beryl was so startled at the question that she didn't know what to say at first. "No! I mean, he's a friend. He's... he's my best friend," she realized. She couldn't remember the last close friend she'd had. Pre-Claire, certainly.

"I only ask because there is a certain glow about you today," Mr. Herrmann said, his eyes twinkling.

"It's sweat," Beryl nearly blurted, but, "He's just a friend, Mr. Herrmann," she insisted.

When they left the shop almost an hour later, Beryl with two books, Ridley with five, it was with a promise to come again soon. Beryl covered a smile as she saw George watching them through the window.

Ridley deposited his books in his car, deciding to leave it in its current parking spot and switching back to his wheelchair to travel the few blocks to the restaurant.

"Did you tell Claire I was coming?" he asked curiously as he wheeled himself along.

"No," Beryl said, "but we'll arrive first –"

"So we can dictate the terms of battle," Ridley finished for her.

She laughed nervously. "This is not war."

*   *   *

A couple of hours later, she wasn't so sure. Dinner had been – "a disaster," Claire would have said, "spectacular," Beryl would have said.

Ridley was gracious enough upon meeting Claire and Leslie, but for the remainder of their meal, he had focused solely on Beryl. *I think he's flirting with me,* she thought, blushing a little, but as she'd never had a man flirt with her, she wasn't certain. He engaged her in conversation, a rare occurrence as she usually sat, silent and excluded, while Claire and Leslie talked around her – "through me," Beryl had often felt.

Beryl could sense Claire becoming sulkier and it only seemed to encourage Ridley more. He avoided mention of their workouts – Beryl had wanted to keep those secret – but kept Beryl talking about the library, research, old books, current world events – topics that highlighted her intelligence and insight.

"He was obnoxious," Claire grumbled as she drove them home. For some reason, Leslie was still with them. She'd started going for the passenger door, but Beryl, newly emboldened by Ridley's attention, pushed ahead and beat her to it, leaving Leslie no choice but to get in the back seat.

I am not going to have this conversation with her sitting back there, Beryl thought. Aloud, she asked innocently, "Where are you dropping Leslie off?"

"I thought she could –" Claire began, but, "My car is at work," Leslie said moodily. "You can drop me off there."

Beryl could feel them watching one another in the rear-view mirror and resolutely turned away, staring out her window and holding tightly to how Ridley had made her feel. "Don't look," she said to herself. "Don't look."

*   *   *

"She didn't like me, did she?" Ridley asked with ill-disguised delight the next day.

"No," Beryl admitted. "Did you have to antagonize her?"

His expression became serious. "I'm sorry if I made things worse for you, but listen," he said, wheeling nearer to her, "don't you see? I didn't say anything unkind to her or Leslie. All I did was concentrate on you, and that, just that, was enough to piss her off. She wasn't the center of attention and she wasn't in control. And she didn't like it."

Beryl couldn't come up with a response. Everything he'd said was true.

"How do you handle arguments with her? The ones you win?" he asked curiously.

"I don't," Beryl said, startled at the question. "Claire always wins arguments." She shrugged. "She sees things, knows things. She's always right."

Ridley's expression was comical as he snorted in incredulity. "No one is always right. It's not possible to always be right."

Beryl looked down at her hands, her hair swinging forward. "Well, I still don't win arguments. It's easier to just let it drop."

Ridley sat back, his head tilted to the side in an expression of bemused disbelief. "You really don't see it, do you? You're brilliant. You're funny. You can discuss anything under the sun. You're ten times the person Claire is." Beryl reddened, but didn't say anything. "That's our next job – getting you to believe in yourself, Marine."

"I'm not a Marine," she reminded him.

"You'd have made a terrific Marine," he insisted, "in every way that counts. I'd have you cover my back anytime, Gray."

"Ooorah," she mumbled.

Ridley laughed and gave her an affectionate slap on the back.

*   *   *

64

Over the next days, Claire continued to denigrate Ridley every chance she got. Beryl didn't respond, though she felt disloyal at not coming to Ridley's defense. Part of the reason she never won arguments with Claire was that she'd learned long ago that arguing only made Claire dig in harder. Ironically, the more Claire tried to tear Ridley down, the less effect it had on Beryl. Ridley's words had seeded a kernel of something in her – a something that had taken root and provided her with a kind of shield she'd never had before. It was as if Claire's words simply bounced off. Claire seemed to sense this also, and changed tactics.

"I don't have anything going on the next couple of evenings," she said over a rare dinner at home with just the two of them. "I could come with you to your parents' for dinner this week."

Beryl nearly choked. "Uh, that's okay. I know you don't really like being around them."

Claire's eyes narrowed the tiniest bit, but her face, instead of becoming angry or upset, became mask-like. *She doesn't even know she does it*, Beryl thought, but it was her signal to tread carefully.

"You don't want me to come?" Claire asked.

Beryl paused. "Don't react the way you always react," she said to herself. "Why do you want to come now?" she asked. "You haven't come with me to see my parents for months. Not since Christmas, in fact."

"You're always after me to go," Claire said. "I just thought –"

"Where's Leslie this week?" Beryl asked unexpectedly.

It was Claire's turn to stammer, "Uh, her in-laws are visiting from Minneapolis."

"I see," Beryl nodded, and she did see, suddenly. Leslie was off with the husband, pretending everything was normal while the in-laws were around, and Claire now had time for Beryl. She picked up her dishes, carrying them into the kitchen.

"You never answered me," Claire said.

"Yes, I did," Beryl said. "I asked you why you wanted to come now, and you couldn't come up with a good reason."

"What's gotten into you?" Claire demanded as Beryl headed toward the stairs.

"Nothing," Beryl shrugged. But as she headed up the stairs, she breathed, "Ooorah."

Chapter 11

"**A**re you sure about this?" asked Aggie's mother, Debbie, as she carried an armful of clothes upstairs to Aggie's new bedroom.

Movers had the bedroom furniture in place in what had been Terrence's room.

"Yes, believe it or not," Aggie said, surprised herself. "It usually takes me ages to make decisions, but this one just fell into place."

Debbie pushed her hair back into place. She was not accustomed to exerting herself except on the tennis court. "Your father doesn't think this will last, not that his opinion matters very much."

Aggie had become accustomed to the sniping each of her parents took at the other since the divorce.

"But then where will you be?" Debbie persisted. "What if she has to go in a nursing home?"

Aggie looked at her mother, knowing full well that she had gone against her parents' wishes when she decided to stand up for Aunt Cory. "Then I'll get another apartment. It's not like I gave up my dream place to do this."

Debbie looked somewhat skeptical, though Aggie couldn't be sure, as her mother had had another Botox session last week. "Your aunt is... eccentric. Are you sure you want to be housemates with her?"

Aggie laughed. "This house is, what? Six thousand square feet? We could wander around for days and not run into one another."

"And," she added, leading the way across the hall to Candace's old room, "Aunt Cory suggested I put my other furniture over here to make my own sitting room. She said we're both so used to having our own space that we might as well spread out so we don't drive each other crazy."

Debbie fanned her sweaty face with her hands. "What are you doing about air conditioning?"

"That is one thing I insisted on," Aggie said ruefully. "I know Aunt Cory doesn't need it; she doesn't feel the heat, but I do. I bought two window units. They're ugly, but they'll make these rooms bearable."

She pulled a sheet from the laundry basket on the floor and her mother helped her make the bed. As Aggie turned to unpack a suitcase of clothes, placing them in drawers, Debbie wandered about upstairs.

"What's this for?" her voice called from down the hall.

Aggie found her in the room at the end. "This was Cory's old room," she reminded her mother. She ran a hand tenderly over the hand-embroidered upholstery of the rocker. "I think she likes to come up here and sit sometimes. Who knows? Maybe it'll be me doing this someday."

"Don't be stupid," her mother said crossly. "We're selling this money pit as soon as your great-aunt dies or goes to a nursing home."

Aggie turned back to the hall, clenching her jaw. *Don't argue with her,* she told herself. *It's not worth it.* But she very nearly fell over as her mother called after her, "And you need to get married. No man is going to want a woman saddled with an old relative."

Downstairs, Cory sat in the study, a book in her lap, the windows open as she listened to the footsteps upstairs. She smiled to herself. It had been a long time since she'd shared this house with anyone, and though she would never have admitted it to anyone, lest the others use it against her, she'd been lonely at times. This house was so filled with memories – "with ghosts, you mean" – that it surprised her sometimes to wander about and realize she was actually alone.

*   *   *

Corinne lies next to Helen, breathing heavily, their naked bodies covered in a sheen of sweat.

"What would your mother say about your, uh..." Helen searches for the right word, "your enthusiasm in the bedroom?"

Corinne laughs softly. "It's not a topic I plan on discussing with my mother," she says.

Corinne knows her hunger for Helen is a surprise – to Helen as well as herself. She thinks of her constantly throughout the day, feeling her body respond, the wetness down there at the thought of what is waiting when she gets back to her – "no, our apartment," she corrects herself.

Their first time, the night Helen had taken her out to dinner, Corinne was shy, not because she didn't desire Helen – she'd thought of nothing else for weeks – but because she was unsure of what to do. It was almost a relief to realize that Helen had done this before, though it made Corinne a bit jealous.

"There are advantages to going to all-girl schools," Helen had murmured, nibbling and teasing Corinne's body into a state of arousal she had not anticipated. *Not that I knew what to expect,* she thought later.

Corinne quickly learned how to please Helen in return. She rolls over now, tracing her fingers lightly over Helen's nipples, watching them harden at her touch.

"Stop," Helen says, chuckling as she holds Corinne's hand to keep her own excitement from building again. "I need to talk to you."

"What?" Corinne asks, resting her head on Helen's shoulder.

"You know that the British have already engaged the Germans and it has not gone well," Helen says seriously. "My supervisor believes we will be involved, fighting alongside the British, within the year."

69

"So?" Corinne asks, her heart beating faster.

"So... I may be sent to England to be a liaison between our office and theirs," Helen says.

Corinne's heart suddenly feels as if it has stopped – suspended in mid-beat – though she can still feel Helen's heart beating, slow and steady, against her ribs. Until this very moment, she has not thought except in vague terms about where the future might be leading, about what she wants for her life, but, suddenly, she sees with absolute clarity that what she wants more than anything is a lifetime with Helen.

She sits up. "Don't go."

Helen looks up at her, a thoughtful smile playing on her lips. "Don't you see how important this is?"

"What I see," Corinne says quietly, "is that I love you." She says these words for the first time and wonders why she hasn't said them before, wonders how she could not have known from the first moment she saw Helen flapping that wet umbrella that this woman would become her everything.

Helen looks up at her, serious again. "I love you, too." She sits also, taking Corinne's hand, "It's because I love you so much that I have to do this. The Nazis pose a very real threat to us." She holds up a hand as Corinne opens her mouth to protest. "I know people say the war will never reach us, but they're wrong. I saw signs of it when I was in Europe, and now, if you'd read and seen some of the things I've seen... the threat is real. It is coming. We must meet it, and not sit back passively."

She speaks with such passion and conviction that Corinne cannot argue. "When would you go?" Corinne asks, her eyes filling with tears.

Helen kisses her eyes tenderly, tasting the salty drops on her lips. "I don't know. Soon perhaps."

Corinne cries in earnest. "What if you never come home?" she sobs.

Helen takes her in her arms, pulling her back down to the bed. "I promise," she says fervently, "I will come home to you. No matter where you are, I will find you."

Corinne cries for a long time before she lies quietly in Helen's arms.

"And just think," Helen murmurs, "you won't have to complain about my mess for a while. You'll have the place to yourself again."

"I don't want to be by myself anymore," Corinne sniffs. "I'd gladly put up with the mess to have you here."

*   *   *

Percival trotted into the study and hopped into his dog bed, positioned near the hearth so he could see the chairs and keep an eye on the comings and goings here. Aggie and her mother followed soon after.

"Well, I think that's everything, Aunt Cory," Aggie said. "I just have to clean my apartment and I'm done there."

"Your landlord isn't giving you a hard time?" Debbie asked worriedly.

"No. I found an in-coming teacher who needed a place, so he's happy to have a new tenant." She sat in the other wing chair and said, "I hope you won't mind if Percival and I clutter up the house more than you're used to. You must promise to tell me if we're bothering you. This is your house."

"It's our house," Cory corrected. "And I learned long ago that a little clutter is a small price to pay for having people you love around you."

"Look at the time," Debbie said suddenly. "I have to go. My bridge club is meeting this afternoon."

"Bye, Mom," Aggie said as her mother blew her a kiss, "Thanks for your help."

She turned back to Cory as her mother left. "I've already talked to Veronica about taking July and August off until school starts again," she said.

"She's not upset, is she?" Cory asked worriedly.

"No," Aggie smiled. "She's going to look after her grandson, so she's glad of the break."

"A break from me, you mean," Cory said wryly.

"Yes, because you're such a pain in the a–"

"Watch your language, young lady," Cory said sternly.

Aggie grinned. "Anyway, she'll be back when school starts. In the meantime, I got someone lined up to come fix our gutters next week."

Cory caught the "our gutters," and hid a smile.

Chapter 12

The start of the second summer term meant less down time for Beryl and Ridley for the next couple of weeks. Every new term was crazy as students acclimated to new schedules and courses, but summer students were already oriented to the university, so life for the librarians was not quite as chaotic as in August.

During a rare lull in their schedule, Ridley turned to Beryl. "Come on," he urged again. "This is killing me. You gotta call."

"All right," she sighed. She found the paper with the Columbus auction house information and looked them up. Pulling out her cell phone, she dialed the number and inquired about the estate sale they'd held on March 20th.

"Oh, yes," said Mrs. Mattingly. "That was the Bishop auction. Sad, it was."

"Why sad?" Beryl asked as Ridley leaned close, trying to listen.

"Oh, the family has mostly died off," Mrs. Mattingly said. She seemed to be a bit of a gossip and was eager to talk. "A huge old mansion, in Bexley. Mostly empty now, except for the old woman who lived there. Never married from what I gathered, no children," she said, getting warmed up. "Only nieces and nephews now. One niece said the old lady wouldn't leave the place. She plans on dying where she was born. But she couldn't afford the taxes, so they had to sell off most everything. Oh, the things we sold: Tiffany lamps,

Chippendale furniture, Persian rugs. Even a Tiffany silver set – that went for thousands. Tons of books, too, but we weren't allowed to sell those. Well, a few got sold, but I expect we'll be going back someday for the rest," she said confidently.

"Is she still living?" Beryl asked. "The old woman?"

"Goodness knows. She must have been over ninety," Mrs. Mattingly said.

"You don't remember her name by any chance, do you?" Beryl asked, holding her breath.

"You're awful curious," Mrs. Mattingly said nosily.

"Well, I bought something I think might have come from that sale, and there was an old letter I thought the family might want back," Beryl fibbed. "So, do you remember a name?" she prompted.

"Oh, let's see... they all called her Aunt something... Aunt Carrie or Aunt Cody or some such thing."

Beryl's hand tightened on the phone. It seemed almost inconceivable that she could have found the Corinne of her book's inscription. "Thank you, Mrs. Mattingly. You've been very helpful."

She hung up and turned to Ridley who grinned and said, "Next stop, Bexley, Ohio."

A few hours later, Ridley was leafing through The Journal of Higher Education while Beryl did an internet search for Corinne Bishop.

"Nothing," she said, slumping back against her chair. "No telephone listing, no record of death, no property tax listing, nothing."

"Well," Ridley mused, only half-listening, "she could be in a nursing home or living with a relative by now, or maybe the house isn't in her name."

"I guess," Beryl sighed.

"Beryl," he said, frowning at the journal, "what's your doctorate in?"

She stared at him. "How did you know I have a doctorate?"

He gave her a rueful glance. "Research," he said, as if this should be obvious. "I am a librarian. I looked you up."

"Why?" she laughed.

He shrugged. "You know too much. Way more than I do, about everything. So I looked up your credentials. You finished your Master's in Library Science from Catholic University twelve years ago, and then you got your doctorate, but it didn't say in what. So... what's it in?"

"Medieval European literature. A highly profitable field of study," she said sarcastically.

Ridley frowned and shook his head. "What are you doing here?"

"What's wrong with here?" she asked defensively.

"Nothing, but," he stared at her, "it's like someone who trained as a surgeon doing family practice. There's nothing wrong with it, but you're not using your training. You should be working somewhere with rare books. I know you do research and appraisals for Mr. Herrmann all the time. Wouldn't you like working in a rare book collection?"

Beryl's face lit up. "I would," she admitted. "I was actually going to apply for a position with the Folger Shakespeare Library about seven years ago, but..." Her face fell.

"But what?" Ridley asked.

"Why would you leave Georgetown?" Claire had asked.

"This is a good opportunity," Beryl insisted.

"You've got job security, you work near your parents' house, we can take courses together," Claire pointed out.

Beryl frowned down at the curriculum vitae she'd been preparing. "You don't think I should do this?"

Claire came to her and wrapped her arms around her. "I just don't want to see you disappointed when you don't get it," she'd said.

"But what?" Ridley repeated, looking at Beryl sharply.

"I... I just decided it wasn't the right move," Beryl mumbled, avoiding his gaze.

"You mean Claire decided it wasn't the right move," he guessed shrewdly.

Beryl flushed crimson, but didn't say anything.

"Excuse me?" said a student, a freshman or sophomore by the look of her. *They get younger every year,* Beryl often thought. "Could you help me with –?"

Beryl jumped up, glad for the interruption.

Ridley chuckled and turned back to the Chronicle where he circled a job posting.

"Hi."

Ridley looked up.

Beryl returned to the desk a few minutes later. "George!" she said in surprise. "What are you doing here?"

"Oh, hi, Beryl," George stammered, nervously adjusting his glasses on his nose. "We got an inquiry on these books." He pulled a cloth-wrapped package from his backpack and held it out to Beryl. "Someone wants to sell them, and Mr. Herrmann was wondering if you would help us, so..." He burned so scarlet, he looked as if he might spontaneously combust. "I thought I'd bring them down to you for a change."

"Thank you," she said, accepting the bundle, and covering a smile as she noted that Ridley seemed a little flustered. "Was there anything else?" she asked innocently when George lingered.

"I... no," George said. "No."

"Please tell Mr. Herrmann I'll get back to him as soon as I can about this," she said.

"I will," George nodded, backing up and nearly falling over the returned book trolley. "Bye, Beryl. Bye, Ridley." He left with a small wave.

"Well, well," Beryl said with a smug smile, enjoying Ridley's discomfort for a change. "I don't think he came here just to drop off a book for me."

Ridley mumbled something indistinct and turned to his computer.

She pulled her chair close so she could speak without being overheard. "You are gay, aren't you?" she asked hesitantly. Sometimes with guys, it was hard to tell.

Ridley nodded.

"George has always seemed like such a nice guy," she prompted gently. "Do you like him?"

To her surprise, Ridley angrily whipped his chair around to face her. "Leave it, Gray," he growled before wheeling away.

Taken aback by the vehemence of his reaction, Beryl kept her distance, coolly pretending to be occupied at her computer when he returned to the reference desk.

"Sorry," he muttered after a few minutes.

She looked over at him. She'd never seen him this upset, but knowing him as she did, she said, "You owe me a beer."

His mouth twitched into a tiny smile. "Insensitive. Right."

"You know," he said several hours later when they were seated at the same booth in the same tavern they'd gone to before, "the people here are going to think we're a couple."

"Couple of misfits," Beryl agreed.

He laughed.

She leaned her elbows on the table, watching the foamy head of the beer in her glass. "So, what was going on today?"

When he didn't answer immediately, she pressed. "Are you with someone? You like the club scene? You took a vow of celibacy?"

"You're getting closer," he said wryly. Looking distinctly uncomfortable, he leaned closer. "I can't date."

She frowned. "What do you mean?"

Embarrassed, he glanced around to make sure he couldn't be overheard and said, "Taking a hit as high as I did... there was... collateral damage."

"Oh," Beryl said, embarrassed also.

"And with guys..." he struggled to explain, "it's sex first, maybe a relationship later."

At Beryl's dubious expression, he asked, "How long before you and Claire had sex?"

Beryl thought. "Two months, I think."

Ridley snorted. "With guys, it'd be more like two hours." He shook his head and took a long drink of his beer. "I'd have to get to really, really trust someone before..." He ran his hand agitatedly through his hair. "In bed, with no legs... and the nightmares..." He swallowed hard. "It's just not going to happen."

Beryl's heart ached for him. "It can't be like that for every man," she said softly. "You're a romantic. Look at your reaction to

77

Corinne and Helen. There have to be other men who feel the same way."

"Maybe," he conceded, "but where do you meet them?"

"I think you've already met one," she reminded him.

Startled, he looked at her. "You mean George?"

"Yes, George," she said. When he continued to look skeptical, she said, "What? He's not your type?"

Embarrassed again, he nodded sheepishly and said, "Yeah. To be honest."

"Listen, Ridley, I'm sure no one's expert on relationships, but if you want to meet someone who can look past the obvious and fall in love with you, you've got to be willing to do the same." She grinned. "Take it from a woman, if the feelings are there, the physical part will grow from that. And it will mean so much more than just sex."

He laughed to cover the sudden wetness in his eyes. "Do they give women a secret lecture about this stuff?"

She raised her glass. "It comes with the estrogen." But she couldn't help thinking how many months it had been since Claire had looked at her with any sexual desire and she felt like a hypocrite offering advice to anyone.

As if he had read her thoughts, Ridley said, "No, I think it's just Beryl," as he touched his glass to hers.

Chapter 13

Aggie startled awake. Lying in the dark, it took her a moment to realize where she was. Though it was her third night in the mansion, she had not yet become accustomed to the unfamiliar shadows and strange noises of the house.

Percival, she saw, was awake also. He lay near the foot of her bed, facing the hallway, his ears pricked. He didn't growl, though, and just as the AC unit cycled off, she heard soft footsteps. Aunt Cory. Aggie had never realized how often she came up to this floor of the house, but she'd been up the night before last as well.

She wasn't sure if Aunt Cory wanted solitude, or if maybe she was hoping for company. Quietly, she stole out of bed and went to the bedroom door which opened silently. Percival hopped off the bed and trotted down the hall to where Cory was sitting in her rocker, his nails clicking on the oak floors. *So much for being quiet,* Aggie thought as she followed.

"Are you all right?" Aggie asked softly, entering the room to find Percival sitting beside the rocker getting his ears scratched.

"I didn't mean to wake you," Cory said.

"I've been sleeping lightly anyway," said Aggie. "Still getting used to this house. You know, I realized, even though I've been coming to this house my whole life, I've never spent the night here until now."

Cory smiled and rocked.

"Would you rather we leave you alone?" Aggie asked.

"No, no," Cory said. She gestured to the window seat and Aggie curled up, hugging her knees to her chest. "It's silly," Cory said sheepishly, "but I like to remember the house as it was, when it was full of people and life. I think it was happier then."

"The house?"

Cory nodded. "There was a book, years ago," she mused, trying to recall, "about a family that belonged to a house, not the other way around. It felt like it could have described our house, our family."

She looked at Aggie, moonlight illuminating one side of her face. "I'm glad you're here, Agatha."

"I am, too," Aggie said quietly.

She hadn't really thought about it, but she did feel a connection to this house, a sense of stewardship.

"Tell me more about Helen and your time in D.C.," she prompted. "How long were you there?"

"Until after the war," Cory said. "The census work was winding down by the time America entered the war, but I wasn't ready to go back to Ohio yet. I got a job at the Navy Yard."

"Doing what?" Aggie asked.

"Building bombs."

"You're kidding." Aggie stared at her great-aunt, trying to picture her as Rosie the Riveter.

Cory smiled again. "I'm not. Our small hands could reach into tight spaces within the casings that men couldn't get to. And it paid a lot better than office work. Of course, it meant putting up with boorish behavior from the men."

"Did Helen work there, too?" Aggie asked.

A shadow passed over Cory's face, visible even in the dim light. "No. She was in England for most of the war."

"Doing what?" Aggie asked again, fascinated at this unknown chapter in her aunt's history.

"I never really knew," Cory said. "It was classified. She was fluent in French, so I always suspected it was something to do with the Resistance." She paused, lost in memories as she rocked. "I only saw her a few times during those years."

*   *   *

Corinne shuffles back to her apartment, exhausted after a twelve hour shift. The collar of her Navy pea coat is turned up against the bitter November cold. Everything she is wearing is men's clothing, oversized with cuffs rolled up, work boots laced as tightly as they'll go. It gives her the appearance of a child playing dress-up, an impression accentuated by her mussed blond hair and blue eyes. Wearily, she climbs the stairs to her apartment and unlocks her door.

Too tired to pull her blackout curtains, she doesn't turn the lights on. Dropping her coat on the couch, she goes straight to the bedroom, unbuttoning her shirt as she goes.

"Well, I must say, that's exactly what I was hoping for," says a familiar voice from the darkness.

Corinne gasps as the bedside lamp is switched on to reveal Helen lying on top of the quilt. Clutching the doorjamb to steady herself, Corinne whispers, "The curtains."

"I'll get them," Helen says, though she is reluctant to tear her eyes from Corinne.

"You're limping!" Corinne cries, rushing to meet her as Helen goes to the window.

"It doesn't matter," Helen says, taking Corinne's face in her hands and kissing her fiercely. She begins pulling Corinne's clothes off.

"I'm dirty," Corinne protests, "I need –"

"You're beautiful," Helen says, her voice husky with emotion, and Corinne sees what she didn't see at first, how deep-set and haunted Helen's eyes have become.

Corinne flings her arms around Helen's neck and kisses her desperately. A short while later, after they have made love, Helen is asleep, the impossibly deep sleep of someone who hasn't truly slept for a very long time. Corinne lies awake, watching her, afraid she will close her eyes and wake to find this was only a dream.

When Helen finally wakes, Corinne is dressed for work, eating a little before she goes.

"What time is it?" Helen asks groggily.

"Ten A.M."

Helen leaps from bed and nearly falls as her injured leg refuses to support her. "I have to catch my plane at two," she says.

"So soon?" Corinne asks in dismay. "You just got here."

"This trip was only to bring some documents that had to be delivered in person," Helen says. "I asked for the job so I could see you."

She sits on the couch and Corinne pours her some coffee – her last coffee, but she doesn't tell Helen that.

"Oh, my God," Helen moans, closing her eyes. "You have no idea how good this is."

"Is it very bad over there?" Corinne asks hesitantly.

Helen nods, staring down at her cup. "Bombings nearly every night," she says. "That's how I broke my leg. Got trapped under some rubble."

Corinne reaches over for her hand. "Can't you come home?" she asks, her eyes filling with tears.

Helen kisses her hand. "Soon. This war has been going on for two years. It can't be much longer now. It will be over soon."

*　　*　　*

"That must have been so hard," Aggie said softly.

Cory nodded. "It was for everybody. We all wrote letters, but they could take months to get through. There was no guarantee that anyone overseas would come home."

"I don't know if I could do that," Aggie said.

"You could," Cory said. "You're made of stern stuff, and you have a good heart." She looked at her great-niece appraisingly. "You deserve better than what she did to you."

Aggie's mouth fell open. "You knew about that?"

Cory looked at her sagely. "I knew. I don't know that anyone else did. Your parents see only what they want to see. But... I knew your heart was broken."

Aggie turned to look out the bay window, blinking rapidly. "It's been three years. I don't know if I'll ever let anyone else close enough to do that to me again."

"You will," Cory said, "when the right one comes along."

Chapter 14

Beryl caught a glimpse of herself in the mirror as she dried off. Normally, she turned from any mirror, especially in the bathroom, but today, she studied herself. She'd lost about ten pounds since beginning to work out with Ridley. She raised an arm – she could actually see some muscle when she tensed up.

Beryl had never been skinny or particularly athletic. Swimming was the only sport she'd really enjoyed. She'd always gravitated toward books, which also separated her from her brother and sister. She'd tried, briefly, to play some sports when she met Claire, but, "this just isn't your thing," Claire had said, not quite masking her frustration after the second time they played tennis together. "Play was not exactly the right word," Beryl would have said as she was more winded from chasing the mishit balls from neighboring courts than from actually playing.

Ridley's routine was working. She felt lighter and stronger than she could ever remember being. She looked at the new clothes laid out on the bed – the first new clothes she'd bought in ages. She was just fastening the button and fly of her pants – pants that fit a little more closely than her usual baggy khakis – when Claire walked into the bedroom.

She stopped and looked at Beryl, her eyes roving up and down. "Are those new?" she asked.

"Yes," Beryl smiled proudly.

Claire shook her head. "I'm sorry, hon, but they just don't look good on you. I don't want you to be embarrassed at work," she said as she went into the bathroom.

Crestfallen, Beryl pulled off the new outfit and dressed instead in one of her ubiquitous over-sized men's shirts and loose-fitting khakis. "That looks better," Claire said as she emerged from the bathroom.

When she got to the library a while later, Ridley looked up in surprise. "I thought you were going to wear your new clothes today?"

Beryl gave an embarrassed smile and said, "I didn't think they looked right."

He looked at her shrewdly for a few seconds, but she wouldn't meet his eye. "What did she say?" he asked.

"What do you mean?" Beryl asked with a telltale reddening of her cheeks.

"You know exactly what I mean," he said, turning to face her. "Claire. What did she say that changed your mind about those new clothes?"

Beryl stared at her computer. "She just didn't think they looked good."

"Bullshit!" Ridley swiveled Beryl's chair around to face him. "You wanted me to trust a woman's point of view on relationships. You've got to trust a gay man about clothes."

Beryl smiled reluctantly.

"Seriously," he said and she sobered up at once. "Claire is threatened by the fact that you're taking charge of your life and making changes. She's not going to give up easily, but don't let her sabotage this, Beryl. You've stuck with it for six weeks and it's paying off. You look great, and I think you feel better." He winked with a wicked grin. "And just wait until you see what I have in store for today's workout."

"Oh, great," she groaned, but inside she glowed with his praise and encouragement. She found herself even looking forward to the workout, *not that I'll tell him that,* she thought ruefully.

Later that day, as their shift was ending, Beryl was gathering up her backpack when Claire came into Lauinger.

"Hey," she said, approaching the reference desk.

"Hi," Beryl said, startled. "What are you doing here?"

"I'm going with you to your parents' for dinner tonight," Claire said.

It did not escape Beryl's notice, nor, she was sure, Ridley's, that Claire was telling her, not asking her.

"But dinner isn't for nearly two hours yet," Beryl pointed out.

"Well," Claire smiled, "we haven't spent much time together lately. I thought we could wander around some stores before heading over."

"Oh... um," Beryl stalled, torn as Ridley and Claire both waited.

"I'm heading to the field house," Ridley interjected. Claire had not even acknowledged him.

"I'll... I'll see you tomorrow," Beryl said, a blotchy flush creeping up her neck.

Claire ignored him as he wheeled away, but Beryl, as if he said it aloud, heard whispers of "sabotage."

Morosely, she followed Claire from store to store, mumbling responses to Claire's animated comments. If Claire noticed Beryl's sullenness, she was ignoring it. She was charming and talkative with Edith and Gerald over dinner. *She hasn't been like this for ages,* Beryl thought, watching her.

"That was nice," Claire said in the car as she drove them home. She reached over for Beryl's hand. "We should do this more often," she said and alarm bells went off in Beryl's head.

When she and Claire met, Beryl had been in the habit of going to the pool early most mornings and swimming a couple of miles. She'd never been lean, but the swimming kept her trim and reasonably toned and she liked the solitariness of swimming laps.

"Stay in bed with me," Claire had wheedled, snuggling up to Beryl under the covers. So, Beryl had switched to swimming after work, though it meant giving up her morning swim buddies. But after a while, Claire started showing up at work as she'd done this afternoon. "Let's go out to dinner," or "Let's go shopping," she'd said. Once Beryl had stopped swimming, Claire seemed to lose interest in doing those after-work things together. Beryl had berated herself a million times for giving up the one thing she truly enjoyed doing, but she hadn't resumed her swimming. Gradually, she gained weight and wouldn't even consider getting back in a swimsuit – "that's when I stopped looking in mirrors," she recalled, "and when you lost your self-esteem," Ridley would have said.

And now, Claire's showing up at work and preventing her from working out felt ominously familiar. "We should do this more often," meant, Beryl knew, "we should do this until you give up this exercising nonsense."

Beryl pulled her hand from Claire's. "No," she heard herself say.

"Excuse me?"

Beryl was nearly as shocked as Claire was. She braced herself. "I'm exercising with Ridley after work," she said. "Which you already know or you wouldn't have come by today," but she didn't say that. "It's something I want to keep doing," she continued aloud, "so... so things like tonight are not going to fit with that schedule."

There was a very tense silence for a few blocks.

"You don't want to spend time with me?" Claire asked at last.

"You only want to spend time with me to ruin this, like you ruin everything that's mine!" Beryl very nearly cried, but she stopped herself, knowing how childish that sounded. *Don't let her manipulate this*, she thought, calming herself before she responded. Clenching her hands tightly between her thighs, she said, "I want to be healthier." *She can't argue with that.* "You play tennis and that doesn't involve me," she pointed out. "We can spend time together after those things if you'll –", but she stopped abruptly.

"If I'll what?" Claire asked icily.

Do it. "We can't spend time together if Leslie's always around."

"Again with Leslie," Claire said waspishly.

"She was with us four evenings last week and all day Saturday after you two played tennis," Beryl reminded her.

"You're keeping count?"

Don't let her do this. "You're the one who just said you wanted to spend more time together," Beryl said as Claire pulled up to the rowhouse. "You figure it out."

She got out of the car and went directly inside where Winston promptly scolded her for getting home so late.

*　　*　　*

"I'm sorry about yesterday," she said brusquely to Ridley the next morning. "It won't happen again."

Claire hadn't said another word to her last evening or this morning, but Beryl was determined she would not back down.

"Okay," Ridley said, looking at her appraisingly. "Nice clothes."

Beryl's mouthed twitched into a pleased grin. She'd felt the unspoken criticism as she came downstairs defiantly wearing her new outfit this morning, but, steeling herself, she had gathered her backpack and left, not even staying for breakfast. She was afraid if she lingered even long enough to make her lunch, Claire would break her silence to begin criticizing her again, and Beryl knew she might not be strong enough to hold firm.

"What's this?" she asked, picking up a page torn from a journal and placed on her keyboard. Looking more closely, she saw, circled there, a job posting for an Assistant Curator in the Rare Books and Manuscripts Library at the Ohio State University.

She turned to Ridley, holding the page.

"What?" he asked innocently, shrugging his muscular shoulders. "It looked like an interesting position."

"I can't... what are you –?" Beryl sputtered incoherently.

"I didn't say you have to take it," he said, "but if you get an interview, you can do some on-site research."

Beryl looked at him blankly.

"For Corinne?" he said as if this should have been obvious.

She frowned. "We have no idea where she is."

He reached over and pulled the page from her fingers. "You know what, never mind. If you're willing to give up that easily, maybe you shouldn't apply. Some rare book historian you'd be."

He turned back to his computer, but grinned a couple of minutes later as Beryl sidled over and, tugging the job posting from under his elbow, took it back to her computer.

Chapter 15

"**O**h, my gosh!" Shannon exclaimed. "What in the hell was I thinking?"

She tried to brush her sweaty bangs off her forehead, but only succeeded in smearing paint which had splattered onto her forearms from her roller.

"You were thinking you'd be a good and faithful friend," Aggie said from the other side of the study where they were applying a fresh coat of a pale silvery blue to the walls and new white paint on the trim – the first fresh paint the room had had in nearly forty years.

Though the lack of furniture still made the mansion seem empty, newly painted walls at least diminished the derelict feel left by all the wall shadows and smudges where paintings had hung for decades on the now blank plaster, still punctuated here and there by hooks and nails.

"Fresh paint is easy," Aggie had said when she suggested it to Aunt Cory, "and it will make the house feel so much brighter. This we can do ourselves," she'd insisted, but, "I didn't realize how big these rooms are," she'd admitted to Shannon once she got started. "Fourteen foot ceilings and all the trim and mouldings."

Cory had helped wipe down all the woodwork and walls she could reach from the floor, but "no ladders," Aggie insisted, images of broken bones working their way into her head.

"No," Shannon recalled now, using a clean rag to wipe the paint smear off her forehead, "you plied me with three gin and tonics before you asked me to help. I wasn't in my right mind."

"You don't have a right mind," Aggie laughed.

"Very funny," grumbled Shannon, holding her roller handle like a spear as she took threatening jabs at Aggie.

"You wouldn't dare," Aggie said, but she didn't look so sure as she circled Shannon, ready to parry the attacking roller, though her only weapon was a paintbrush.

Just then, Cory walked in. "Oh, it looks so cheerful," she said, clasping her hands together in delight and pretending she hadn't noticed Aggie and Shannon threatening one another with their painting implements. "You girls are doing a wonderful job. How about some lunch?"

Shannon lowered her roller, beaming. "She called us girls."

Cory chuckled. "You could be seventy and you'd still be girls to me."

Aggie grinned as they wrapped the brush and roller in plastic wrap to prevent them from drying out.

Approaching the kitchen, they smelled bacon frying.

"BLTs," Cory announced. "My favorite summertime meal."

"It smells heavenly," Shannon said as she washed up at the sink.

"And I'm starving," Aggie added. "Even Dad won't be able to complain when he sees how much better the house is looking."

As they began eating, Cory said, "Your father is not happy about this arrangement, is he?"

Aggie took her time chewing and swallowing before replying, "No, he isn't."

"What the hell are you thinking?" Edward Bishop had said to Aggie the week previously when she had gone to visit him at his home in Muirfield. His new wife, Clarissa, younger than Aggie by five years, and already surgically enhanced in several places, had poured him a cold beer as he came home from his round of golf. "Not only are you giving that crazy old aunt of mine false hope that she can stay there," he'd said angrily, "but now you're throwing your money away on that dinosaur of a house. Money you don't have, I might add. She wasted all hers, and now she'll bleed you."

Aggie tried hard not to roll her eyes. Her decision to become a teacher had always been a sore point between her and her parents. "You could have done anything," had been a frequent refrain when she was in college and for several years after. "Your brothers were smart! They went into fields that pay, for God's sake," she'd heard time and again.

"I like spending time with Aunt Cory," Aggie said in her defense. "And that house is worth fixing up. It's your family home," she'd reminded her father. "Don't you care about it?"

Edward scoffed as he put his feet up. "This house is bigger than that one, and it's new. Why in the world would anyone want to hang onto something old and past its usefulness?"

Aggie stared at him and bit her lip just in time to keep herself from blurting, "And just when do you think Clarissa is going to find you old and past your usefulness?" She knew there was no way her brothers or their wives would take care of him or their mother if anything happened, and that they would expect her, as the only daughter and the one who didn't have an important job, to be the one to take care of them. *The hell with that,* she thought, watching Clarissa stroke his sweaty hair, what was left of it, off his forehead, and trying not to shudder in disgust. *You'd better have good long-term care lined up.*

"He thinks you're wasting your time and money here, doesn't he?" Cory guessed slyly over their sandwiches.

Aggie met her eyes and nodded. "Yes. But he's wrong," she said defiantly. "I don't understand how he can just walk away from this place."

"Ah," said Cory, her eyes growing misty, "some of that may be his father's fault."

"Grandfather Terrence?" Aggie asked in puzzlement. "How?"

*   *   *

Corinne runs through a freezing February rain, up the walk to the main entrance of Walter Reed General Hospital. At the front desk, a

93

severe-looking woman is typing something with several carbons, pounding the typewriter keys to make all her copies legible.

"Excuse me," Corinne says breathlessly, "can you help me? I just got this telegram..." She digs in her coat pocket and holds out a crumpled piece of paper. "My brother is here. Major Terrence Bishop."

The woman, looking irritated at the interruption, pauses her typing to consult a clipboard. "Ward 10, that way –" but before she can finish, Corinne is rushing down a long corridor, scanning signs, looking for Ward 10. Skidding to a halt outside the entrance to the ward, she sees a dozen white iron-railed beds lining each side of a long, dimly-lit room.

A white-capped nurse wearing a white shawl against the chill is sitting at a desk half-way down the ward.

Corinne, dismayed as she scans the beds, does not at first see Terrence among the occupants.

"May I help you, Miss?" asks the nurse in a whisper.

"My brother, Major Terrence Bishop," Corinne whispers back, her eyes brimming with tears as she fears the worst.

"This way," the nurse says, leading Corinne to a bed she's passed, not able to recognize the man lying there, most of his head wrapped in heavy white bandages, only one eye and his mouth exposed. His arms and torso are also heavily bandaged.

"Shrapnel and bullets," the nurse whispers. "He's sedated. I don't know if he'll be able to tell that you're here," she says kindly, pulling a straight-backed chair near, "but you may sit with him awhile."

She resumes her work, writing in the patient charts as Corinne sits and waits. From time to time, one man or another moans or shouts out, bringing the nurse hurrying over to whisper soothingly, sometimes offering an injection or a pill after which they quiet.

Dusk is falling as dinner trays are brought to the ward, and some of the men sit propped against pillows to eat. Others can't sit up, or can't bend casted arms to feed themselves. Terrence doesn't awaken.

"May I help?" Corinne asks, watching helplessly as the nurse tries to get to those who require assistance.

"Oh, yes, please," the nurse says gratefully. She looks about

Corinne's age. "If you could feed Lieutenant Cooper, in the bed next to your brother?"

Corinne turns to the man she'd had her back to and realizes, with a shock, that he has no arms. Fumbling in her embarrassment and uncertainty, she moves the dinner tray to the bedside table and asks, "May I help you?"

"You sure can, honey," the young soldier says with a rakish grin. Corinne pulls her chair near the bed as he sits up and wiggles his rear-end back so that he can sit against the bed's headrails.

Corinne hesitantly lays a napkin across his chest.

"Oh, come on closer, sugar," he coaxes. "It ain't like you gotta worry about wandering hands."

Corinne is so shocked that she drops the fork, its clatter echoing loudly in the room. He laughs, which makes Corinne blush even more.

"Lieutenant, please be kind," the nurse admonishes. "Miss Bishop has only just arrived."

The change in Lieutenant Cooper's attitude is instant. "Bishop? Terrence's sister?" he asks, looking abashed.

"Yes," Corinne says, retrieving a clean fork from the meal trolley.

He glances over at Terrence's still figure. "We were together at Anzio. He pulled me to safety. I didn't hear he was hit until later." He shrugs his shoulders. "Sorry about before."

Corinne holds out a forkful of beef stew. "It's okay," she smiles. "But something tells me my brother's going to have plenty of stories to tell about you when he wakes up."

*   *   *

"Poor Terrence," Cory said, dabbing at her eyes with her napkin. "He was never the same after the war. Father was so disappointed. He had counted on Terrence taking over the bank, but Terrence wanted no part of it. He said he'd seen enough of hurting people to last him a lifetime, and all he wanted to do was read or maybe work in a store somewhere. And that's what he did. Margorie, his wife, tried to make it work, but... she and Edward left within a year of Terrence's return home. I don't think Edward has ever forgiven his father for not having more ambition, not being ruthless enough to survive in business. Even as a boy, he had that hunger to prove himself, and he still does."

Cory looked at her niece. "You probably remind him too much of his father, being content to do something you love instead of something that will make lots of money."

Aggie sat with her head tilted to one side. "How could I live my entire life in this family and not know any of these things?" she mused. "Someone could write a book about this."

Chapter 16

"**M**r. Herrmann? This is Beryl. I have an estimated value on that trilogy," she said. "No, I'd rather tell you in person. Will you be at the store later this afternoon? Good... I'll see you then."

Ridley glanced over. "You sound like you're sitting on a golden egg."

Beryl grinned. "I am, kind of. This was Asimov's Foundation Trilogy, all first editions from the early 1950s. Should be worth somewhere between four and six thousand."

"You're kidding," Ridley said, stunned.

"For science fiction," Claire would have scoffed in disbelief.

"I'm not kidding," Beryl said happily. "These just rarely come up in this condition. So, if Mr. Herrmann can find a buyer, he'll get a very nice commission."

Ridley looked at her quizzically. "What do you get out of this?"

Beryl shrugged. "The thrill of the hunt, mainly. He always offers me books in trade, but for something big like this, he usually shares his commission with me."

"Mind if I go with you?" he asked casually.

"Not at all," Beryl said. "Claire's away at a conference this week and won't be home until tomorrow night, so we can grab something to eat, too, if you like." She tried not to think about the fact that Claire was at her conference with Leslie.

Ridley left the desk for several minutes to restack a trolley of books. When he returned, Beryl was sealing a large envelope.

"That isn't by any chance going to Ohio State, is it?" he asked.

"Maybe," Beryl shrugged with a sly smile.

"You're really applying?" Ridley asked in surprise.

"Just to see what happens," Beryl said noncommittally. "They probably won't call. I'm sure they'll get plenty of applicants more qualified than I am."

"I doubt that," Ridley said, "but if they do call, you'll have a chance to look for Corinne."

"I know," Beryl said, looking over at him. "I just hope she's still around to find." She dropped the envelope in the outgoing mail box.

Several hours later, Beryl and Ridley were heading toward his car.

"Oh, my gosh," Beryl grumbled shakily, "I can barely lift my backpack, my arms are so wiped out."

Ridley grinned wickedly. "Aren't arm workouts great?"

As he wove through traffic on their way to the book store, he said, "Beryl, I've been thinking about what you said... about dating and... relationships and... George."

She looked over at his hands clenched tightly on the steering wheel. "What would you think," she said, "if I were to ask George if he could join us for a bite to eat when we're done at the book store? That way –"

"It won't feel like a date," Ridley finished, relieved that she understood. "And then, I can kind of... see how it goes." He glanced over and said gratefully, "That would be great."

Mr. Herrmann was so pleased with Beryl's news about the Asimov Trilogy that he insisted on taking them all out to eat. Placing a small "Be Back Soon" sign in the door, he led the way to the Tabard Inn. There, they had an animated discussion that eventually got around to how George had come to work at The Scriptorium.

"After I got out of the Navy, I wanted something as far away from the military as I could find," he said quietly. "I wandered into the store and Mr. Herrmann and I started talking, and..."

"You were in the Navy?" Beryl asked, astonished that she had never known this.

George nodded. "Naval Academy and then fifteen years in."

"Then discharged, just like that," said Mr. Herrmann indignantly with a snap of his fingers. "Under that Don't Tell rule."

Beryl's heart lifted a bit as she saw Ridley's eyes meet George's in unspoken recognition. When she and Mr. Herrmann took their leave over an hour later, George and Ridley were still talking.

"Good night, my dear," Mr. Herrmann said with a knowing smile.

"Good night."

Beryl waited for a bus, feeling a nagging melancholy that she couldn't explain. It wasn't until she was nearly home and remembered with a guilty feeling of relief that Claire wouldn't be there, that she realized she missed the anticipation of coming home to someone who wanted to be with her, eager to share her day, having waited all day to hold her and kiss her. Ridley and George, if it worked out, were just beginning all of that – the thrill of discovering someone, finding out how much you have in common, the excitement of having that relationship in your life.

"You wanted forever," she reminded herself.

"I wanted happily ever after," herself retorted. "There's a difference."

Claire's car was parked in its usual spot in front of the rowhouse. She remembered that tomorrow was garbage day, and the car would have to be moved. Winston greeted her with yowls of hunger as she unlocked the door.

"Okay, okay," she said, patting him and trying to make her way to the kitchen without tripping over him.

A few minutes later, as Winston ate contentedly, she looked for a spare car key. It had been months since she'd needed it as she so rarely drove Claire's car. It wasn't in any of the kitchen drawers, nor was it on any of the hooks on the bulletin board. Claire used to keep a spare in her briefcase, though Beryl had no idea if it was still there. Retrieving the briefcase from its cubby, she carried it to the couch. There was no key in any of the outside pockets. She unzipped an inside pocket and slid her hand in. There was a leather key fob along with some cards. A few of the cards pulled out as she withdrew her hand with the key. One of them flopped open as it landed on the carpet.

As she bent down to pick it up and return it, her eye was caught by the words written inside – "your beautiful body" and "the way you make me feel" and "when you kiss me"....

Beryl clapped a hand to her mouth as she stared at Leslie's handwriting. Numbly, she opened and read the other cards to find more of the same. Her heart was pounding so rapidly it felt as if it had cramped into one sustained, painful spasm.

"Breathe," she told herself. She got up, the cards falling to the floor as she began pacing aimlessly, trying to force her brain to engage.

"How many times have I apologized?" she said out loud as she paced. "How many times has she lied to me? Insisted Leslie's just a lonely friend?"

Winston, who had been cleaning his whiskers, paused in his ablutions to watch her as she walked back and forth, muttering to herself, rubbing her knuckles against her forehead or clutching her hair with both hands. After several minutes, she paused her pacing.

"This is getting you nowhere," she said. "She's due back tomorrow night. Calm down and think."

But as soon as she stopped moving, her brain was immediately flooded with unbidden images of Claire and Leslie together and she began pacing again.

The room darkened as the late summer twilight fell, but she didn't notice. She was startled by the ringing of her cell phone. Half-afraid it would be Claire, she glanced at the screen. It was Ridley.

"Hey," she said.

"What an evening," he said happily.

"What?" It took several seconds to recall that she'd left him with George not even an hour ago. This interlude of shock and betrayal felt as if it had been going on for an eternity.

"What's wrong?" he demanded.

A wave of tears choked her unexpectedly and she couldn't answer.

"I'm only a few blocks away," he said. "I'll be right there."

"No, Ridley, I –" but he had hung up.

Within a few minutes, the doorbell rang. Beryl opened the door to find him standing there on his crutches. He came in and, bracing himself on one crutch, held her with his other arm as she sobbed.

When she quieted a little, she led the way upstairs. Turning on a light, she realized Claire's briefcase and the telltale cards were still lying on the floor. Wordlessly, Ridley picked up a few and read them.

Though his expression was sympathetic, he said, "If this was really a surprise, then Claire isn't the only one who's been lying to you."

Beryl blew her nose and dried her eyes. "I guess you're right. Part of me did know, and another part wanted to believe her lies, so I did."

He tossed the cards back to the floor and said, "Okay. So what now?"

"What do you mean?"

"You said she's going to be back tomorrow evening sometime." Beryl nodded. "So? Are you going to be here? Are you going to lock her out of the house? Are you going to make up? What?"

"I don't know," Beryl said, looking around in a stupor. "I can't even think."

Ridley watched her for a moment. "Take tonight," he suggested. "Call in sick tomorrow – I think you can truthfully say that. Think about what you want to do. If you want to leave, you'll have time to get some things packed. I can come get you after work."

"Tomorrow's Thursday," she remembered. "Dinner with my parents."

"Cancel," he said. "Unless you want to move back home?"

"Never," she said with a shiver of distaste. "They'd never let me hear the end of that." She could just imagine Marian's reaction.

"You can move in with me," he said. "I've got two huge bedrooms and two bathrooms. You can commute with me until you figure things out. No mess, though," he warned. "That place is ship-shape and I want it kept that way."

Beryl grinned sheepishly. "That's very generous of you, but I –"

"Hey," he interrupted. "Marines stick together. We never leave one of our own behind." He glanced back down at the scattered cards. "Unless you want to stay."

She looked at him gratefully. "Could you put up with a cat?"

Chapter 17

"You could just answer, you know," Ridley said as Beryl covertly peeked at her cell phone when it vibrated yet again.

She had finally turned the ringer off at Ridley's request as Claire began calling, seemingly as soon as she got home.

"You sure you want to leave those?" Ridley had asked after work on Thursday when he came by the rowhouse to get her. He nodded toward the briefcase and cards still lying on the living room floor.

Beryl looked around, and briefly considered how satisfying it would feel to trash the entire room, knock over all the dining chairs, leave all the kitchen cupboards hanging open and dump all kinds of stuff to dry in the kitchen sink.

"I'm sure."

To Ridley's surprise, Beryl had packed not only her clothes, which fit into two small suitcases, but she had boxed up all of her books as well. "I don't trust her with these," was all she said.

"You're not planning on coming back, are you?" he asked.

Beryl shook her head, but didn't trust herself to speak as Winston meowed piteously from his carrier.

As promised, Ridley's second bedroom was large and airy. Beryl stacked her boxes of books along one wall and still had plenty of room.

"I'll get those out of here soon," she promised.

"No hurry, Beryl," Ridley assured her.

His apartment was indeed immaculate. Located on the second floor of his building, it felt even roomier thanks to its sparse, masculine furnishings in contemporary leather and chrome .

Winston explored tentatively, sniffing everywhere. To Beryl's surprise, he leapt up into Ridley's lap and settled, purring loudly.

"It's official," Ridley grinned. "I pass muster."

"I guess you do," Beryl said wonderingly. "He's never that friendly with new people. He never did take to Claire."

"Good judge of character," Ridley said ruefully.

"Should have been a clue," Beryl realized.

To her surprise, she wasn't dissolving into a puddle of tears. *I think maybe I've been more prepared for this than I knew,* she thought.

She listened to Claire's messages, but wasn't ready to talk to her. "I didn't want you to find out like that," said one message. She sounded contrite. Another, "There are so many things we need to talk about; please call me." Still another, "Please don't throw away eight years."

"I'm not the one who threw it away!" Beryl exploded when she heard that one. "I was there, the faithful one, no matter what she did."

That was the thing that was actually bothering her as much as Claire's betrayal.

"How could I have let myself be so brainwashed?" she asked Ridley Saturday night, her third Corona in her hand.

"It happens," Ridley said philosophically. "We need to believe in the things we love. If they have faults, we can look past them. If they ask too much of us, we can accept that. If they betray us, we can forgive." Even through the beer haze, Beryl could hear the edge creeping into his voice, see the hard line of his jaw. "Up to a point," he added. "But then, they cross a line – a different line for each of us. Then you can't forgive any more. Then you've had enough."

"What happened?" Beryl asked in a hushed voice, knowing they weren't talking about Claire anymore.

"Same thing that's happened a million times before," he said harshly. "It was the early days after 9/11. We all naïvely thought we'd blow Bin Laden away and be home in a few months. We got a new commanding officer who thought he had some unique plan for success." His jaw worked back and forth. "He sent my unit back into a section of mountains perfect for an ambush. Only one road in... high cliffs on either side."

He shook his head. "We knew it was most likely a suicide mission, but... we were Marines. We loved the Corps. We followed orders." He pressed his fingers to his eyes as Beryl listened, horrified. "The bomb was just the beginning. A few of us were trapped inside the wreckage of our Humvees. The ones not injured in the blast tried to find cover, but snipers cut them down from the cliffs. We couldn't get a shot and we had nowhere to go."

His voice cracked as he said, "Eighteen went in. Only three came out." He scoffed. "I should say two and a half," he said bitterly.

He looked at her, his eyes shining. "I do understand how it feels to be betrayed by something you believed in."

Beryl sat helplessly, unable to speak. If Ridley had been a woman, pouring out such an emotional experience, she would have gone to her, held her, consoled her. But with Ridley, none of that felt right.

As if he had read her thoughts, as he so often seemed to do, he said, "You don't know how to react, do you?" Beryl shook her head. "It's okay. No one does. We're expendable. Penises and muscles. The only two things men are good for."

"Well, having no need for the former," Beryl said, clearing her throat to ease the tightness there, "I've always appreciated the strategic placement of fig leaves."

Ridley sat silently for a few seconds before he burst into laughter, shaking his head and wiping his eyes.

"I mean," she continued, "I can admire Michelangelo's David, but I don't want him in my living room."

Cracking up now, Ridley reminded her, "You don't have a living room. And I would love to have David in here. No fig leaf."

*   *   *

Beryl had a hard time remembering later how she got through that first weekend. She was certain she wouldn't have if it hadn't been for Ridley. Though she wasn't crying or blubbering, she felt physically ill. Ridley gave her time to herself, but made her emerge from her room to eat, saying, "Just a few bites. C'mon, I slaved in the kitchen for hours." On Sunday, he suggested a workout. I know you don't feel like it now, but you'll feel better after." And she did. A little.

When they got to work on Monday, Beryl still had not talked to Claire.

"Are you afraid to talk to me?" Beryl actually laughed late-morning when she heard that taunt on her voicemail. *I knew it wouldn't take her long to make this my fault,* she thought.

Ridley glanced at the clock. "Time for lunch," he said. Beryl opened her mouth to protest that she wasn't hungry, but he cut her off, saying, "You need to eat. Here." He wheeled into the staff office and produced a small sealed container from the refrigerator. "Some leftover lasagna. Go warm it up."

Beryl nodded gratefully and was just opening the container when Claire appeared in the doorway, having stepped uninvited behind the reference desk.

Ridley stood from his wheelchair and said protectively, "Showing up at work is below the belt."

Even standing on one leg, he was imposing and Beryl felt immensely glad of his presence. Claire looked at him, her dislike of him transforming her face into something ugly. *She blames him,* Beryl realized. It only lasted a moment before she recovered herself and turned back to Beryl, but Beryl had seen it.

"We need to talk," Claire said.

Beryl stood there for a moment, torn about letting Claire dictate when and where they would talk for the first time, but she said to Ridley, "It's okay. Heat up the lasagna. I won't be long."

She came around the desk and Ridley was glad to see that she took command, walking assertively as she led the way outside so that Claire had to hurry to follow.

Not wanting their conversation to be overheard, Beryl led the way to a nearby tree providing some shade in the continuing July heat.

"Can't we go sit somewhere cool?" Claire asked.

She's actually smiling, Beryl saw in surprise. "No," she said. "We're not going to be that long."

There was a bench, but she remained standing. "What do you want, Claire?"

Claire's smile faltered as she perceived that her charm wasn't working as it typically did. "I want to explain... "

"Explain what?" Beryl cut in. "How you've been lying to me for who knows how long? Explain why I was the one apologizing over and over again for suspecting that there was something going on with you and Leslie?"

"You misunderstood what you read," Claire said, grinning her crooked grin. "It was nothing..."

Beryl stared at her, not quite sure she was hearing what she was hearing. Those alarms were going off in her head, signaling one of those encounters where Claire would twist and smooth everything over in a way that would leave Beryl tongue-tied and unable to rebut.

"Don't let her do this!" Beryl cried silently. "Well, enjoy your nothing," she said coldly, turning away. "I'm not listening to anymore of this."

"What about the rent?" Claire called after her.

Beryl stopped and turned slowly. "Excuse me?"

"Rent is due next week," Claire said, that ugly something flitting across her features again.

Beryl felt as if she had never seen Claire clearly before. She laughed. "I suggest you ask Leslie," she said as she resumed her walk back to the library.

Ridley was waiting at the reference desk. "I'm fine," she said brusquely. "Let's eat."

As they waited for the microwave, Beryl's cell phone buzzed, indicating a voice mail.

"Oh, sorry," Ridley said. "I forgot – your phone rang while you were outside."

Frowning, Beryl listened, expecting to hear Claire's voice again. Her frown turned to an expression of incredulity.

"What is it?" Ridley asked.

"It's Ohio State. They want to schedule an interview."

Chapter 18

Corinne sits on the steps of the Lincoln Memorial, the collar of her coat pulled snugly around her neck, her face uplifted to the weak February sunshine as she enjoys a few moments to herself. After nearly a year at Walter Reed, Terrence is still recovering. He'd had many operations to remove most of the shrapnel and bullets, but "some are too perilous to go after," the doctors have said. "The pieces in his brain are in too deep." His head is misshapen, the right side caved in slightly where a large fragment of bomb casing had pierced his helmet and fractured his skull. The injury had paralyzed his left side, though "he's getting movement back with the help of his therapists," she wrote home.

Her work at the Naval Yard continues full-tilt. From all reports, the Allies have gained the upper hand and the Germans are on the defensive.

"At last, there's hope," Helen wrote in her last letter. Corinne pulls it out and re-reads it, though she has it memorized. "And we desperately need hope. Every time I look up to see our planes flying east on bombing raids, my heart rises, urging them on to bring an end to this God-awful war, but I wait to see how many will come back, knowing some won't."

Helen had been re-assigned to a new posting, somewhere "not in London," was all she could write.

"But through everything, the one thing I cling to, my talisman, is you – your love, your faith. If I didn't have that, I would have nothing," Helen wrote.

Corinne sighs and looks out at the reflecting pool before her, much of it still skimmed in a thin sheet of ice. Carefully refolding the letter, she presses it to her heart. She glances at her watch and anxiously scans the people below her.

Helen, in a rare bit of pre-arranged travel, is due in Washington today. She is to deliver some documents when she first arrives and then will have two entire days' leave before she has to fly back. Corinne has taken time off work, her first time off in over two years, as she reminded her supervisor when he started to object.

She nearly doesn't recognize Helen standing there, gazing up at her. *She's so thin,* Corinne thinks as she rushes down the granite steps to throw her arms around her, but Helen's thinness gives her face a more chiseled handsomeness.

"I can't believe you're here!" Corinne exclaims, holding Helen as tightly as she can. Though her appearance has changed, she still smells like a summer garden.

"I'm like the proverbial bad penny," Helen grins, pulling back to look into Corinne's eyes. "I keep turning up. Hope you don't mind."

Corinne has to fight to prevent herself kissing Helen on the spot. "No, I don't mind," she says, her eyes shining. "Where would you like to go? What do you want to do?" she asks as she picks up Helen's bag.

"Do you have to ask?" Helen says as her eyes drink Corinne in. "I don't know if I can even wait to get back to the apartment," she says, linking her arm through Corinne's as they walk.

Corinne notices that Helen has kept her limp, a remnant of the war that will remain with her for the rest of her life. As they walk, she tells Helen about Terrence. "I'll probably have to go home with him when he's released," she says, glancing worriedly at Helen. "Mother and Father came out to visit him at Christmas, with his wife Margorie, but... he wouldn't talk to them. I'm the only one who can do anything with him."

Helen doesn't answer. Corinne isn't even sure she's listening. When they get to the apartment, Corinne barely gets the door closed before Helen has taken her in her arms, kissing her hard. There is an urgency to her love-making, a desperation that makes her almost rough. Gasping, Corinne feels her body respond as Helen nearly rips her clothing off, carrying her along as Helen brings them to a crescendo that leaves them both spent and trembling.

Helen lies on her stomach, her face turned from Corinne who props up on one elbow, rubbing her back.

"You've been shot!" Corinne exclaims as her fingers probe the small indented scar over Helen's right shoulder blade.

"It's nothing," Helen assures her.

"They've been sending you on missions to France," Corinne says accusingly.

Helen doesn't answer and her silence confirms Corinne's fears, the things she has long suspected. Corinne gets abruptly out of bed, pulling on a robe, and goes out to the kitchen where she busies herself making coffee with the French press Helen had bought when she first moved in. "I don't know how Americans can stand this boiled sludge," she had said with a shudder of distaste when she had her first cup of percolated coffee. Corinne uses the coffee she has been hoarding for weeks, just for this visit.

Helen follows her out to the kitchen wearing only a chemise and underpants. Corinne turns her back, not wanting Helen to see the tears on her cheeks.

"I'm sorry I can't tell you more," Helen says. Corinne sniffs, but doesn't answer. "I'm not really in danger most of the time. I'm only a courier. It's not like I'm infiltrating Nazi installations," she tries to joke, but Corinne still doesn't respond.

She steps up behind Corinne, wrapping her arms around her and nuzzling into her fragrant blond hair. "It will be over soon."

"That's what you said two years ago," Corinne says angrily. "It's now 1945 in case you hadn't noticed, and the bloody war is still going on!"

She tries to pull away, but Helen holds her tightly.

111

"Don't be angry," Helen whispers, desperation in her voice. "I don't think I could bear all this if I didn't have you to hold tight to."

"Are you sure I'm the only one you're holding tight to?" Corinne asks, knowing it sounds childish, but unable to stop herself.

She turns and, for the first time since she has known Helen, she sees tears in her eyes.

"I'm sure," Helen whispers. She blinks, brushing a hand over her eyes. "I have something for you," she says brightly, changing the subject. She limps to the couch and retrieves a small package from her purse. "I passed this quaint little bookstore run by an old man from Budapest," she says. "And I found this. This is by one of my favorite authors. Happy Valentine's Day."

Corinne's throat is tight as she says, "I don't have anything for you."

"You are my Valentine's present," Helen says.

Corinne holds the little book out. "I want you to inscribe it."

*   *   *

Percival sat up suddenly down at the foot of the bed. Groggily, Aggie woke, watching his scruffy head tilt from side to side as he listened to something she couldn't hear.

She glanced at the bedside clock and saw that it was five A.M.

"I am going to start locking her in her bedroom," she groaned as she threw the covers back. "Come on."

Percival hopped off the bed and waited for Aggie to open the door. When she did, to her surprise, he did not go down the hall to Cory's old room as she expected, but went the other way, down the stairs.

Aggie followed him and as she came down the curving expanse of the staircase, she saw light thrown out into the foyer from the study. There, she was surprised to find Aunt Cory up on the library ladder in her nightgown and slippers, shuffling through the books there. Small piles of books were scattered about on the floor.

Speaking calmly so as not to startle her aunt, Aggie said, "Is there something I can help you find?"

As if she hadn't heard, Cory was muttering, "I've lost it. I've lost it," as she slid books to one side, scanning each one as she did so.

Worried now, Aggie said, "What have you lost, Aunt Cory? Let me help you look."

"The book," Cory said, almost frantically. "The book about the house."

"I remember you telling me about it," Aggie said. "We'll find it. Come down, please, and I'll help you look."

Cory blinked down at her, seeming to just realize she was there. Slowly, she descended the ladder.

"How long have you been looking?" Aggie asked, looking around the room at all the displaced books.

"I don't know," Cory said, wringing her hands and looking near tears.

Aggie wrapped a protective arm around Cory's thin shoulders. "Let's get some breakfast, and then we'll start looking again," she suggested.

In the kitchen, Cory still seemed agitated and a little confused. Aggie kept glancing at her as she got the coffee going and pulled out a griddle.

"I'm losing track of the days now that I'm out of school," she said. "What do we have going on today?"

"It's Tuesday," Cory said at once. "You said you would help me trim the hedges today."

"Oh, that's right," Aggie said, breathing a sigh of relief as Cory calmed down. She cooked up a batch of pancakes for them and set a plate in front of Cory as she took her own seat.

"So, what made you think of this book all of a sudden?" Aggie asked as she poured syrup over her pancakes.

"I dreamed about it," Cory said.

"You dreamed about a book?"

Cory ate a bite of her pancakes before saying, "I dreamed about the day Helen gave it to me. I realized I hadn't seen it in a long time."

Cory looked askance at her niece. "I'm not losing it."

"Yes, you are," Aggie said. "You just told me you lost it." Her joke was rewarded with a smile from Cory. She reached out to lay a hand on her aunt's arm. "I can understand being upset at losing something that was really special. Don't worry, we'll find it."

They spent the remainder of the day searching methodically through the bookcases in every room of the house. Cory couldn't remember the title, but "you'll know it by the inscription," she insisted.

But by the end of the day, Aggie had to admit the book was nowhere in the house. "It must have been in the books that got sold at the auction before we stopped them," she said apologetically.

"It doesn't matter," Cory said, but she seemed distraught at the loss.

Late that night, Aggie heard her going down the hall to her old room. "Let's leave her be for tonight," she murmured to Percival.

Chapter 19

"What do you mean you won't be here this weekend?" Edith asked.

When Beryl had returned the call to Ohio State, they had wasted no time in scheduling her interview.

"I know this is short notice," said Dr. Bartholomew Hudspath, the head of the Rare Books and Manuscripts Library, "but could you be here this Friday? Your qualifications are just what we were hoping to find in a candidate."

"I... I think so," Beryl stammered.

She'd gone to her supervisor to request the time off while Ridley did an internet search for flights to Columbus. She chose one from his list that would leave at a reasonable hour on Thursday morning and get her back to National Airport Sunday afternoon. "I still can't make myself call it Reagan," she muttered as she clicked through the reservation links.

"Staying until Sunday is good. You'll have extra time for some detective work," Ridley said with a wink.

"Now, I have to face my mother," Beryl said, not looking forward to this at all.

"You do remember we're celebrating your nephew's birthday this Saturday, don't you?" Edith asked when Beryl stopped by after work on Tuesday.

"That's why I'm dropping off a card and present today," Beryl explained patiently.

"I don't understand," Edith persisted as she resumed icing a cake. "You've never been to a conference before."

"I don't want to tell anyone it's an interview," Beryl had said to Ridley.

"Well, I'm going to one now," she said to her mother.

"This seems very last minute," Edith said, clearly suspicious.

"The opportunity came up at the last minute," Beryl said, a trifle impatiently. "Why are you giving me a hard time about this? Nick and Marian always have things come up and can't come to some function or other. You don't argue with them."

"I'm not arguing with you," Edith argued. "Besides, that's different."

Thursday morning, as they ate an early breakfast, Ridley insisted once again that he would drive Beryl to National to catch her flight.

"I can take a cab," she protested.

"I want to do this," he said.

"You're sure you don't mind looking after Winston?" she asked worriedly.

"We're buds now," he grinned. "We'll be fine. Unless you'd rather take him to Claire."

Beryl's expression darkened. "It seems impossible it's only been a week," she said.

Ridley's eyes narrowed. There had been moments when he could sense Beryl's resolve wavering. "It hasn't been a week; it's been months," he reminded her. "It's only been a week since you said, 'enough'."

The previous day, a card had come to Beryl in the campus mail. It was beautiful, full of emotional sentiments of love and forgiveness. Claire had signed it, "I'll never stop loving you."

"What?" said Ridley when Beryl passed it to him to read. He tossed it back to her. "You're not falling for this, are you?"

Beryl didn't know how to answer. She couldn't honestly say she still loved Claire, but, "I promised. I said forever," some stubborn part of her kept insisting.

When she admitted those doubts to Ridley, he said, "She knows you. She knows how to work you." When she didn't look convinced, he said, "She's all sentimental and sorry now. And it'll last precisely as long as it takes to get you back. Then she'll start taking you for granted and treating you like shit again."

"Maybe I shouldn't go on this interview," Beryl worried as they left the apartment Thursday morning. "This is all happening so quickly..."

"The timing is perfect," he countered. "You're not tied to anything here. Except me, of course," he added with a grin.

Traffic was heavy getting to the airport. Ridley kept quizzing her as they crept along, "Got your directions and maps? And your suit for the interview?" He had talked her into shopping for a new suit, something professional. "The new Beryl is going on this interview, not the old one," he'd reminded her. He tilted his head as they left the store, garment bag in hand, scrutinizing her. "And I think a haircut would be a good idea, too."

Beryl nearly panicked. "My hair is fine."

"Not so much," he said not so gently. "You use your hair as camouflage when you want to hide from people. No more hiding, Gray."

"I feel naked," she'd grumbled an hour later, as she left the hair salon with her hair shorter than it had been in years, but he grinned as he caught her appraising her image in mirrors as she passed. Not that she'd admit it to Ridley, but this looks better, she thought grudgingly.

"Got the book?" he asked as he pulled into the drop-off lane outside the terminal.

Beryl patted her backpack as she opened the car door.

"All right. Go get 'em, Marine," he said, offering her, not a hug, but a fist bump.

"Ooorah," they said at the same time, laughing as she waved him off.

*   *   *

She was in Columbus by lunchtime. She found the car rental kiosk at the Columbus airport and, ditching the rental's GPS after it sent

117

her the wrong way on I-670, pulled out the maps Ridley had printed for her off the internet. Eventually, she found her way to the hotel where the university had reserved a room for her for Thursday and Friday nights.

"Plan on being here all day Friday for the interview," Dr. Hudspath had said over the telephone.

"I may need to stay an extra night, at my expense," Beryl told the young man at the reception desk.

"No problem, Dr. Gray," he said with a smile as she did a double-take. It caught her by surprise to be addressed by her title.

She dropped her bags off in her room and went to explore a bit of the campus on foot. She found the Thompson Library and grinned at the irony that the oldest and rarest books on campus were housed in one of the most modern buildings, its bowed glass façade reflecting the brilliant summer sky.

Once she was confident she knew where she was to report the following morning, Beryl's thoughts turned to Corinne Bishop. She walked back to the hotel where her rental car was parked, and, consulting her map again, she headed toward Bexley, now engulfed by the larger city of Columbus. She found parking on Main Street and wandered around the quaint downtown area.

Curiously, Beryl explored the shops, searching for one which looked as if it had been around long enough for the owners to know the history of the area. She went into an antique shop and made some inquiries, but the owners had only been there a couple of years and didn't know the name Bishop. As she exited, she nearly ran into a blond woman walking arm in arm with a thin elderly woman.

"I'm so sorry," she mumbled, and continued down the sidewalk. She turned to look again at the blonde, and was mortified to find her looking back also. Red-faced, but smiling to herself, Beryl made her way across the street.

Spying a barber shop which looked as if it had been around for the last hundred years, Beryl ducked inside and felt as if she had stepped into another era. Only one man was in a chair getting a haircut, but four others sat along the wall, holding magazines or newspapers. All of them, the barber included, were elderly gentlemen who looked up in surprise as she entered.

"Hello," she said uncertainly.

"Hello," came a chorus from the men.

"I was wondering if you could help me?" she said. "I'm looking for a family that, I think, has been in the Bexley area for a long time. The Bishops?"

Beryl had expected nothing more than blank stares, so she was more than surprised when all the men broke out at once with reminiscences of the Bishop family.

"I knew poor Terrence Bishop. Remember him at Long's Hardware?"

"I worked there as an assistant gardener when I was a kid."

"Who's in the house now? Anybody know?"

"Terrence's sister, I think."

"My aunt was one of their cooks."

Excitedly, she interrupted them to ask, "Could you tell me where the house is?"

Again, she got a chorus of conflicting directions as all the men tried to be helpful, but finally, the barber stepped forward and gave her definitive directions. "You're only four blocks away. Go to the next corner, turn right and straight ahead three blocks, then left one block," he said, pointing her in the right direction.

"Thank you so much," she said gratefully.

Beryl decided to leave her car where it was and walk. The barber's directions were good, and in a few minutes, she was standing on the sidewalk at the entrance to a long drive flanked by stacked-stone walls that extended along the sidewalk in either direction to the borders of the property. The drive curved around a large oak tree blocking her view of the house. She was surprised at how her heart was pounding at the thought that she had at last discovered Corinne's home.

A car beeped behind her, scaring her to death. Beryl jumped aside in time to see an older Honda pulling into the lane as the driver, a blond woman, stared at her curiously. Someone was in the passenger seat, but she couldn't get a clear view of that person.

Embarrassed to be caught standing there like a voyeur, Beryl hurried away.

"Who was that person?" Cory asked as they pulled into the drive.

"I have no idea," said Aggie. "But we saw her. On Main. She almost ran into us. Probably just someone curious about the haunted house."

"If the house is haunted, you realize what that probably makes us," Cory quipped.

Aggie laughed. "Okay, I'll have to rephrase." She parked the car. "Are you okay getting inside? I want to go see if she's still standing there."

She jogged quickly back down the driveway, scanning the sidewalk in both directions, but the woman was nowhere in sight.

"That's curious," she muttered. It took her a second to realize she was disappointed.

*　　*　　*

"What do you mean you found the house?" Ridley asked excitedly later that evening when Beryl called him. "Did you go up to the door? Speak to anyone?"

"No," she admitted sheepishly. "I was standing in the entrance to the driveway and almost got run over by a car pulling in, and then I scurried away."

"You scurried?" Ridley laughed, trying to picture this.

Beryl heard another voice in the background. "Do you have someone over?" she asked.

Ridley was quiet for a few seconds and then said, "George is here."

Beryl's mouth fell open in surprise. "Oh, well... tell him I said hello."

"It's not what you think," he said in such a low voice that Beryl had a hard time hearing him. "We're just going out for dinner."

"I'd... I'd better let you go, then," she stammered.

"Would you mind if I tell him about our quest?" Ridley asked in a more normal tone.

"No," she said. "I'll keep you posted."

"Call me tomorrow after the interview," he said. "I want to hear all about it. Good luck."

"Thanks. Talk to you tomorrow. Bye."

Beryl felt a tumult of mixed emotions as she hung up. Ridley had been her lifeline these past weeks and through all the crap with Claire. She hadn't realized how much she had come to count on him being there. If he and George became a couple, that would change... It always did.

She pulled down the covers on the bed and settled back to watch some television. She had no idea how to prepare for the interview, not really knowing what they would want to talk to her about as she had no actual experience working with a rare book collection. Really, besides her doctorate and library work, her only practical experience was her research and appraisal work for Mr. Herrmann.

Her cell phone rang unexpectedly. Expecting to hear Ridley asking some forgotten question, she answered without looking at the display.

"Hi," came Claire's voice.

"Hi," said Beryl automatically as she groaned internally, cursing herself for not looking.

"Did you get my card?"

"Yes." Beryl closed her eyes, trying to bolster her resolve, picturing Ridley mouthing reinforcements.

"Can we meet and talk?" Claire asked.

Beryl was quiet for several seconds. "We really have nothing to talk about."

"I don't think that's you talking," Claire said. "That's Ridley."

"Why don't you think it's me?" Beryl asked, getting a little angry.

"Because you're always willing to talk things over," Claire said warmly. "That's one of the things I love about you."

Don't let her do this, Beryl thought. Aloud, she said, "Well, maybe you should have been more willing to talk back when I wanted to – before you cheated."

She expected an angry outburst from Claire, and was surprised when Claire was quiet for a few seconds before saying in a conciliatory tone, "You're right. I was... I've been so confused. I don't know why I did what I did."

This was not going well. Beryl knew she had never been able to stay angry if Claire backed down. She had told Ridley she never won arguments, and this was one of the reasons why. It had become one of Claire's strategies to get around her, and, though Beryl had seen it, knew Claire used it when she needed to, she had never been able to muster enough righteous anger to hold her ground. *That's probably the only reason we stayed together for eight years,* she thought as all these things ran quickly through her head.

"Where are you staying?" Claire asked as she sensed Beryl's weakening and pressed her advantage. "I can come to you."

"NO!" Beryl nearly shouted. Staying with Ridley had felt safe precisely because Claire didn't know where she was, couldn't just show up unannounced. And she certainly wasn't going to tell Claire where she was at the moment, or why. Taking a deep breath to calm herself, she said, "Claire, I do not want to see you. I do not want to talk to you." She looked down and saw how tightly her fist was clenched. Giving up on calm, she said firmly, "I'm going to hang up now. Please don't call back."

She could hear Claire's voice protesting as she pressed the button to end the call. She immediately silenced her ringer and set the phone on the bedside table along with her glasses.

Slowly, she sank down into the pillows as tears came, unbidden and unwelcome. *What am I doing here?* she asked herself, feeling utterly alone and lost as she sobbed for the first time since the night she had found the cards in Claire's briefcase.

She very nearly packed up and left that night, sorely tempted to run back to D.C. as fast as she could. The only thing that prevented her from calling the airline was the thought of leaving Dr. Hudspath hanging after he had been so kind to her when they arranged the interview. That and facing Ridley.

*   *   *

"Well?" Ridley demanded Friday evening. "Tell me everything."

Beryl decided not to tell him about Claire's phone call. Or the crying. Or the sleepless night that followed as she checked the clock nearly every hour, afraid she would sleep through the alarm. When she did sleep, it was with disturbing dreams about Claire... dreams in which she stood there hurt as Beryl shouted and cursed at her until Claire turned and walked into a house where Leslie closed the door in Beryl's face....

"I think it went well," she said. "I met with the Rare Book faculty and staff throughout the morning, then had meetings with a dean and someone from HR in the afternoon. They showed me around campus. Oh, Ridley, you wouldn't believe the collections they have, and some of the medieval prayer books and manuscripts," she moaned. "They call me Dr. Gray," she added with a delighted giggle.

"Well, of course they do," he said, and she could picture him shaking his head. "We should all be calling you that."

"I've just never..."

No one had called Beryl by that hard-won title – not Claire, not her family. Her family had given her the barest nod of acknowledgement when she completed her degree, and that was the end of it. Claire, when she learned that Beryl had a doctorate, had only talked more about her own master's and how she might pursue a doctorate one day.

"You sound like this is something you would like," Ridley said, snapping Beryl back to the present.

Beryl bit her bottom lip. "I think I would," she admitted for the first time, not having wanted to get her hopes up. Echoes of Claire's old warning, "I don't want you to be disappointed when you don't get it," had played over and over in her head, keeping her from acknowledging, even to herself, how much she wanted to be offered this job.

"Of course, being offered the position and accepting it are two different things," she said, but only to herself. She would think about that later.

Chapter 20

Beryl woke Saturday morning, determined to make contact with the inhabitants of the Bishop house. Part of her resolve was due to having watched *Sleepless in Seattle* in her hotel room the night before, thinking how like Meg Ryan she would be if she went back to D.C. without having even said hello.

"I don't think Ridley would get it," she chuckled to her reflection as she dried her hair.

She decided to drive back to Bexley and have breakfast at a restaurant there before going to the house. She lingered over breakfast, having a third cup of coffee before paying her check and walking out into the bright August morning.

As she had the last time, she walked the few blocks to the Bishop house. Peering around the corner of the stone wall as she stood on the sidewalk, she saw no traffic in the lane, and no signs of movement in the bit of the yard that she could see. Taking a deep breath, she entered the gravel lane. As she walked, she took in the huge old trees, their canopies providing deep shade for large clumps of rhododendron and hostas and hellebores, the spaces between them filled with an enormous variety of ferns, some of which Beryl had never seen before.

As she rounded the oak tree she had seen from the sidewalk, she got her first glimpse of the house and stopped dead in her tracks for a moment. It was enormous, made of brick, but as she got closer, she could see that the brickwork around the windows and chimneys was laid out in intricate patterns she doubted any bricklayer could duplicate now. She noted the shiny, new copper gutters and saw some scaffolding set up where it looked as if some roof repairs were ongoing. A deep covered porch seemed to wrap all the way around the house.

A brick walk veered off to the right, heading as if it led to the front door, though its path was obscured by overgrown hedges, while the drive continued around to the back of the house. Beryl decided to follow the drive, and came around to a door on the back porch of the house. Off to one side, she saw a garage, but no car. Stepping nervously up to the screened door there, she raised her hand and knocked.

*   *   *

"What do you mean you had a visitor?" Aggie demanded when she got back from doing some shopping with Shannon. "Who was it? What did they want?"

Cory smiled a bemused smile and said, "I think we'll find out tonight. I invited her back for dinner."

"You what?" Aggie nearly shouted. "Who did you invite for dinner?" She was totally confused and was worried that Cory had done something foolish. She looked around quickly. "Was this person in the house? Are you sure they didn't take anything?"

"Agatha, sit down," Cory said calmly. "You're getting all worked up for nothing."

Aggie took a deep breath and sat down. "All right," she said, holding both hands up. "I'm sitting. Now, start at the beginning and tell me what happened."

"Well," Cory smiled, "there was a knock at the back door. I thought it was one of the workmen, but when I answered, it was a young woman. She asked if she had the Bishop house, and when I said she had, she looked so happy. She asked me if I was Corinne."

"What?" Aggie asked again. This was so weird. She frowned. "How did she know your name?"

"I don't know," Cory said, looking totally unconcerned. "When I asked her that same question, she said she had something of mine and asked if I would mind if she came back later today to return it to me. So, I invited her for dinner."

Aggie sat with her mouth open, staring at her aunt. "You invited a total stranger for dinner? Just like that?"

Cory nodded happily. "Just like that. I had a good feeling about her. And she's not a stranger. Her name is Beryl."

*　　　*　　　*

Beryl nearly ran back to her car. She'd found Corinne! Oh, she couldn't wait until tonight to tell Ridley. She drove back to her hotel, feeling so energized that she changed and headed out for a run around campus.

I couldn't have done this two months ago, she thought proudly as she jogged along easily.

She couldn't believe she'd been invited back for dinner tonight. Dinner with Corinne. "Please be the woman I've believed you to be," she breathed in rhythm with her footsteps.

Wine. She would pick up a nice bottle of wine to bring tonight. She wondered who the blonde was that she had seen with Corinne. Smiling to herself, Beryl hoped she'd be there tonight, too.

By six o'clock that evening, she was back at the Bishop house, freshly showered and refreshed from a much-needed nap. She had dressed carefully, wearing some of the newer, closer-fitting clothes Ridley had helped her pick out. This time, she drove to the house, parking along the curb out front. It seemed impertinent somehow, overly familiar, to drive down the lane to the back door. "Just because you feel like you know her, doesn't mean you do," she reminded herself. She paused as she walked up the drive, her backpack hanging from one shoulder, unsure whether to take the brick walk to the front door or continue around back. She finally decided on the front door.

Pushing her way through the overgrown boxwoods and yews, she followed the brick walk to the ornately carved mahogany door. She raised her hand to knock, but then let it fall back to her side. "What are you doing?" she asked herself.

"This isn't you," she could hear Claire's voice say mockingly. "You barely talk to people you know, much less going into a stranger's house."

Beryl actually turned and started to walk away when she stopped, picturing herself having to explain to Ridley that she'd finally found Corinne and had left before getting a chance to give her the book or talk to her.

Closing her eyes, she took a deep breath and went back to the front door. Raising the heavy brass knocker, she let it fall once, triggering a series of frantic barks from inside the house. A moment later, the door was opened by the young blond woman she'd seen earlier, holding a struggling terrier mix.

"It's you," said the blonde.

Beryl nodded stupidly. "It's me."

"Why are you smiling?" asked the blonde self-consciously, glancing down at herself.

"Nothing," Beryl said, shaking her head. "I'm Beryl," she forced herself to say, holding out a hand. "Beryl Gray."

"Aggie – Agatha Bishop," Aggie said, taking her hand. "Please, come in." She stepped back to allow Beryl in, eyeing her curiously as Beryl entered the foyer in open-mouthed delight. She set Percival down.

"This is incredible," Beryl murmured admiringly, bending to pet Percival who was dancing on his hind legs. "Just how I imagined."

"Sorry?" Aggie said. "Why would you have imagined this house?"

But just then, Cory came into the foyer. "Good evening, Beryl," she said warmly, holding out her hand in greeting.

"Hello, Miss Bishop," Beryl said.

Cory smiled at the grudging approval on Aggie's face at Beryl's manners.

"Thank you so much for inviting me into your home," Beryl continued. "I brought some wine."

"That's very thoughtful of you," Cory said. "I can open this and pour while Agatha gives you a tour."

She left the two younger women standing awkwardly in the foyer as Percival sniffed Beryl's legs curiously.

"I'm afraid I'm a little confused," Aggie confessed. "I don't understand how you know my great-aunt?"

"I don't," Beryl said, stepping forward and looking upward through the oval of the staircase. "Not really. But I feel like I do."

Before Aggie could ask another question, Beryl turned to her and asked, "Did your family build this house?"

"Um, yes," Aggie said, distracted from her other questions. "In 1860, I think. My great-great grandparents."

"It really is incredible," Beryl said, forgetting her shyness as she caught sight of the study with its bookshelves. "May I?" she asked, turning back to Aggie.

"Uh, yes," Aggie said again, feeling completely off-kilter. "Who are you?" she wanted to blurt, but that seemed incredibly rude. She'd gotten nothing further from Cory about why she felt such a connection to this Beryl person.

She and Percival followed as Beryl explored the contents of the bookshelves.

"Who collected all these?" Beryl asked excitedly, pulling book after book off the shelves and then replacing them carefully before moving on.

"All of us," Aggie said. "I mean, my great-great grandparents already had an extensive library, but it's been added to over the years. I think it means more to Aunt Cory than anything. The books were the only things she really insisted on keeping..." Aggie stopped as if realizing she was revealing too much to a stranger.

Beryl looked around at the nearly empty room. "Oh, yes. The auction. Mrs. Mattingly was right, it is sad that your great-aunt had to let so many things go, but I'm so glad she was able to keep the books, mostly because –"

"Here you are," Cory said, bringing two wine glasses into the study and offering them to Aggie and Beryl. She beamed at them.

"What do you think?" she asked, gesturing around the room.

"The house is beautiful, but the books are really fantastic," Beryl said.

"Well, dinner is about ready. If you girls would come to the kitchen, I could use some help," Cory said.

Beryl and Percival followed Cory, with Aggie bringing up the rear, feeling as if she had stepped through the proverbial looking glass.

"Oh, it smells good," Beryl said appreciatively as she stepped into the kitchen, delighting again in the details: the classic marble floor tiles, laid out in a basketweave pattern in black and white, with a large porcelain sink and marble countertops.

"I hope you don't mind eating in the kitchen," Cory said as she opened the oven and pulled out a covered roasting pan and a baking sheet of rolls and setting them on the stovetop. "I always enjoyed eating in here with the staff as a child, but now... there's no dining room furniture, so we don't have a choice," she laughed.

"I'm definitely more kitchen than dining room," Beryl smiled. The long wooden table was already laid with three place settings at one end.

"Agatha," Cory said, "would you mind carving the roast for us? And, Beryl, could I impose upon you to place these dinner rolls in this basket?"

Beryl set her backpack down in a corner and did as Cory asked.

Within a few minutes, they were seated with Cory at the end of the table and Aggie and Beryl on either side while Percival settled under the table, ready to pounce on any dropped bits of food. Throughout, Aggie kept staring at Beryl suspiciously, still completely non-plussed as to what exactly was going on. Cory made small talk, asking Beryl where she was from and what she did.

"So, what brings you to Columbus from Washington?" Cory asked at last.

"Well, two things, actually," Beryl said, taking a sip of her wine. "I had an interview with Ohio State yesterday, but I've been looking for you for some time."

"Why?" Aggie burst out, unable to contain herself any longer.

Beryl swallowed and went to her backpack, where she squatted down and retrieved a small paper-wrapped package. She returned to the table and handed it to Cory.

"I think this may be yours," she said hopefully.

She watched Cory's face carefully as she unwrapped the paper.

"Oh." Cory's hand fluttered to her mouth as her eyes blinked rapidly. Aggie leaned over to see what lay in the tissue paper. "You don't know..." Cory said in a strangled voice, "I've been looking..."

"Is this the book?" Aggie asked. "The one you were so upset about losing?"

Cory nodded, her eyes shining with tears.

Aggie reached over and gently picked it up, opening the front cover. Her eyebrows raised as she read the inscription, blushing a little. "Aunt Cory," she said in a scandalized tone.

Cory laughed, looking not the least abashed. "I told you you'd know it by the inscription."

Beryl was watching her reaction with bated breath. "So you are this Corinne?"

Cory nodded, wiping her eyes. "I am."

"Can you... would you mind telling me a little about Helen?" Beryl asked hesitantly.

*　　*　　*

Corinne and Terrence wend their way through Union Station, making their way to the train that will take them home to Ohio. The war is finally over in Europe, though not yet in the Pacific. Terrence's doctors say he will most likely not recover fully. Physically, he is still weak in his left arm and leg, but more critically, he has not recovered mentally.

"He's not the same," Corinne wrote to her parents, trying to prepare them. "He's easily upset, and cannot bear any yelling or arguments. And he has spells," – "seizures," the doctors called them, episodes during which Terrence would stare, muscles rigid, sometimes for several minutes before he would look around blankly, not aware of what had happened.

Corinne has quit her job and given up her apartment in D.C., knowing that once she is home, she will most likely not be able to leave again.

"You simply must come home to help me with Mother and Father, especially if Terrence is to live with us," Candace, who never married, had written. "With the war over, your lark is also over and it is time you accept your responsibilities."

This is the bitterest thing of all. "I feel I have no choice but to give up my independence, my life here," Corinne has written in a letter to Helen, who is still in Europe, helping coordinate post-war efforts.

"Please, please come to me when you can," she wrote. "My life will not be complete without you."

She has sent trunks on ahead, one of hers and one of Terrence's. She glances up at him now as they walk arm in arm through the train station. He is very handsome in his uniform, and with his cap pulled low over his right eye, he looks devil-may-care. Only she knows he does it to cover the scars that are still visible. *What about the invisible ones?* she wonders a short while later as the train chugs slowly out of the station and they head back to a world where she and her brother no longer belong.

*   *   *

Aggie, who spent most of the evening observing Beryl as Cory talked to her, felt somewhat mollified by the time Beryl took her leave late that night.

She doesn't seem like a lunatic, she thought as she cleared the dinner dishes.

Aggie and Cory had both been astonished to hear Beryl's tale of how she came to have the book in her possession.

"I'm not sure how much those three boxes of books went for at the original auction," she said seriously. "But if you ever want to sell any more of these, please call me. We should get you in touch with an auction house that specializes in rare books. You have tens of thousands of dollars of books here. And they don't sell these by the box."

"My dear," Cory said as they got up from the table at last, having exchanged addresses and telephone numbers, "all I can say is you must have been led here somehow. I cannot thank you enough for returning this book to me."

"Miss Bishop," Beryl said, glancing again at the silver-framed photo of Corinne and Helen that Aggie had retrieved from the mantel, "would it be all right... would you mind if I wrote to you?" She carefully folded the piece of paper with Cory's address and phone number and tucked it into one of the pockets of her backpack. "I would like to know more about you and Helen, as much as you feel you can share."

"Why would you care so much about the relationship between two people who were so much ahead of your time?" Cory asked.

A curious expression passed over Beryl's features, but she said only, "I feel like you've become friends."

"I would be delighted to write to you," Cory said, "but if your interview went well, you may find yourself living nearby and we can continue our correspondence in person."

Beryl smiled. "That would be nice." She picked up her backpack. "Thank you again, Miss Bishop."

Cory surprised her by giving her a hug, and left Aggie to walk Beryl to the front door.

"You must think I'm nuts," Beryl said sheepishly as they stood in the foyer.

"Maybe a little," Aggie admitted with a bewildered smile. "But I have to ask, why did you really feel such a strong need to find my aunt?"

Beryl looked at her and Aggie could see the sudden hurt, the vulnerability in those eyes. "I just needed to know," she said, and it sounded as if she were having a hard time speaking. "I needed to know a relationship could last a lifetime and beyond."

Chapter 21

For Beryl, the flight back to D.C. was something of a blur. Ridley was waiting for her at the baggage claim, the first time she had seen him wearing both prosthetic legs.

He stood when he saw her. She rushed to give him a hug, laughing to herself as she caught the envious looks on other women's faces. *If you only knew,* she thought.

"So," Ridley said, insisting on carrying her small suitcase, "tell me everything."

She filled him in on more of the details of the interview and her dinner with Corinne and Aggie.

"Corinne and Helen lived in D.C.?" he asked in surprise.

"For a while," Beryl said. "Then Helen got posted to England during the war. That's as far as we got, but Corinne - Aggie calls her Cory - said she would write to me, tell me more."

"And when will you hear from OSU?" Ridley asked.

Beryl shrugged. "I really don't know," she said. "Dr. Hudspath said they can't make a formal decision until the posting period is over and all candidates are interviewed, but he implied they would like to make a decision soon. So, it could be as long as a few months yet, I imagine."

Ridley nodded. "Good. I don't want to lose my roommate too soon."

She looked over at him as he drove. "So, how was your evening with George?"

A tiny smile played on his lips. "It... it was nice." She waited. "And I think he feels the same. We do have a lot in common, and... like you said... he's not into the typical sex first, talk later thing. We never seem to run out of things to talk about." He nodded. "I like him."

Beryl beamed.

"Tell me more about this Aggie," Ridley said, glancing over at her.

Beryl laughed. "Well, she's very protective of her great-aunt. I think at first she must have thought I was a stalker or something. I almost bowled them over, literally, on the sidewalk and then later, she was the one who almost ran me over when I was standing in their driveway."

"You like her," Ridley observed, smiling.

"What? No," Beryl protested.

"Yeah, you do," he grinned. "I can tell."

"Well, maybe... she seems nice," Beryl admitted, "Under different circumstances, but there's no way, right now. I'm not jumping into anything with anyone," she said a little bitterly, recalling her telephone conversation with Claire.

When they got home – home, Beryl thought. *I've only lived with him a little over a week, and it feels more like home than the rowhouse did after all those years* – Winston greeted her loudly, winding his way through her ankles, nearly tripping her as she carried her backpack in.

"It was only a few days," she crooned, picking him up and cuddling him to her. She immediately frowned, hefting him. "He's heavier," she said, looking at Ridley accusingly.

"Well," Ridley waffled, "he was hungry. What was I supposed to do?"

"He's always hungry!" Beryl said. "You're supposed to say 'no.' What kind of parent are you?"

The look on Ridley's face made her laugh.

"What? You never thought of yourself as a parent, did you?" she asked.

Her cell phone rang. She pulled it out of her pocket and, looking at it, saw that it was her sister. Grimacing, she answered.

"Hey, Marian."

Ridley watched curiously as he moved about the kitchen, laying out fixings for sandwiches as Beryl listened to whatever her sister was saying, mumbling occasional responses.

"All right," Beryl was saying glumly. "I'll get over there this week. Bye."

Ridley didn't say anything until they were seated at the table with sandwiches and drinks. "What just happened to you?"

She looked up at him. "What are you talking about?"

He shook his head, staring at her. "As soon as you picked that phone up, it was like watching you shrink. You turned into a completely different person." He watched her watching him, thinking about this. "That's what you're like with Claire, too. It's like seeing two personalities in one person. You're not like that at work and with me, or with Mr. Herrmann and George."

Beryl ate, saying nothing.

"What did she want?" Ridley asked after a little while. "Your sister?" he added when Beryl stared at him blankly.

"Oh, she said Mom needs some help clearing out boxes of old stuff from the basement," Beryl said.

Ridley sat back. "And why is that your job?" he asked, trying not to sound accusatory.

Beryl looked at him. Her mouth opened and closed a few times.

"I mean, it's fine if you want to help," he hastened to add, "but why is there this expectation that you will always be the one to do these things? What's going to happen if you take the OSU job and aren't here anymore? Who's going to be Beryl?"

*　　*　　*

"Who's going to be Beryl?"

That question ran through Beryl's head frequently over the next few days. Ridley had given her a lot to think about. She had never realized how much she changed when she was with Claire or with her family, but she knew when he said it that he was right. "Realizing it and stopping it are two separate things, though," she could have said.

She honestly had no idea what her family's reaction would be if she was offered the Ohio State position and decided to accept it. Probably not good, but... as much as she would have liked to think it would be because they would miss her, she strongly suspected it would more likely be because she wouldn't be there to do everything anymore.

"What's the matter with you?" her mother asked on Thursday as they shuffled boxes in her parents' basement.

"Nothing," Beryl muttered, opening yet another box of Nick's old high school trophies, sports letters and scrapbooks of newspaper clippings Edith had put together.

She tried not to think about the reason why there were no boxes of hers down there... tried not to remember that her one box of mementos, consisting mainly of letters and yearbook remembrances from her few close friends had been tossed unceremoniously in a misguided attempt to prove to Claire that she and she alone had Beryl's affections.

"Why do you want to hold on to these if you weren't in love with them?" Claire had asked, her voice casual but her eyes narrowing the way they did when she was angry or upset as she leafed through Beryl's high school yearbook, reading the sentiments inscribed there. "If they didn't mean anything, you don't need them, do you?"

Beryl had lost count of how many times over the past several years she had regretted letting Claire manipulate her like that. *Those memories are gone, lost forever,* Beryl thought bitterly, *and here are boxes and boxes of things Nick and Marian don't ever look at.*

Edith eyed her shrewdly. "How's Claire?"

Beryl's face drained of all color as she realized with a shock that she hadn't told them about breaking up with Claire. Of course, it would be hard to tell them about breaking up when she had never told them she and Claire were a couple. Not in so many words.

"Why bother?" Claire had said when Beryl first brought the topic up. "I'm not out to my family. Sorry, but it's not worth the hassle. They would never understand anyhow."

"You're not going to tell them about me?" Beryl had asked, trying to hide her disappointment.

Claire scoffed. "I've never told them about any of my other girlfriends."

But Beryl's family was not like Claire's. Even if they hadn't been told, they included Claire, invited her to holiday dinners, birthday celebrations. Claire had gone at first, but then less and less frequently. Beryl knew her mother wasn't stupid. As much as Edith seemed oblivious in regard to the interactions among her children, she had some sixth sense when it came to Claire. Maybe because she had seen in Claire what Beryl never had, Beryl realized now.

"Um, I really don't know how Claire is," Beryl said to her mother, digging through the box in front of her. "I... I moved out. I'm staying with Ridley."

"I see," Edith said.

Something snapped in Beryl's brain and she turned to her mother.

"Do you, Mom? Do you see?" She could feel her heart pounding. "Do you see that my heart is broken?" It was hard to breathe. "Do you see that I am the one helping you clear out Marian and Nick's stuff? None of this is mine. They're not here; I am. I do things and they get the credit. They get the thanks. I get nothing. I got nothing from Claire and I get nothing from you." Beryl knew she should stop, but now that she had started, she couldn't. "You might as well know that I wasn't at a conference last weekend. I was interviewing for a job at Ohio State University, and if they offer it to me, I'll probably accept."

She could feel sudden tears stinging her eyes. *I will not cry in front of her*, Beryl thought fiercely.

"I have to go," she said, turning to the basement steps.

"What about dinner?" Edith asked.

"I'm not hungry," Beryl said as she nearly ran up the steps.

Beryl was blocks from the house, wiping her cheeks angrily when her cell phone rang. Expecting it to be her mother, she nearly didn't look. To her surprise, it was an unfamiliar number, but she recognized an Ohio area code.

"Hello?"

"Beryl? This is Aggie Bishop."

"Hi." Beryl stopped in her tracks.

"I hope I'm catching you at an okay time," Aggie said uncertainly.

Beryl gave a half laugh. "This is perfect timing, actually," she said. "What can I do for you?"

"Well, your visit got Aunt Cory reminiscing, and…" Aggie paused, sounding hesitant, "before I start back up with school, she would like to visit D.C., so… we're coming out there tomorrow. I got a hotel room for a few nights. We'll be doing some museums and monuments, and… we would love to see you if you're going to be around."

Before Beryl could respond, Aggie blurted, "I know this is last minute, and if you're not available, we understand, I just –"

"I'm available," Beryl cut in. "And I'd love to play tour guide. I live here and I don't take advantage of the things D.C. has to offer. How are you getting here?"

"I'm driving," Aggie said. "It's only seven or eight hours by car, and I think I can find my way to the hotel."

"Well, pack comfortable shoes because once you're here, we'll be walking or taking buses or the Metro," Beryl said. "Driving and parking is a nightmare. Will Corinne – I mean, Cory – be up to walking, do you think?"

Aggie laughed and it made Beryl smile to hear it. "She could run circles around both of us, probably," Aggie said.

"Okay, well…" Beryl didn't really want to end the call, but didn't know what else to say.

"Can we call you tomorrow when we get to the hotel?" Aggie asked.

"Yes, and after work, I could meet you for dinner?" Beryl suggested.

"That would be great."

"Can I bring my friend, Ridley?" Beryl asked. "He has been as interested as I have in the mystery of Corinne and Helen. He'll never forgive me if he finds out you were here and he didn't get to meet you."

She could hear Aggie chuckle. "I had no idea my little great-aunt had generated so much intrigue."

"You have no idea."

Chapter 22

Cory chatted as they left Columbus, I-70 stretching out in a flat ribbon before them. Aggie smiled. Beryl's visit, or the return of the book, or the renewal of the memories associated with it – perhaps all of those things – had been a tonic to Aunt Cory. As soon as the idea of a visit to Washington had taken hold, she had wanted to look up things they could see and do while there. She had never been on the internet, and was fascinated at the images that popped up on Aggie's laptop, as many of the monuments hadn't existed when she was last there.

"The Roosevelt Memorial," she had said. "I want to see that." She smiled. "And the Lincoln. I haven't seen the Lincoln in almost seventy years."

What must it feel like to say that? Aggie wondered now during a lull in the conversation as she drove. *To want to go see something you haven't seen in seventy years?*

Shannon was watching Percival for the weekend. She'd been properly astonished at Aggie's tale of Beryl's unexpected appearance. "You're kidding," she kept saying.

"Would you stop saying that?" Aggie said.

"Sorry, it just seems incredible, the whole idea of the book surviving, falling into the hands of someone who would hunt down the owner," Shannon said, eyeing Aggie closely. "She sounds like she must be... special," she added, not so subtly.

143

"Oh, don't even," Aggie said, shaking her head. But in spite of her gruffness, an unwilling smile played on her lips, and she said, "But it was kind of sweet. I don't know what happened to her, but something... something drove her, made her search for Aunt Cory. And Helen. She said she needed to know a relationship could last a lifetime and beyond."

Shannon watched Aggie's face closely, and she could see the wistfulness there. Wisely, she kept quiet.

Aggie mused on that conversation as she drove. She glanced over at Aunt Cory who had fallen asleep before they got to Cambridge. She would never admit it to Shannon or Cory or anyone else, but Beryl had touched something inside her. "You're being stupid," she scolded herself. "You don't know anything about her," but it didn't stop her from smiling as she remembered the way Beryl had turned to look back at her after almost mowing them over on the sidewalk, or Aggie's disappointment as she had nearly run down the driveway hoping to find Beryl still standing there, or the surprise when she had opened the front door to find that Aunt Cory's mystery woman and her own mystery woman were one and the same.

*　　　*　　　*

Ridley rolled his eyes as Beryl checked her cell phone for about the tenth time since lunch. "I think we'll hear it when it rings," he said.

Beryl blushed and put her phone down. "It's just a long trip by car. Cory is in her nineties."

"Right," he smirked.

"Oh, shut up," she said, getting up to restack some journals. She could hear him chuckling as she walked away.

When her phone did ring mid-afternoon, she snatched it up. "Hi."

"Hi," said Aggie warmly. "We made it. We're at the hotel, and I think you're right. I will be perfectly fine not driving any more in this city."

Beryl laughed. "Well, why don't you rest for a couple of hours? You must be tired. Ridley and I get off at five, and we'll come meet you at your hotel. There's a wonderful Mexican restaurant only a few blocks from where you are, if you like Mexican. They have great margaritas. Do you mind an early dinner?"

"We love Mexican and we prefer early," Aggie said. "We'll meet you in the lobby at... five-thirty? Does that give you enough time to get here?"

"Sounds good," Beryl said. "We'll see you then."

"Bye."

The rest of the afternoon crawled by for Beryl, who kept looking at the clock and then at her watch.

"They're not broken," Ridley said, shaking his head.

Beryl glared at him. "You're really enjoying this, aren't you?"

"Kind of, yeah," he admitted happily. His expression became more serious. "It's nice to see you happy for a change, that's all."

When five o'clock finally came, Beryl and Ridley hurried to his car. Traffic snailed along as Beryl sighed impatiently at every red light.

"You're really going to like them," she said for about the hundredth time.

"I know I will," he smiled. "What do you think? Chair or crutches?"

She glanced over at him, surprised that she had never realized what a consideration that choice must be. "At least I have a choice," Ridley would have said. "Most people don't."

Deciding this was a chance for a little pay-back, she said, "Well, crutches show off your arms more."

He looked over quickly. "Yeah," he admitted sheepishly. "But I think I'll slow us down if we have to go more than a few blocks."

"Strap them to your chair, so you can switch when we get to the restaurant if you like," she suggested.

When at last they arrived at the hotel, Ridley found a parking space in the lot. Beryl nervously smoothed her clothes as she got out.

"You look great," he assured her. She noticed that he himself had chosen his clothes carefully that day, wearing a close-fitting shirt the exact same blue as his eyes. He looked very handsome.

They entered the lobby and immediately spotted Cory and Aggie. If they were surprised to meet Ridley in his wheelchair, they hid it well. Under the pretext of getting out of the traffic flow, Beryl discreetly steered them toward a half-wall in the lobby that separated the reception area from the lounge so that Ridley could stand for introductions, balancing against the wall as he shook hands.

"I've wanted to meet you for so long," he said sincerely to Cory who beamed up at him. Her head barely came to his chest. "Are you hungry?" he asked.

"I'm ready for a margarita," she said as he laughed.

Beryl and Aggie followed behind while Cory walked alongside Ridley as they made their way down the crowded sidewalk.

"The drive was okay?" Beryl asked.

"A little tiring," Aggie admitted, "but not bad."

They walked half a block in awkward silence.

"Where do you work?" Aggie asked, looking around curiously as if she expected a library to pop up.

"Georgetown University," Beryl replied. "Ridley and I work together at the Lauinger, it's the humanities library."

"Why do you want to leave?" Aggie asked.

"I don't, really," Beryl admitted, "but I love old books, and Ohio State has an opening in its Rare Books and Manuscripts Library, so..." She shrugged. "We'll see. I've lived in D.C. my entire life. It would feel strange to leave."

"I know how you feel," Aggie said. "I've lived in Columbus my whole life. Went to OSU. It's not great, but it's familiar."

"Ohio State is great," Beryl laughed. "Your only problem is it's too close to home. Speaking of home, your home is beautiful," Beryl said enviously.

Aggie chuckled a little. "That's not my home," she said. "It's Aunt Cory's. Actually, it's held in some kind of trust in her name. I don't really understand it. My great-grandfather arranged it all so she could stay with Grandfather Terrence until he died... it got complicated," she said apologetically.

"How long have you been living there with your aunt?" Beryl asked.

"Only a few weeks," Aggie said. "My family – my father and

brothers – wanted Aunt Cory to move to an assisted living facility so they could sell the house. We had to have the auction to pay back taxes on the property. There was some kind of family scrap years ago about bad investments or something, but... Aunt Cory didn't want to leave, and I don't blame her, so... I agreed to keep an eye on her." She watched Cory laughing with Ridley up ahead. "Sometimes I wonder who's keeping an eye on whom."

A little while later, they were seated at a table as a fresh pitcher of margaritas was delivered by their server. Ridley poured for everyone and raised his glass in a toast.

"To Dr. Beryl Gray," he said, "whose determination to solve the mystery of Helen and Corinne made this meeting possible."

Beryl blushed furiously as Aggie and Cory raised their glasses and chimed in, "To Beryl."

"And now," Ridley said, turning to Cory, "I have been dying to hear more of your story. What happened after the war?"

*   *   *

Corinne carries a breakfast tray up to Terrence who rarely leaves his room. He accepts the tray silently, but as she turns to leave him, he reaches out to squeeze her hand, and she smiles in understanding. She pauses on the landing on the stairs, looking out the stained glass window at the gardeners who are pruning back the roses.

Corinne had hoped, once Terrence was back in familiar sur-roundings, that he would be better, but it has been almost six months and he is the same. Margorie tried to get him to come home, "our home," she insisted, "with our son," but Terrence just smiled and shook his head. She left in tears.

"It's not right," Candace insists frequently since their return home. "You're coddling him," she says accusingly to Corinne.

But Candace tried to coddle him. When he and Corinne first ar-rived home, Candace tried to embrace him, tried to be the one to take care of him, but he recoiled at her touch, turning instinctively to Corinne for protection from Candace's smothering.

Candace, in her hurt, lashes out at Corinne instead, belittling the work she did in Washington. "Yes, the entire war turned on the efforts of our little Corinne," she says waspishly.

Corinne, who understands Candace's bitterness, her littleness, smiles serenely and refuses to respond, which only serves to make Candace's heart colder and more bitter still.

This particular morning, as she comes down the stairs, Corinne hears the early mail bell and goes to collect the post from the tray hanging below the mail slot. Leafing through the envelopes as she carries the mail to the dining room, there is a letter for her. From France.

Corinne hands the remainder of the mail to Mother who is still at breakfast with Candace, going over committee assignments for the church bazaar. Father is already at the bank.

Corinne's face, as she reads Helen's letter, has a telltale flush of excitement that attracts Candace's attention like a shark to blood.

"Who is that from?" she asks.

Corinne's face is radiant as she looks up and says, "From Helen. My friend Helen. You remember, Mother, I told you about her. She was in England during the war and is just now coming home. I have invited her to stay."

"Stay?" Candace asks sharply, with a quick glance at their mother to gauge her response.

"That's nice, dear," Mary Bishop says sweetly, but "How can you be so thoughtless?" Candace butts in. "Now? When Terrence is so... so addled? To have a stranger in the house?"

"She isn't a stranger to me," Corinne says coolly. "And I think she may be able to help Terrence."

Candace laughs cruelly. "How can some woman whom he has never met help him?" she asks.

"Because she fought and was injured," Corinne says proudly, "working with the French Resistance. She's terribly brave. She and Terrence have things in common."

"Things you would never understand," is implied, but not said aloud.

Candace, who can think of no response to this, sits silently through the remainder of breakfast, but Corinne, who knows her sister well, knows that she is stewing, building up a new volley of protests.

As soon as Mary goes to her study to begin writing the morning's letters and make up a new week's menu with Cook, Candace launches a new attack against Helen's coming.

"It's too late," Corinne says, cutting her off. "The invitation has been extended, and I will not rescind it now."

Candace looks outraged. "Without so much as a 'by your leave'?"

"Yes," Corinne smiles. "Where I am, she will be."

Candace's expression changes and Corinne is immediately wary.

"And where do you think she will stay?" Candace asks with an acid sweetness.

Bracing herself, Corinne responds, "She will stay with me," and she knows then that her sister guesses at the true nature of their relationship, but she will not be deterred. She folds her letter and stands, and there is an unaccustomed forcefulness to her presence that even Candace has to acknowledge. "She will be here with me or I will quit this house. Believe me when I say this, Candace, because I swear by everything I hold dear that I mean it."

And Candace, who wants more than anything to feel loved and yet has not the slightest idea of how to love, feels instead a cold rush of envy for her sister who easily does both – though Candace would have been astonished had someone told her it was envy. "It's not!" she would have cried. "I'm not!" but inside, her heart hardens and withers a bit more as Corinne floats happily from the room.

*   *   *

"Oooh," Cory said as she drained her third margarita over dinner, "I haven't talked this much in a long time!"

Beryl and Ridley both chuckled in delight, but Aggie said protectively, "Remember, we have to walk back from here."

"Was the food okay?" Beryl asked anxiously.

149

"It was delicious," Aggie said appreciatively.

Beryl paid the dinner bill. "You fed me a wonderful meal," she reminded Cory and Aggie when they tried to protest.

The restaurant was crowded as they rose to leave, but Ridley, thanks to his crutches and broad shoulders, cleared a path for the others to follow in his wake. He retrieved his folded wheelchair where he had left it near one of the front windows. He could see that there was now a line of patrons waiting to be seated.

"Oh, shit," he muttered as he glanced through the glass. He tried to stop Beryl, but before he could call her, she had opened the door for Cory and nearly walked into Claire and Leslie as they stood in line.

It only lasted a few seconds, but Aggie, not understanding the reason for the sudden stop in their progress out the door, placed a hand on Beryl's shoulder and asked, "Is everything okay?"

Claire's eyes immediately zeroed in on her, communicating an instant and obvious animosity that left Aggie feeling totally confused.

Cory stepped forward, taking Beryl by the arm and saying, "What a delightful dinner. Could we walk around for a bit or I'll never be able to sleep tonight." She steered Beryl past the queue of people and out onto the sidewalk.

Beryl's gaze was fixed on the pavement as Cory guided her, with Ridley and Aggie trailing along in their wake.

"What just happened?" Aggie asked, non-plussed.

"Later," Ridley muttered, back in his chair, keeping a worried eye on Beryl as he wheeled along.

"I'm all turned around. Which way to the Mall?" Cory asked over her shoulder to Ridley.

He responded by taking the lead, leaving Beryl to walk silently beside Aggie as Cory chatted, exclaiming when the Mall came into view, "This looks so completely different. There were still ugly concrete munitions buildings here the last time I saw this place."

Beryl gradually pulled out of her preoccupation, pointing out the various museums lining either side of the Mall, lit up dramatically now in the dusk. When Cory saw the Carousel, she insisted on riding, giggling like a little girl as she rode a garishly painted horse, sitting sidesaddle.

Aggie kept glancing worriedly at Beryl who still seemed to be only partially with them.

When at last Ridley and Beryl dropped Cory and Aggie off at their hotel, they had made plans to spend Saturday visiting several of the monuments that Cory particularly wanted to see.

"See you tomorrow," Aggie said as Beryl and Ridley bade them good-night. Turning back to Cory, they made their way to the elevator. "What happened when we were leaving the restaurant?"

"I think Beryl ran into an ex-lover," Cory said.

"What?" Aggie asked in surprise. "That woman who was looking at me so hatefully?" She glanced down at her great-aunt. "How do you know?"

Cory smiled up at her. "I may be old, but I remember enough to recognize a broken heart when I see one."

Chapter 23

If Beryl and Ridley had any concerns about Cory's energy level, they were dispelled by mid-morning on Saturday. They had already begun a huge loop from the Vietnam Memorial to the World War II, with plans to continue on to the Korean and then to the Lincoln.

"Good thing I thought to pack snacks," Beryl said to Aggie, retrieving her backpack strung to Ridley's wheelchair as they completed a tour of the World War II Memorial.

The two of them went outside the circle of granite columns and located a shaded bench while Cory and Ridley lingered inside despite the continued August heat.

"You were right," Beryl said as she handed Aggie a bottle of water. "Your aunt has more energy than I do."

Aggie smiled. "She is amazing." She took a long drink. "Thanks for thinking of this," she said, raising the bottle. She glanced over at Beryl. "Are you okay?"

Beryl met her eyes for a second, and saw that there was no point in pretending she didn't know what Aggie was referring to. She gave a small shrug. "It's getting better. I just didn't expect to run into her like that."

They sat in silence for a few seconds. "Her idea?" Aggie asked. "She discovered a new love and just had to see where it would go?"

Beryl heard the bitterness in Aggie's voice. "Uh, no," she said. "My idea – when I found out the truth about her and the woman we saw her with last night."

"Oh. I'm sorry," Aggie said. "That stinks."

Beryl gave a half-laugh. "Yes, it really stinks." She took a drink, and said, "It had actually been going on for quite a while. I just didn't want to see it." She could see Cory talking to Ridley as they pointed to something inside the memorial. "Ridley's been a life saver for me. He let me move in with him. Let me sulk. Made me eat." She smiled. "I'm not sure what I would have done without him."

She turned to Aggie. "What about you?"

"It shows?" Aggie said sheepishly. "It's been three years for me. My ex met her soul-mate after we'd been together for five years. And that was that."

Beryl could see the hurt still etched on her features even after all this time. "Did you have a clue?"

"No," said Aggie and she was mortified to feel sudden tears spring to her eyes. "We were happy. We were good together. I... I think that's been the hardest part. It's bad enough to break up when you know things are starting to go sour between you." She blinked hard. "How do you ever trust someone else again when you didn't see it coming the last time?"

Beryl didn't know what to say, but Cory and Ridley came to find them at that point. They also accepted bottles of water and some granola bars that Beryl had packed.

"What a beautiful memorial," Cory said, pressing her hand to her heart. "And the Vietnam. There just aren't words."

"I know," Ridley said. "No matter how many times I go, I'm in awe."

She laid a gnarled hand on his shoulder. "One day, there will be a memorial to you and those who fought with you," she said.

He looked at her, and Beryl could see the emotions churning in his eyes.

"Another granola bar, anyone?" she asked to break the tension.

"I'll take one," Aggie said, giving Ridley an opportunity to occupy himself with an adjustment on his chair which gave him an excuse to turn away for a few minutes.

"Ready?" Cory asked enthusiastically after only a couple minutes' rest.

She and Ridley led the way toward the Korean Memorial. It also stunned them into silence as they walked among the larger-than-life figures. It felt like an outdoor church as no one there spoke more loudly than a whisper, looking up into the bronze faces, each one unique, real.

When they left to head toward the Lincoln, Aggie sidled over to Beryl, and, as if she was carrying on an uninterrupted conversation, asked "So, is your break-up the reason you interviewed at OSU?"

Beryl considered for a moment how to answer. "It helped make the timing right to think about a move," she said in measured tones. "One factor of many."

"What are the others?" Aggie asked casually. "If you don't mind talking about this."

"I don't mind," Beryl said. She took a deep breath. "Have you ever... have you ever found yourself looking in the mirror and realizing you don't like the person looking back? It's... you had dreams for what you would do with your life, with your career, and somehow, without knowing exactly how it happened, you're stuck in a place you never wanted to be. And you feel as if everyone in your life is holding you in that place, almost like holding you underwater, only letting you up long enough to gasp for air and then pushing you back under, because it suits them to have you here. And the only way to break free is to do something kind of drastic. But then, you're afraid you're only reacting to the negative stuff, and how do you figure out if the drastic thing is the right thing?"

She realized how much had just come spilling out and grinned in embarrassment. "I'm not normally this much of a mess," she said with a wan smile.

Aggie looked at her and said, "I don't think you're a mess." They walked on for several yards. "What about your family? Won't they object to your leaving, if you accept?"

"You forget I haven't been offered the position," Beryl reminded her. "But, they're part of why I'm thinking of going." Aggie waited as Beryl chose her words. "I don't know if I can really describe the dynamics... it's kind of like being invisible, but being expected to do everything. I feel like Cinderella sometimes." She shook her head. "I just had an argument with my mother – the evening you called, as a matter of fact – during which I blurted out that I had interviewed at OSU. Not how I wanted to tell them."

"I thought you sounded upset over the phone," Aggie said. "Maybe being farther away will make them appreciate you more."

Beryl grinned ruefully. "It would be nice to think so, but..."

When they got to the Lincoln Memorial, Cory didn't want to go up to the Memorial itself.

"I would just like to sit here on the steps," she said. "This was the last place Helen and I met in Washington before I took Terrence home." She looked at Beryl. "Valentine's Day, 1945," she smiled wistfully.

The younger people left her to herself for a while, lost in her memories as they climbed the steps. Ridley took his crutches, leaving his wheelchair where Cory could keep an eye on it.

"What happened to Helen?" Beryl asked when they got to the top and looked back down at Cory's tiny figure.

Aggie shook her head. "She died before I was born, but I'm not sure what she died of, and Aunt Cory never speaks of it." She glanced over at Beryl. "She's been talking more since your visit, and if you two continue to write, maybe she'll talk to you about it."

*   *   *

Corinne sits in the rocker near her bay window, watching Helen sleep in the grey pre-dawn light. Her heart is full to bursting with the joy of having Helen with her again, and not just for a few hours or a day, but forever.

Mary and Eugene had blithely welcomed Helen as Corinne's special friend when she arrived a couple of weeks previously. Candace was polite, but Corinne knows it is only a matter of time before the mask of politeness cracks and Candace's spitefulness spills forth, and so she remains on guard.

Terrence, as Corinne had known he would, took to Helen immediately.

"I like her," he said to Corinne a few days after Helen's arrival. "She doesn't talk all the time."

Indeed, Helen has changed. She is kinder. Corinne has been surprised to hear her thanking the maids and the kitchen staff; she no longer leaves her things lying about for someone else to pick up. She is quiet for long periods of time, holding a book in her lap, but often not reading it.

"You don't know how wonderful it is," she says to Corinne, "to be able to sit and relax, without the sounds of bombs or planes or guns..."

Yet, despite Helen's insistence that the quiet of the Bishop house is peaceful for her, Corinne cannot shake the feeling that Helen is brooding about something.

"No, I don't miss it," Helen laughs when Corinne asks her if she misses the war, but she doesn't meet Corinne's eyes as she says it.

Corinne holds her when they are in bed, after they have made love, holds her tenderly as she falls asleep, breathing in her flowery scent, thinking that she will never take for granted the gift of having Helen with her again. But deep in the night, when she is no longer in Corinne's arms, Helen's sleep is disturbed, restless, and Corinne lies in the dark wondering what it is that Helen dreams of.

*   *   *

"Is she okay, do you think?" Ridley asked, looking down at Cory sitting far below them.

"I'll go check on her," Aggie said as she began to descend the steps.

"I thought we could have lunch somewhere nearby and then drive over to the Roosevelt," Beryl called down to her. "It's too far to walk. And then, I had somewhere special I thought you might like to see."

Aggie smiled back up at her. "That sounds good."

"I like them," Ridley said, hopping over to stand next to Beryl as they watched Aggie and Cory talking.

Beryl sighed. "Me, too."

Chapter 24

"Tell me everything," Shannon insisted eagerly when Aggie came to her house Monday evening to pick Percival up.

"Well, let me show you," Aggie said, pulling out her camera.

"Oh, my God," Shannon moaned as Aggie began clicking through the photos she had taken at the various monuments and memorials. "Who is that?"

Aggie grinned. "That's Ridley, Beryl's friend, and he's gay."

"Damn," Shannon muttered. "Is he really gay, or...?"

"He's really gay," Aggie assured her.

Sighing in resignation, Shannon took the camera to get a better view of Beryl. "She's attractive," she said, looking up at Aggie. "Not beautiful, but very nice-looking."

"She is," Aggie agreed. "She wouldn't say so, but she is."

Shannon frowned at one of the photos. "Where is this?"

Aggie leaned over to see which image she had on the camera. "That's the Folger," she beamed. "The Folger Shakespeare Library?" she added at Shannon's blank look.

"Did she know you teach Shakespeare?"

"She didn't then," Aggie smiled. "She just knew we liked books and wanted to take us to one of her favorite places. It was sweet."

Shannon watched Aggie's face for a moment. "So," she said,

clicking back through the photos again, "she's attractive, she loves old books, including Shakespeare, she likes your great-aunt... she is single, isn't she?" she asked, glancing sharply over at Aggie.

Aggie's shoulders slumped a little. "Well, kind of."

"What do you mean, 'kind of'?" Shannon asked with a frown.

"She and her partner just broke up a few weeks ago," Aggie explained. "We bumped into her as we left a restaurant."

"You're kidding," Shannon said. "In a city that size? What are the chances?"

Aggie shrugged. "Anyway, she's definitely not over that situation yet."

"What happened?"

"The partner cheated and Beryl found out," Aggie said.

"Sounds familiar," Shannon said darkly.

Aggie shook her head. "I don't understand why being faithful and loyal is so hard."

"It isn't hard to do," said Shannon. "It's hard to find."

*   *   *

"Aunt Cory? We're home," Aggie called out a short while later. She and Percival couldn't find Cory anywhere on the main level of the house. "Go find her," she whispered to Percival, and he trotted to the kitchen door where he barked to be let out.

Aggie opened the door and Percival raced down the path to the garden. Aggie followed, and found Cory sitting on her bench as dusk fell a little early in the shady depths of the garden.

"Hey there," she said, sitting beside her aunt. "Aren't you getting eaten up by mosquitoes?" She looked closely when Cory didn't respond. "Have you been crying?" she asked in alarm. "What's wrong?"

Cory sniffed, but didn't respond immediately. Aggie noticed a bundle of letters, tied with a ribbon, lying in her lap.

*   *   *

Corinne pulls on her Navy pea coat – "Why on earth do you keep that dreadful thing?" Candace had asked in disgust when Corinne first pulled it out of her closet – and goes out to the garden. Snow is falling lightly, the small flakes twirling lazily in the cold air, and landing lightly on the dark green leaves of the holly and nandina bushes just off the path. She finds Helen sitting on a bench where she is mostly sheltered from the snow by the overhanging branches of an oak still clinging to its dried, brown leaves.

"Here you are," she says, sitting close to Helen who smiles and wraps an arm around Corinne's shoulders.

Helen has been with them for six months, six glorious months. Corinne has never been so happy... except she can see the growing restlessness in Helen's eyes. Sometimes, when she looks at Corinne, Corinne knows she isn't really there.

"What are you reading?" she asks, picking up the book lying in Helen's lap.

"Rilke," Helen says.

"In German," Corinne smiles. She snuggles closer. "Aren't you cold?"

Helen looks around as if surprised to find that it is winter and it is snowing. "I hadn't thought about it." She tilts Corinne's face up and kisses her tenderly. "I'm never cold with you around," she says with a hint of her old roguish grin.

"Flatterer," Corinne scolds. "It's almost sunset."

"Sunset?" Helen asks, puzzled.

Corinne looks at her uncertainly. "Doesn't Chanukah begin at sunset tonight?"

"Oh, that," Helen smiles. "You don't have to do this."

"But I want to," Corinne insists. "You've been with my family all this time, and you'll have to live through Christmas. I want to do something for you."

Helen laughs softly. "I can't remember the last time I set foot in a temple," she says, and her eyes suddenly lose focus as the smile slides from her face.

"Don't!" Corinne wants to cry. "Don't see them!" but she knows

Helen cannot forget the scenes she witnessed after the Allies entered Germany. Her office was charged with helping to get food and clothing and medical supplies to the survivors of the camps.

"I don't go to temple," Helen repeats quietly, "but that wouldn't have stopped them from taking me away." She looks at Corinne, looks into the open, innocent face she loves so. "They would have locked us up, also. For this," she says, kissing Corinne softly. "Just for this."

Corinne feels hot tears run down her cheeks as she nestles into Helen's shoulder, tears that quickly become icy trails on her skin.

Helen pulls away after a moment and stands, her hands thrust deep in her pockets as she says, "I have to go back."

"What do you mean?"

Helen turns to look at her, and Corinne can see the storminess in those changeable hazel eyes. "I have to go back. See how things are now. Maybe... maybe go to the Mediterranean from there."

She is so restless, she is ready to explode, and Corinne wonders how she didn't see it before now.

"Come with me," Helen says, looking back down at her.

"But... Terrence," Corinne says, biting her lip.

Helen comes back and sits next to her. "I think he's ready to be on his own more," she says gently. "Talk to him. We could leave in the spring."

There is an urgency to her voice, and Corinne knows that Helen must go, whether Corinne goes or not.

"You should go," Terrence says when Corinne does talk to him. "Helen needs you."

Unlike Candace, who sees and resents, or her parents, who see only what they wish to, Terrence sees and understands. He and Helen have spent long hours talking and walking together, increasing Candace's resentment – sentiments echoed in her angry pounding on the piano in the parlour as she plays moody pieces by Bach and Beethoven.

"Why does he talk to her?" she asks jealously.

"Because she listens," Corinne says. She suspects that much of

Helen and Terrence's time together is spent in a companionable silence, both of them lost in their own memories and thoughts.

"But don't let her make you parachute in," Terrence smiles as he wraps his good arm around Corinne's shoulders.

"What do you mean, parachute?" Corinne demands. "Helen has never parachuted. She was a courier."

Terrence laughs, a sound Corinne hasn't heard from him since before the war. "And how do you think she was getting behind enemy lines to deliver her messages? How did you think she broke her leg?"

Corinne frowns. "She told me she broke it when she was caught in rubble in a bombing in London."

Terrence nodded. "I expect she didn't want to worry you," he says, and he limps away, chuckling.

*   *   *

"What's wrong?"

Cory wiped her eyes and smiled a tremulous smile. "I'm just being silly. Silly and old."

"You're anything but silly," Aggie said, wrapping an arm around Cory's shoulders.

Cory took a deep breath. "Live your life, Agatha. Live your life, every second of it. You can't live without regrets, but don't let the regrets be from not living."

Later that evening, alone in her room, Aggie sat in her bed, clicking repeatedly through the photos from their weekend in D.C. Glancing at the bedside clock, she saw it was nine-thirty. *It's not too late,* she thought, biting her lip. She picked up her cell phone and scrolled through the numbers. Clutching the phone to her chest for a second, she thought about what Cory had said, and pushed the call button.

"Hello, Beryl?"

163

Chapter 25

Beryl yawned as she and Ridley finished a set of pushups.

"Tired?" he asked.

"Yeah."

"I heard you talking late last night. Claire or Aggie?" he asked.

She rolled her eyes. "Aggie, thank God."

Claire had been calling frequently since the night they had run into her outside the restaurant.

"No wonder you don't want to see me," she'd said the first time Beryl had answered the phone.

"What are you talking about?" Beryl had asked, not understanding.

"You've already got someone," Claire said accusingly. "How long has this been going on?"

Beryl was so astonished that she could only laugh. "You are amazing," she said. "You cheat on me, for who knows how long, and now, you're trying to make this my fault?"

"Why do you even talk to her?" Ridley had asked in total incomprehension.

Beryl shrugged. "I'd hate to think we can't even be friends, after all that time."

Ridley snorted. "The only way Claire will be friends is if she can put you back where you belong."

"Well, that's not going to happen," Beryl insisted.

"You've been having lots of long conversations with Aggie," he said now. "Things are going well there?"

"Yes," she said with a small smile. She looked at him and noted the dark circles under his eyes. "Why were you up? You didn't sleep again last night, did you?"

He shrugged and didn't answer. "Come on, next set," he said.

Beryl let it go. Ridley hadn't been sleeping well in the few weeks since Cory and Aggie came to visit. She could hear him sometimes, yelling in his sleep in the middle of the night. Other times, she would hear him out in the kitchen and knew he hadn't gone back to bed.

"So, how is Aggie?" he asked during their next break between sets.

"She's good," Beryl panted. "Getting ready for the new school year."

He smiled. "It always feels exciting, doesn't it? The start of a new year? Makes me want to go buy notebook paper and pens. Next set."

"She said Cory's been different since their visit here... seems to have stirred up lots of memories for her," Beryl said, watching Ridley from the corner of her eye as she took a drink from her water bottle.

His expression darkened, but he didn't say anything.

"Have you talked to George lately?" she asked as they moved to the pull-up bars.

"No," he said curtly.

"You want to go by the bookstore tonight?" she asked, delaying the start of her pull-ups.

He pumped out a set before saying, "No, I don't think so." He wiped his face with a sweat towel and said, "Why don't you go, though? It's been a while since you were there. Get up."

Standing on a chair to reach the bar, Beryl grunted through eight pull-ups before she dropped back to the ground, panting.

Ridley grinned. "Remember when you couldn't do one?"

*   *   *

When Beryl got back to the apartment later that night, there was one light left on for her, but Ridley was in his room with the door closed.

She had gone to The Scriptorium where George was thankfully working alone, giving Beryl the opportunity to talk to him.

"Are you two... talking?" she had asked hesitantly, feeling a little guilty about going behind Ridley's back.

George flushed. "Well, we talk on the phone, but he hasn't wanted to get together lately, so..." He shrugged.

Beryl bit her lip, wondering how much to say. "Do you like him?" she asked.

George met her eyes. "I really like him," he admitted.

"Then don't give up," she urged. "Something's bothering him, I don't know what, but you probably have a better chance of getting through to him than anyone else."

Beryl shushed Winston, who was meowing loudly as she came into the apartment. She picked him up and held him to quiet him. She listened at Ridley's door, but couldn't hear any sounds. She turned off the living room light and went to her room. She and Aggie had already talked – their conversations had become a nightly occurrence, the part of her day she looked forward to the most. It seemed they never ran out of things to talk about. As much as she knew she was getting to like Aggie – "more than like," said an insistent voice in her head – she was grateful for the distance separating them. *I am not going to drop back into that same old pattern of falling for someone too quickly,* she often thought. In her talks with Aggie, as they compared notes on their breakups, she was embarrassed to realize how much she had subjugated herself to Claire without even realizing she was doing it.

"You blame me, but you let it happen," she knew Claire would have said, and she knew, too, that there was a kernel of truth in those words.

"Never again," she replied harshly to that voice, deathly afraid of making the same mistakes again if she got involved with Aggie, or anyone else.

167

She got changed and slid into bed, Winston curling up next to her, purring loudly.

She wasn't sure what time it was when she was startled awake by a shout. Leaping out of bed, she raced out into the living room where she could hear more shouts coming from Ridley's room. Hesitating just a second, she opened his door to see him thrashing about, tangled in his sheets.

"Ridley! Ridley!" Beryl called, trying to wake him. She reached for his shoulder to shake him awake and, without warning, he grabbed her by the throat and the arm, pulling her off-balance as he yanked her across the bed where she crashed into his wheelchair before landing heavily on the floor. The impact drove the air from her lungs, but her gasps for breath were further inhibited as his weight crashed down on top of her and his fingers closed like a vise around her windpipe.

"Ridley," she rasped in panic, "it's me, Beryl..." but he seemed deaf.

The strength of his grip on her throat was terrifying. In desperation, she began kicking and clawing at him. Not until she scratched at his face did his pressure lessen as he seemed to realize where he was.

"Beryl?" he gasped in horror. He rolled off her. "Oh God, oh God... did I hurt you?" He helped her sit up, gulping air painfully into her lungs.

"I'm okay," she managed to croak. She looked up at him, barely able to make out his features in the dark. "Are you all right?"

Without warning, he began weeping, clutching his hands around his abdomen as if he were in physical pain. Beryl scooted closer to him and he let her pull him into her arms. She could feel him trembling as he sobbed. She didn't know how long they stayed there, but eventually, he quieted.

"Every night, it's the same," he whispered, sitting up and taking a deep, shuddering breath. "I'm trapped in the wreckage; my legs are pinned and I can't move. My weapon is just beyond my reach, and all I can do is wait. I hear the sounds of my buddies screaming, hear shots being fired and laughter... and I'm waiting... waiting for that face to come around the corner of the Humvee and point a gun in my face..." He pressed his fists into his eyes. "And I am so fucking scared." She could feel his shame at that admission.

He looked up at her. "If I hurt you, I'll never forgive myself," he said, his voice cracking.

"I'll be fine," she assured him shakily, reaching out to lay a hand on his arm. "Serves me right for trying to wake a Marine in the middle of a bad dream," she tried to joke, but he was having none of it.

"I'm not safe to be around," he said.

"We need a drink," Beryl said hoarsely. "Come on. Neither of us is going back to sleep after that."

She winced as she tried to get up. She wasn't sure she didn't have a couple of cracked ribs, but she wasn't going to say so to Ridley.

He uprighted his chair, pulling it near the bed so he could place one hand on the seat, the other on his mattress and hoist himself up into the wheelchair. Beryl realized she had never seen him without his below-knee prosthesis on, or without his shirt.

When they got out to the kitchen and turned the lights on, she was startled by the number of scars marring his trunk. What she could see of his right leg below his shorts was horribly scarred also.

Turning to the frig, she asked, "What do you want?"

"Milk."

"Milk?" she asked, turning to stare at him. "Not a beer?"

He shook his head. "I don't think alcohol is a good idea right now."

By the time she poured two glasses of milk, he had wheeled up to the table, his head resting on his hands.

"Here you go," she croaked.

He looked up at her worriedly, an expression of utter remorse on his face as he saw the bruises beginning to show on her neck. She could see marks where her fingernails had raked his cheek.

"Don't," she said. "We're both okay. But someone may report us for domestic violence." He didn't smile. She took a drink of her milk and said, "When was the last time you talked to someone about your PTSD?"

He shrugged one shoulder. "It's been a while."

"Don't you think maybe you should?" she suggested hoarsely.

Chapter 26

Aggie filled her coffee cup and carried it out to the veranda where she sat, enjoying the early morning coolness while Percival inspected the garden. Closing her eyes, she savored both the coffee and the solitude.

Who would've thought, she wondered with a droll smile, *that in a house this large, Aunt Cory and I could get in each other's way?*

With so little furniture left now, there really were not many areas in the house where one could sit, with the end result being that they frequently found themselves together in the study or the kitchen. Aggie often retreated to her sitting room upstairs, but then found she was constantly worrying if Cory was okay by herself downstairs, so that she couldn't really relax there, either.

A smile returned to her face as she thought of Beryl, something she found herself doing more and more frequently. She was past denying the flutter in her stomach when she saw it was Beryl calling in the evenings. She had no idea how things between them might change if Beryl were to be offered and accept the OSU position, and she kept reminding herself that Beryl wasn't ready for a new relationship yet, but... in her most honest moments, she had to admit she was starting to care deeply for Beryl. "That doesn't mean you have to be stupid," she reminded herself sternly, determined to never again act the fool over some woman.

Inside, Cory sat in her chair in the study, with the windows open, an old leather-bound journal on her lap. Beryl's return of the lost book and her questions about Helen had triggered a desire in Cory to revisit old thoughts and memories – things she hadn't really thought about in decades. Aggie had relaxed a bit since moving in, and was not nearly as bossy as she had been. Cory smiled. Maybe that was Beryl's influence, too. Beryl freely admitted she had felt as if she had come to know Cory without ever having met her, but in so doing, had imagined Cory as a twenty-something, a deeply-in-love young woman with passions and an interesting life waiting to be lived... It made Cory feel as if the clock had been turned back to be thought of that way, to be looked at by a young person and know that she wasn't being seen as an old woman or someone's great-aunt – someone whose life was over and done with.

*   *   *

"How many times are you going to re-pack?" Helen asks with a laugh as she enters the bedroom to find Corinne yet again re-organizing her trunk.

On the dresser sit their first-class tickets for an ocean liner leaving from New York in four days.

"We'll have to stop and see my parents while we're in New York," Helen had said as they made their travel arrangements. "They'll love you," she repeatedly reassures an anxious Corinne.

The past few months have wrought a wonderful change in Helen as she was able to focus her energies on planning their tour of Europe. Corinne is excited beyond words to think she is finally going to see places she has always dreamed of.

"You may be disappointed," Helen cautions her. "England continues to be under rations, and my friends write that London is still devastated by the bombing."

"What about Paris?" Corinne asks. "We will be able to go to Paris, won't we?"

Helen's expression darkens and Corinne wonders what memories will be stirred by a visit to France. She has never asked where in France Helen's missions were. "We can if you like," Helen says. "I think you'd prefer a visit to other places in France." Corinne knows she is silently adding, "Places not occupied by the Nazis."

Though Corinne is afraid of what she will see in Germany, she knows she must stand by Helen as she goes. "It's the strangest thing..." Helen has said to Corinne more than once since her return, "I have never thought of myself as Jewish or lesbian," – Corinne squirms uncomfortably at that word – "I was just... me. But knowing that people like me, like us, were rounded up and tortured and killed – it makes me feel a connection to them that I've never felt before."

But what Corinne is looking forward to the most is the Mediterranean. "You've never seen anything like the blue of the water," Helen says to her as they lie in bed at night and plan. "Sitting on warm Italian stone, and looking out at the sea as you smell the dust and the olive trees and the sun..."

"You can't smell sun," Corinne laughs.

"You can in Italy," Helen assures her.

Corinne is just closing the lid of her trunk again when they hear shouts from below. She and Helen fling open the bedroom door and race down the stairs into the den to find her father lying on the floor next to his chair.

"What happened?" Corinne cries.

"I don't know, Miss Corinne," says the maid who found him. "I was bringing him his afternoon tea – you know he likes it promptly at three o'clock when he gets home from the bank – and he was just there."

Helen rushes over to him. "Send someone to get Mrs. Bishop from the garden," she says authoritatively as she places fingers on his throat, "and then call the doctor. Ask him to come and to send an ambulance."

"Yes, Miss Helen," says the maid, running to do as Helen asks.

As they wait for the doctor to come, Helen loosens Eugene's tie and shirt collar and fans him. "Why don't you go wait for the doctor?" she suggests to Corinne, refusing to meet her eye, and Corinne knows why Helen wants her out of the room. Dumbly, she nods and goes to the front entry where she paces anxiously.

"It's his heart," the doctor tells the family a short while later as Eugene is whisked away by an ambulance, lights flashing and sirens blaring. He finds it difficult to meet Mary's tearful eyes as she wrings a lace handkerchief. He glances at the three grown children – Terrence sits in the Morris chair in the corner, withdrawn into his own world, while Candace fans herself melodramatically, looking as if she might swoon. Only Corinne, the young, pretty one meets his eye stoically, demanding the truth. Her friend, somewhat mannish but attractive, stands behind her. *She seems most sensible,* he thinks and he is gratified that she will be there, lending her support through what is to come.

"I'll know more when I can examine him at the hospital, but it is doubtful he will live more than a day or two," the doctor says to Corinne. "I told him three years ago, he had to take it easy, turn over more responsibilities at the bank, but..." He remembers why Eugene couldn't take a lesser role and casts a troubled glance at Terrence who is very white.

He clears his throat, and speaks directly to Corinne. "I'd like for you to come with me to the hospital."

The vigil lasts for nearly two days. Eugene is agitated and demands Corinne summon his lawyer to his hospital room. The three of them are huddled in there for hours as nurses and the rest of the family are barred from entry.

"I'm the eldest," Candace complains petulantly. "Why is she in there instead of me?"

"I suspect because Eugene trusts her to carry out his wishes." Wisely, Helen does not say this.

Instead, she paces ceaselessly, knowing that this turn of events will almost certainly spell an end to their plans for travel. Her heart sinks as she contemplates having to stay here indefinitely, for "I can't leave now," Corinne sobs in Helen's arms after her father dies. "I promised him... I'd stay to settle his affairs. He was adamant that Terrence be taken care of and he knows Candace wouldn't do it.

And there was something else... he couldn't bring himself to say... he was almost incoherent with worry. He kept stammering something about 'the wall, in the wall.' I have no idea what he meant. All I could do was promise him I would take care of it."

She raises her beautiful tear-stained face. "I know you have to go," she whispers. "I see in it in your eyes."

Helen kisses her tenderly. "I don't want to go without you."

"But if you don't, you'll come to hate being here, and I couldn't bear that," Corinne says, laying a hand tenderly on Helen's cheek. "I'll join you if I can... but if I can't, I'll be here waiting for you to come back. I'll always be waiting."

*   *   *

Aggie came into the study. "Are you ready for breakfast?" she asked, but stopped short as she saw Cory wiping her cheeks as she closed her book.

She sat down in the other chair, her face concerned as she asked, "Are you sure you're all right? It's just that lately, there seem to be so many painful memories."

Cory looked up at her. "Some of them are," she agreed. "But just because it's hard doesn't mean it isn't good."

Chapter 27

Beryl looked up from her computer as George came to the reference desk.

"Hi," she said brightly.

"Hi," he smiled, but the smile faltered a bit as his eyes slid down her face to her neck. She tugged up the collar of her shirt, trying to hide the bruises.

"Thanks for doing this," she said. "I don't think he'd go if he had to go alone."

"I don't mind," George said.

Ridley wheeled out of the staff room. "Hey," he said.

"All set?" George asked, glancing at his watch. "We should have plenty of time to get to the VA and find parking before your appointment."

"Kumbaya time," Ridley said sarcastically, looking down as he fiddled with his backpack.

George laid a hand on his shoulder and said, "It won't be like that."

"I'll see you at home later," Ridley said to Beryl.

"If I survive my mother," Beryl joked. Her eyes met George's for a few seconds before he followed Ridley to the door.

If Beryl had thought being tackled by Ridley in the midst of his nightmares was tough, it was nothing to facing her mother for the first time since her outburst in the basement. "That was always the problem," Beryl had tried to explain to Aggie. "I always held everything in until I was ready to explode, and then my family just laughed off my 'dramatics,' as they called them." Edith's typical response, a response copied by the rest of the family, was to ignore Beryl's dramatics. The tactic usually worked as Beryl almost always quailed from pursuing whatever had triggered her outburst in the first place. "I just learned to keep my mouth shut." Edith had apparently decided to act as if Beryl had never spoken of Ohio State or another job, and no further mention of the topic had been made over the phone the past few weeks.

When Beryl got to her parents' house, she found Marian there also, flipping through the newspaper. "What are you doing here on a weeknight?" she asked in surprise.

Without looking up at her, Marian replied with a slight edge to her voice, "I heard that the basement was full of boxes of my stuff, so I came to clear a few out."

Beryl flushed, but, rather than stammer or apologize, she simply said, "Good."

Marian looked up at that, but Beryl turned to her mother asking if she needed help with dinner preparations. Gathering plates for the table, Beryl asked her sister if she was staying for dinner.

"You know," Aggie had said gently when Beryl was trying to describe her interactions with her family, "you sound like a lot of my teacher friends who complain that their husbands and kids take them for granted and never help them around the house. They don't ask directly for help; they expect the husband and kids to see that they need help because they themselves would notice and jump in. And then they're repeatedly disappointed when it doesn't happen. They turn into martyrs."

Beryl had opened her mouth immediately to protest that that wasn't what she did, but now, thinking back on that conversation, she had to wonder.

"Here," she said, forcing herself to adopt a light tone as she set the stack of plates down in front of Marian. "If you'll put these on the table, I'll get the silverware."

Marian blinked up at her, but Beryl didn't stay to see whether she would protest. By the time she brought the silverware out to the table, Marian had the plates laid and was going back to get water glasses.

Quickly deciding that whooping would not be the appropriate response to this small victory, Beryl contented herself with a tiny smile of satisfaction.

"What happened to your neck?" Edith asked as they all sat, her eyes probing.

Knowing better than to deny anything had happened, which would only raise her mother's suspicions, Beryl said, "I thought I'd play a joke on Ridley and snuck up on him. He reacted. It was stupid of me to startle a Marine."

Gerald blinked and looked up. "I remember one time…" and he launched into a narrative that no one really listened to about his time in the Air Force.

They were just clearing away the dinner dishes when Beryl's cell phone rang over where it lay next to her keys on the kitchen counter. To Beryl's intense irritation, Marian answered.

"Just a moment," she said to whomever was on the other end. "They want Dr. Gray," she said mockingly.

If Beryl had thought getting Marian to help set the table had signaled a shift in their relationship, she was wrong. Beryl snatched the phone from her sister, and said, "This is Dr. Gray," before she walked into the den and shut the door loudly.

Never in her life had Beryl been able to make decisions easily, without second-guessing herself, largely because everyone else her entire life had second-guessed for her. Perhaps things wouldn't have been any different this time if she hadn't been so angry with her sister, but she was as surprised as anyone when she returned to the table where her family was eating dessert and announced, "I am the new Assistant Curator in the Rare Books and Manuscripts Library at the Ohio State University."

*   *   *

"You're kidding!" Ridley exclaimed when she got home later that evening to find him and George seated at the table over Chinese and gave them the news.

She hugged both of them delightedly.

"This deserves a toast," Ridley said, going to the refrigerator and pulling out three bottles of Sam Adams.

He and George raised their bottles and said, "To Dr. Gray."

Beryl took a long drink and sat back, exhaling at last. "Well, your reaction was a lot more positive than my family's," she said. "My mother didn't speak to me for the rest of the evening. And my sister..."

"Do you really care what she thinks?" Ridley asked sardonically.

Beryl grinned. "Not really."

Her expression sobered as she considered the consequences of her decision. "Wow," she murmured. "I start October first. I've got a boatload of stuff to do." She looked up at them in dismay. "I've got to find an apartment in a city I don't know. Will I need a car? I've never owned a car. Why the hell didn't I think about that before?"

Ridley could see the panic building in her eyes. "Calm down," he said. "We'll tackle this one thing at a time. Tomorrow, you'll hand in your notice to Georgetown. We can go to Ohio over Labor Day if you like and spend the weekend looking for apartments. And we can check out the bus situation. Does Columbus have a train?"

No one knew.

"Anyway, it will be fine," he assured her.

Beryl looked at him, suddenly hit by how very much she was going to miss him. "Maybe –"

"Don't," he cut in. He reached across the table and took her hand. "You worked hard for this. You deserve it. It's a good thing, Beryl. A good thing." He sat back. "Why don't you call Aggie and give her the news."

*   *   *

"Beryl, that's wonderful!" Aggie said when she heard.

Beryl was biting her lip as she waited for Aggie's reaction. "You're sure?"

Aggie laughed. "I'm very sure." She hesitated for a second, then said, "It's what I was hoping for."

Beryl suddenly found it hard to breathe. "Really?"

"Really."

Sitting there, Beryl found herself filled with a warmth she hadn't known in a very long time.

Chapter 28

"**A**gatha, it's only ten o'clock," Cory said. "They can't possibly be here yet."

Aggie turned from the front windows where she was looking for any sign of Ridley's car.

"If you'd be more comfortable staying at a hotel, I'd understand," Aggie had said nervously as Beryl made plans to come to Columbus to scout for an apartment, "but we have lots of empty bedrooms right here... I mean we don't have beds, but –"

"We'd love to stay with you," Beryl interrupted. "Are you kidding? Stay with friends instead of at a hotel? We can get air mattresses if you don't mind us camping out with you."

She smiled at the warmth in Aggie's voice as she said, "We're looking forward to having you here. Both of you."

"I know they're not here," Aggie said now. "I was just dusting the window sill."

"I see," Cory said with a knowing smile as she herself ran a damp mop over the foyer floor. "I remember when there was an entire crew of maids and gardeners to take care of this old place," she called.

"Well, one benefit of a mostly empty house," Aggie said as she ran her cloth over the mantel, "is that it's easy to clean around here."

* * *

183

Corinne is preoccupied as she comes home and goes directly to her father's den. The sound of Candace's piano fades as she closes the door. The handsome mahogany paneling creates a quiet, meditative atmosphere and she understands why her father liked it in here so much. The den still smells faintly of his pipe tobacco. It has taken her weeks to make sense of the bank's books, and she is exhausted. She looks up at a soft knock on the door. Her mother comes in, closing the door behind her.

"Is it as bad as you thought?" Mary asks, noting the dark circles under Corinne's eyes.

Corinne looks at her mother, wondering how much to tell her. "Father –"

They are interrupted by the maid bringing in a tea tray. "Just like we did for Mr. Bishop," she insists each day when Corinne comes home from the bank.

"Thank you, Frances," Mary says as she accepts the tray and pours tea for her daughter and herself.

Waiting until they are alone again, Corinne resumes, "As nearly as I can tell, Father... 'borrowed' funds from depositors' accounts for some rather... questionable investments. Things related to post-war recovery projects, but..." she glances worriedly at her mother, "they haven't paid off as he expected, and the money isn't there to replace what he took."

Mary's hand flies to her mouth. "Are we in danger of closing?" she asks in a horrified whisper.

Corinne stares into her tea cup. "Not immediately. Not if I can find a way of making up what he took, but... if word of this gets out and a run starts, we'll be ruined."

Mary takes a bracing breath as she steadies herself. "I'm so sorry you have to deal with this, my dear," she says. "We will do what we must."

Corinne looks at her mother searchingly. "Do you mean that?" She knows her mother has always been spared the necessity of dealing with anything outside the running of the household.

Mary blinks. "Of course, I do."

184

Corinne sets her tea cup down and leans toward her mother. "Then I think we may be able to salvage the situation, but it will not be easy. It will mean scrimping here at home in order to free up funds that we can use to replace what Father borrowed."

Mary nods. "We can do that."

"Yes, but," Corinne says seriously, "I do not want Terrence or Candace to know why we are doing this. I don't want Father's reputation sullied, and Candace would use this to make Terrence feel guilty about not returning to the bank. That would kill him. All we have to say is that, as the current keeper of the household accounts, I have decided that we spend too lavishly, and we must be thriftier."

"You know this will draw your sister's ire," Mary says, looking at Corinne appraisingly. "She will blame you."

Corinne meets her mother's gaze unflinchingly. "I know, but it must be done, and this will be the easiest way."

Mary draws herself up. "Then we will do what we must. We survived the Depression when others went under. We will not be closed down now." She tilts her head sympathetically. "I want you to know how I appreciate your giving up your travel plans to stay. I don't know how I should have dealt with your father's funeral and all of this without you. I hope that you and Helen will be able to travel together one day soon."

Corinne digs her fingernails into her palms painfully in order to stay the tears threatening. "I hope so, too," she says stoically.

After her mother leaves the den, Corinne opens a desk drawer and pulls out a small lockbox. Pulling a tiny key from a chain around her neck, she unlocks the box and pulls out a packet of letters and postcards – the Swiss Alps, Vienna, Geneva. Each one is filled with brief descriptions of the sights, but always, "I'm saving Italy for you," Helen writes.

*   *   *

"They're here!" Aggie said excitedly when Ridley's car pulled around back.

She and Cory rushed outside to greet Beryl and Ridley with hugs of welcome. Aggie held Beryl a little longer than necessary, but noted that Beryl returned the embrace just as tightly.

"What a house!" Ridley said appreciatively as he stood with his crutches, looking up at the enormous structure. Cory proudly took him on a tour, leaving Aggie to help Beryl with their small suitcases and sacks containing air mattresses.

"How was the trip?" Aggie asked as she led the way up the sweeping staircase to two empty bedrooms.

"It was good," Beryl said. "Seemed to fly by. Luckily, we have similar taste in music, so when we weren't talking..."

"How are his nightmares?" Aggie asked quietly. She set down the things she was carrying and turned to face Beryl, scanning her neck for any remaining bruises.

"He still has them some nights," Beryl said, "but not like that night. His therapist thinks our visit to the memorials triggered stronger flashbacks for him. I didn't even think about that," she added guiltily.

"I don't think most of us would," Aggie said sympathetically, reaching a hand out to Beryl's shoulder, but immediately withdrawing it.

They were interrupted by Cory and Ridley's voices drawing near.

"Do you want to rest before dinner?" Cory asked solicitously.

"No," Beryl and Ridley replied in unison.

"Good!" she smiled. "Aggie, why don't you call Shannon, and let's get the grill fired up."

"Oh, my God," Shannon whispered a few hours later as she and Aggie stood near the kitchen sink. "He's gorgeous!"

Aggie rolled her eyes. "Stop. I told you, he's gay," she whispered back.

"I don't care," Shannon said emphatically. "He's eye candy. I'm just going to drink him in while he's here." She glanced over at the table where Ridley, Beryl and Cory were huddled over a map of Columbus as she scraped plates in preparation for placing them in the sink. "And Beryl seems really great."

Aggie, unable to hide how she felt, beamed as she looked at Shannon. "She is," she said simply.

When she and Shannon had the dishes done, they joined the others at the table, pouring fresh glasses of wine for everyone. They now had a newspaper spread out, circling likely-sounding apartments for Beryl to check out. Aggie got out her laptop and brought up more real-estate listings on-line.

"Well, I don't need to worry about how big it is," Beryl joked as they read descriptions of square footage and number of bedrooms. "Since I don't have any furniture. All I need is a kitchen, a bedroom and a bathroom."

"Then why don't you just stay here?" Shannon suggested innocently, getting up to go outside with her wine.

Ridley grinned and followed her on his crutches, leaving a silent, shocked trio at the table.

"Think they ever would have figured that out on their own?" he asked conspiratorially.

"I doubt it," Shannon said, feeling very satisfied with herself.

*　　*　　*

Beryl lay awake on her air mattress, unable to sleep. Shannon's suggestion, once voiced, made it seem so obvious, but... they had all continued looking through the ads as if she hadn't spoken. Neither she nor Aggie nor Cory seemed to know how to broach the topic. She didn't want to push her way into their home, and she honestly didn't know if their silence was due to not wanting a stranger here or not wanting her to feel backed into a corner where she felt she couldn't say no without offending them.

"You barely know them," she reminded herself.

"I know that."

"What if you don't like it once you're here? How are you going to move out without hurting their feelings? Or what if they get tired of you? How are they going to say so?"

"I know," she said to herself irritably.

Frustrated, she got up and crept to her door. It opened silently. Barefoot, in her t-shirt and shorts, she went down the broad staircase to the study. Moonlight was streaming in through the tall windows, making it almost bright enough to read by. She sat in one of the wingchairs, drawing her knees to her chest, trying to think through how to handle this.

She was startled by the click of dog nails on the wooden floors as Percival trotted in and jumped up, placing his front paws on her chair and nuzzling her gently.

"Hi, there," she smiled, giving his ears a scratch.

She jumped when Aggie followed him a moment later.

"I'm sorry," Beryl apologized immediately. "I hope I didn't disturb you."

"I wasn't asleep," Aggie said, taking the other chair as Percival curled up in his bed. She looked over at Beryl in the moonlight. Screwing up her courage, she said, "I suspect we weren't sleeping for the same reason."

Beryl realized how fast her heart was beating. She didn't know what to say.

"Or maybe not," Aggie corrected, cursing herself for assuming.

"No," Beryl blurted. "You're right, I think." She swallowed, but it was hard to do. "I... I would love to live here with you and your aunt, but..."

"But you're not sure if we want you," Aggie finished for her. "I know Shannon thinks it's simple, but it isn't. This will only work if we promise to be honest with each other."

Beryl looked at Aggie, wondering what "this" she was referring to. Hoping she wouldn't pass out from hyperventilating, "I agree," she managed to croak.

Aggie shifted to face Beryl. "I don't want to scare you away, but... I care about you. A lot. It's the first time since Rachel left that I've felt this way about anyone, but I know it's too soon for you, after Claire..."

Beryl took a deep breath. "Aggie," she bit her lip. "I... I care about you, too. You are the best part of my day, but... I used to feel that way about Claire, and... I just don't trust myself..."

Aggie bravely came to Beryl, and held out her hand. Beryl took it

188

and let Aggie pull her to her feet. "Both of us need to learn to trust again – ourselves and each other – but... one thing I'm learning from Aunt Cory is that there's nothing worse than getting old and realizing your regrets are from not taking the chance on happiness when it was right there in front of you."

She came closer until her lips met Beryl's in a kiss, tender and wounded and soft. Tentatively, they held one another, savoring this first kiss, both afraid to yield to the tumult of emotions coursing through them. When at last they pulled apart, both aching for more, Aggie murmured, "Just so you know, without any doubts... I would like to have you to live here, if it's what you would like."

Calling Percival, she went back upstairs, leaving Beryl standing in the moonlight.

Chapter 29

"I don't know what we'll do here without you," said a heavy-set woman with Coke-bottle glasses.

"Thank you, Doris," Beryl said, giving her a hug. "I'm going to miss all of you."

As word slowly got round that Beryl was leaving, colleagues sought her out to wish her well.

"I had no idea so many people even knew who I was," Beryl confided to Ridley.

He shook his head. "You way underestimate how much you've done around here," he said. "I knew who you were even when I worked over at Dahlgren."

Beryl didn't know what to say to this, so she said nothing. With two weeks left here at Georgetown, she would have one week for her move before starting at Ohio State.

"Do you want to buy any furniture?" Ridley had asked.

"I don't think so," Beryl had replied. "I'd just have to move it. I may as well wait until I'm in Columbus and get stuff there."

"How about a car?"

She shrugged. "Aggie said buses run near their house to campus, so transportation shouldn't be a problem, and then if I find that a car would be more convenient, I can take my time looking for one."

She expelled a deep breath. "I just can't believe I'm actually doing this."

Neither could her family. They had gathered for a niece's birthday the weekend after Labor Day.

"This is a joke, right?" Nick scoffed when he was told.

"No joke," Beryl said.

He turned to Marian. "What did you do to piss her off this time?"

"Why is this my fault?" Marian retorted.

"Because Beryl would never do something like this on her own," Nick said as if this should be obvious.

His wife, Julie, who had been watching Beryl's face during this exchange, said smugly, "Maybe you don't know your sister as well as you think you do."

Beryl shot her a grateful smile. She got up from the table, leaving Nick and Marian sniping at one another. *I'm really not going to miss this,* she thought as she carried her dishes into the kitchen.

Her father followed her a moment later. "I'm proud of you, Beryl," Gerald said, giving her a kiss on the cheek.

For getting this job, or for breaking away? Beryl wondered, but all she said was, "Thanks, Dad."

Much more difficult than telling her family or her colleagues was telling Mr. Herrmann that she was moving.

"I have to tell him in person," Beryl insisted. She looked up at Ridley, and said, "Unless George already did?"

Ridley shook his head. "I asked him not to. I knew you would want to tell him yourself. Want to go today after our workout?"

Beryl nodded. Ridley wasn't letting up on the workouts. "I've only got a few more weeks to whip you into shape," he declared. "I want to turn out a finished Marine. And you'd better keep it up once you're out there," he said threateningly.

When they got to The Scriptorium later that evening, Beryl tried to savor everything – the musical tinkle of the bell, the slightly musty scent of the books, Mr. Herrmann's cologne.

"Oh, my dear," Mr. Herrmann said when she told him, his eyes growing bright. "How I will miss you! But it makes me so happy to know you will be working to preserve and collect old books. This is what you should be doing." He leaned close. "I just wish you were doing it here."

Beryl smiled. "Part of me does, too, but I think it will be good for me to live somewhere else for a while."

He looked her up and down. "Maybe you are right, but," he gestured at her, "you already look like a new person!"

George came over to give her a hug. "Congratulations again."

"Thanks," she said, squeezing him tightly.

*   *   *

"You don't have to take all these," Ridley said, pointing to the boxes of books stacked in Beryl's bedroom. "It's not like the Bishop house is bereft of books. Sort through them, take the ones you really want with you, and leave the rest here for now. They won't be in my way at all, and, once you're sure you're settled, then we can make arrangements to get the rest to you."

His suggestion was reasonable, and Beryl caught his subtle hint that maybe, moving in with Aggie and Cory wasn't the smartest thing to do.

"It just seems," he said, picking his words carefully, "that maybe it's moving a little fast."

"This whole thing was yours and Shannon's idea," she reminded him.

"I know," he hedged.

"And you were the one encouraging me to explore things with Aggie."

"Yeah, in terms of sex, which I still think would be good for you," he said, "not in terms of moving in together."

"We're not 'moving in together'," she told him. "I'm renting a room from her and her ninety-something great-aunt – a room in a huge mansion. And I don't intend for the sex thing to happen for a long, long time, if ever."

"Whatever," he said, shaking his head in total incomprehension.

"You're such a guy," she laughed.

"Thanks for noticing," he said sarcastically.

"Speaking of which, what's happening with George?" she asked nosily, deciding that, as she was leaving, she didn't need to be so cautious anymore. "He's been over here a lot lately."

"Things are... moving along," Ridley said vaguely. "It's weird, Beryl. I've never been with anyone like him. He's not pushy. He's been willing to let me set the rules. It's just so different."

Beryl smiled. "This sounds very promising," she said with a superior air.

"Do you need to see your parents one more time before we leave in the morning?" he asked, changing the subject.

Beryl sobered up at once. "No."

Her last visit with her mother and father for their last Thursday evening dinner together had been tough. Edith, never a demonstrative or emotional woman, had actually apologized to Beryl.

"I never meant to ignore you or take you for granted," she tried to explain. "It's just that you were the steady one, the one I never had to worry about getting into trouble, or doing anything foolish. And I suppose... I can see how that could appear to you as if I didn't care as much..."

Her voice cracked, and she turned away. Beryl went to her and said gently, "Mom, I know I made it sound as if I'm doing this as some kind of reaction, but I'm not. I worked hard for my doctorate, and I've never done anything with it. I let Claire talk me out of applying for other positions that I would have loved, and then this one came along out of the blue. I'm not going to let life slide by me anymore. I'm only a few hours away. I'll be home for visits."

"It won't be the same as having you so nearby," Edith insisted, *and that,* thought Beryl, *is a very good thing.*

*   *   *

"Is this everything?" Aggie asked in surprise as she, Cory and Percival greeted Beryl, Ridley and Winston when they arrived the last weekend of September.

"I travel light these days," Beryl quipped, as she and Aggie carried her one box of books and her two small suitcases of clothes up to the room she had used before where the air mattress awaited. They set Winston's carrier down and supervised Percival as the two animals sniffed curiously at one another through the grated door.

"Didn't you take anything from the place you shared with Claire?" Aggie asked gently.

Beryl shook her head. "I didn't want any of it," she said firmly. Everything she had once liked now had negative connotations attached to it, real or imagined – a bed Leslie and Claire had had sex in... a sofa they had curled up on together... "Let it go!" she'd told herself harshly back when she had decided to leave with so little.

"I like that. A fresh start," Aggie said, and Beryl had the strong feeling that she had read her mind. "We can go furniture shopping after school or this coming weekend, if you like," Aggie offered.

Beryl smiled gratefully. "That would be great. Thanks."

The next morning, Ridley prepared to drive back to D.C. by himself after breakfast, and Beryl found herself choking up as she tried to say good-bye.

"I honestly don't know what I would have done without you," she whispered as she held him tightly while he leaned against his car.

He held her just as tightly as he murmured, "Or I without you. You've done more for me than you know. You made me believe I don't have to be alone anymore." He gave her a kiss on the cheek. "I'll be out to visit," he promised. "And you'd better come back to see me, too."

"I will."

Settling behind the wheel, he reached over to the glove compartment and pulled out a fat envelope which he pressed into Beryl's hand.

"What's this?" she asked.

"The rent you've been paying me," he said. "Don't argue. I don't need it, but I appreciate that you wanted to share expenses. You'll need it here. You're starting over."

Tearfully, she waved him off as he drove away. She felt something at her elbow, and turned to find Cory taking her arm, steering her toward the garden.

"Good-byes are never easy," Cory said softly.

"I don't know how you and Helen did it," Beryl said.

*   *   *

Corinne stands on the outdoor observation deck at the Columbus airport. She knows Helen's plane isn't due for at least an hour, but she likes to watch the planes taking off and landing, eagerly anticipating the time when she can be on one of them, taking off with Helen for exotic locales. The chill October air has a bite to it, and she draws the collar of her old Navy pea coat more closely around her neck. She smiles to herself, remembering how it irritates Candace that she will not throw it away.

"I can't believe you would embarrass us by going about in that ratty old thing," Candace declared only this morning as Corinne prepared to leave for the airport. "And are those men's pants you're wearing?"

Constrained by the roles she has been forced to assume as bank president and community leader, Corinne feels a rush of exhilaration now as she stands, feet wide apart, feeling the wind in her hair, whipped to a higher velocity by the propellers of passing planes. For this bit of time, she can pretend she is just Corinne again, living on her own, independent and free to do as she wishes. But she is not. Even as she stands there, she recalls that there is a board meeting this week for which she must prepare.

When Helen's plane lands at last, Corinne catches sight of her descending the plane's steps. Waving madly, she pushes her way inside to rush into Helen's arms. Ignoring the curious stares of the other passengers, she and Helen hold one another tightly as Corinne breathes in the flowery scent she has missed so.

"Oh, I can't believe you're here," she murmurs.

Helen's throaty laugh sounds in her ear. "I'm here." She pulls back to look into Corinne's eyes. "Let's get out of here."

"Where are we going?" she asks a few minutes later as Corinne drives them from the airport in the Bishops' 1946 Chrysler Windsor, Eugene's last big purchase before his heart attack.

"Not home," says Corinne. "Not yet."

She drives them out of town, out into the country, where harvested fields full of stubble run to the horizon. Parking on the side of the road, she turns to Helen and says, "Tell me everything, everywhere you've been, everything you've seen."

Helen laughs again. "I've told you in my letters and postcards." She sees the desperate look in Corinne's eyes and says, "But I'll tell you again, later. For now, tell me what you've been dealing with. Your letters alluded to problems, but you never said what exactly."

Corinne tells her about Eugene's financial indiscretions and her efforts to fix everything before any of it could become public knowledge.

"Only Mother knows," she says. "I've had to put everyone on a strict allowance, which Candace, of course, protests. But, the hardest part was having to let some of the staff go. They'd been with us for years, most of them. I kept the oldest ones, and have done all I could to help the younger ones find other work, but... the house and grounds are suffering. We can't keep things as they were."

Helen takes her hand, noticing the worry lines newly etched upon Corinne's forehead. "I know how capable you are," she says. "I know you'll get everything worked out. Have you been able to pay back what Eugene took from other accounts?"

"Nearly. I think with another six or seven months, I'll have everything square, and then I can leave and we can do as we please."

Helen leans to her and kisses her passionately. "Six months," she murmurs when they part. "Then I'll show you the world."

*   *   *

"As I look back," Cory said, "I'm not sure how we did it, either. It broke my heart every time we had to say good-bye. It's a wonder I still have a heart."

She and Beryl walked along the garden path, strewn with early fallen leaves and acorns that crunched as they walked.

"I think," Beryl said, taking Cory's hand, "that you must have the biggest heart of anyone I've ever known."

Cory smiled. "Bless you. And bless you for coming to us. We needed you, Beryl Gray."

"Not as much as I needed you, Corinne Bishop."

Chapter 30

There was a loud shuffling and scraping of chairs as the bell rang.

"Remember, have the second act of *Romeo and Juliet* read by next week," Aggie called to the students as they pushed to the door. All except Becka.

"I've already read the whole thing, Miss Bishop," she said as she remained seated at her desk, her book still open, clearly signaling that she was ready for a long talk.

"That's great, Becka," Aggie said, trying to hide her consternation at having Becka in the last period of the day, which allowed her to hang out after the bell rang. Aggie had already found it tough to get away, and they were only a month into the semester.

"Hey," Shannon's head popped around the doorway. "Aren't you ready yet? We have to go."

"Hi, Miss Callahan," Becka said glumly.

"Hello, Becka," said Shannon. "Sorry, but we've got to run."

"Have a good weekend, Miss Bishop," Becka said as Aggie nearly ran out the door.

"You, too. Bye."

Aggie released a pent-up breath as they escaped into the parking lot. "Whew! Thank you!"

"No problem," Shannon grinned. "You have got to get tougher."

"It's just hard because I usually do need to stay and get things done at the end of the day, and she takes it as an invitation to sit and chat."

"It's only going to get worse if you don't cut her off somehow," Shannon warned.

"You're right."

"I know I am. You don't see anyone hanging out in my classroom, do you?" Shannon asked.

Aggie looked at her ruefully. "You teach algebra, and you're a bitch."

Shannon spread her hands apart, eyebrows raised, as if to say, "See? Problem solved."

Aggie laughed. "I'll figure something out. My way."

"Whatever."

"You coming to dinner tonight?"

"And miss the chance to see the incredible Dr. Gray?" Shannon teased. "Of course, I'm coming."

Aggie stopped abruptly as she tossed her bag into the back seat of her car. "You do like her, don't you?"

Shannon tilted her head. "Yes. I do like her. I was prepared not to, but so far... I can't find anything to dislike. Damn it. How are things going, by the way?"

"It's barely changed our routine. We've hardly seen her," Aggie replied. "She's been working late, and when she is at the house, she spends most of her time up in her room. I'm going to take her shopping for some furniture tomorrow."

Aggie got in her car and rolled the window down. "See you at six. It's the end of her first week at OSU."

"Should I bring champagne?" Shannon called sarcastically as she went on to her car.

"I already have some," Aggie returned with a wave as she pulled away.

*   *   *

"The collections are amazing," Beryl was saying a couple of hours later over dinner. "I've been familiarizing myself with them this week. But the medieval documents – manuscripts and prayer books mostly – you really have to see them. It's incredible to think of the work that went into preparing the vellum, grinding and mixing the ingredients for the inks – you should see the colors, even centuries later – and then the painstaking work of inscribing the actual text."

She was animated in a way that she never was when talking about herself, and her enthusiasm was contagious. Her eyes behind her glasses were bright, and the way her hair changed color, depending on how the light hit it... Aggie caught Shannon watching her watch Beryl, and turned back to her plate, her face burning.

Aggie popped the champagne she had bought, and poured for everyone, raising her glass in a toast to Beryl and her new position. Embarrassed by the focused attention, Beryl changed the subject, asking Aggie and Shannon how the new school year was going.

"Well, other than Aggie being cornered three days a week by an obnoxious student who –" Shannon began.

"She's not obnoxious," Aggie protested. "She's just lonely. She doesn't have any other friends, and I've been elected."

"You're too nice," Shannon insisted, her attention caught as Beryl got up from the table to take some empty dishes to the sink for rinsing.

"Sorry," Beryl muttered, pausing to return to the table to carefully push her chair back into position first.

"That dinner was excellent, Aunt Cory," Shannon said appreciatively while Beryl brought a plate of brownies to the table.

"I'll have to make you a hundred dinners to thank you for all the help you gave Agatha with the painting," Cory said.

"It's a good thing she ran out of gin, or I'd still be painting," Shannon grumbled good-naturedly.

"Well, I'd be glad to help with things like that, too," Beryl offered.

"Thank you, Beryl," Cory said. "As a matter of fact, the garden and yard need a serious raking and cleaning up, so if you're willing...?"

"Of course," Beryl smiled.

"How about we go furniture shopping tomorrow morning, and tackle the garden in the afternoon?" Aggie suggested.

"Oh, girls, that would be wonderful," Cory said.

"I'll clean up. You cooked," Beryl insisted when they were done with the brownies and rose from the table.

"I'll help you," Shannon said. "You and Aunt Cory go sit on the porch and relax. We'll be out in a few minutes," she said to Aggie, giving her a playful shove. "Don't worry, I'll behave."

She put the leftovers away and dried the dishes, chatting about football, which Beryl knew nothing of, while Beryl washed the pans and utensils. Shannon went to wipe down the table, still watching Beryl covertly as she rinsed the sink and then scrubbed it clean, followed by wiping it dry with a clean towel.

Unable to stand by any longer, Shannon went to her. "Beryl, stop. Just stop."

Beryl looked up at her.

Gently, Shannon took the towel from her hands and hung it on the oven door handle to dry. "You don't have to do that anymore. No one here will care that the sink isn't perfectly clean and dry. No one cares that the chairs aren't all pushed in," she said, gesturing to the table where the chairs were somewhat haphazardly left sitting about. "You don't have to do that anymore," she repeated.

Beryl raised her gaze to Shannon's, and knew that she understood. To her shame, she felt sudden tears spring to her eyes, and she rushed out the back door into the garden.

Shannon let her go, and made her way out to the front porch where Cory was rocking and Aggie was sitting on the topmost step as dusk fell. She sat heavily next to Aggie.

"Where's Beryl?" Aggie asked.

She looked at Shannon more closely when she didn't receive an immediate reply. She hadn't seen that look on Shannon's face in a long time, not since....

"What's wrong?" she asked in a low voice.

Shannon pressed her forehead to her hand. "God, that trigger is so strong. You think you're over it, and then..." She took a deep breath. "I don't know if her partner ever hit her, but I know abused behavior when I see it. She's out back. Go to her."

Aggie had to wander to the far corner of the garden before she found Beryl near an old grotto, long since dry. Darkness was descending in earnest as she sat next to her on one of the granite benches, carved with elaborate acanthus leaves. For long minutes, she simply sat there.

At length, she said, "Shannon's ex-husband used to beat her. For years, I stood by, knowing it was happening, but not sure what to say. I felt like such a coward, pretending it wasn't happening, and letting her pretend all her bruises and black eyes were accidents. I can't remember what happened to make me finally say something, but... all it took was one person acknowledging to her that they knew the truth, and she said it changed everything. Even so, it took her a long time to stop reacting to the things that reminded her of her life with him."

She shifted closer and laid one hand over top of Beryl's where it tightly gripped the edge of the bench.

Beryl's head was bowed. "I'm just so ashamed, and so angry. I let it happen," she whispered. "She never touched me. She didn't have to. I... I was so infatuated in the beginning that... and then, later, I didn't want arguments. Somehow, without even knowing how it happened, I was doing everything her way. All she had to do was point or say one word and I would jump." She removed her glasses and swiped her sleeve angrily across her eyes. "I don't know who I am anymore."

Looking down, she flipped her other hand over and twined her fingers with Aggie's, resisting the urge to kiss the hand of this woman who had become her savior.

"No!" said another voice in her head immediately, the one that used to try and warn her about Claire, the one she never wanted to listen to. "You've got to be your own savior. No one else can play that role."

"I don't think you're that person anymore, Beryl," Aggie said softly. "I know you're not over it completely, but you'll never be that person again. And I wouldn't want you to be. You will find yourself again. I think you've already started to. Remember, you're just one of the walking wounded in this house."

Beryl's mouth twitched into a smile. "That's what Ridley used to say."

Aggie shrugged. "For a man, he's pretty smart," she admitted grudgingly.

Beryl laughed. "That's what I used to say."

Aggie tugged on Beryl's hand. "Come on. I'm afraid to leave Aunt Cory alone with Shannon too long. It's hard to tell what stories she'll get Cory to spill when I'm not there to defend myself."

Chapter 31

"Well, how are you settling in?" Bart Hudspath asked, his eyes widening a little in surprise at the lack of any kind of personalization of Beryl's office – not even her framed doctoral degree on the wall.

He looked very like what Beryl had expected from their initial telephone conversations: wire-rimmed glasses, salt and pepper hair and beard, tweed jacket. His genial manner seemed a contradiction to his prestigious accomplishments: faculty positions at Columbia and Yale, including a stint at the Library of Congress before coming to Ohio State as the head of the department.

"I'm doing just fine, thank you," she said, reaching over to clear a stack of folders off the seat of the extra chair next to her desk.

"HR got you all set up with your benefits paperwork?" he asked, sitting and crossing his legs comfortably.

Beryl nodded. "No problems," she said.

"And you don't mind helping with the cataloguing of our new acquisitions?"

"Not at all," Beryl hastened to assure him. "I did some of that at Georgetown, so I know the complexities of cataloguing will help me be that much more familiar with what we have."

"Good," he smiled. "Well, I'll let you get back to it. Oh, a few of us are going out for drinks this Friday after work. We'd love to have you join us."

"Thanks, but... I have plans for Friday," Beryl said, trying not to look too pleased.

Just a couple of evenings ago, Cory had come to the study with an envelope in hand. Standing there, she'd said, "Agatha's birthday is this Friday, and I got these tickets for *West Side Story* quite a while ago. I'd like you to use them."

"No," Beryl protested immediately. "You got those for the two of you."

"I insist," Cory had said, pushing the envelope into Aggie's hands with a smile that made her look suspiciously like Shannon. "You two go and have a good time."

"Well, some other time then," Dr. Hudspath smiled. Picking up on Beryl's shyness, he reassured her, "We're all just a bunch of old-book geeks."

"Thanks," Beryl repeated as he left.

Her new colleagues really were nice people, even if they were a bunch of old-book geeks to others. "But so am I," she smiled to herself. It had just been a long time since she'd had to get to know a new group of people, geeky or otherwise, and the constant newness of the social interactions left her mentally exhausted most evenings, so that she'd been going upstairs and crashing on her new bed almost as soon as she got home.

The mansion was starting to feel like home, now that she had a bed and dresser. She had also bought an over-sized leather club chair and ottoman for the study, along with an extra side table and a couple more lamps.

"You can't keep hiding in your room," Ridley had said knowingly during one of their early phone conversations. "It sounds like Winston spends more time with them than you do. You're not intruding on them," he added, anticipating her objections. "They invited you to live there; they want to spend time with you."

She sighed. "I guess."

"Have you been working out?" he demanded.

"Yes, sir," she replied. "I found the campus rec center and I've been going right after work."

"Good Marine," he said.

She heard a voice in the background. "Say hi to George for me." George had been there a lot lately as she and Ridley had talked. No word yet on whether he had spent the night, but Beryl took it as an encouraging sign that Ridley was trusting him enough to spend this much time with him.

"Trust," she sighed as she hung up. "Why is it so hard?"

*   *   *

Beryl waited for the bus, sweaty from her workout, her backpack slung over her shoulder. As she had promised Ridley, her workout routine was something she was determined to hang onto. *I'm not stopping for anyone this time,* she thought fiercely, though Aggie had not uttered the first hint that Beryl shouldn't be doing this. Quite the contrary, Beryl thought she'd caught Aggie furtively eyeing her a few times when she was wearing a t-shirt and jeans.

The cool October evening felt good on her flushed face. She was almost disappointed when the bus arrived.

"Don't you want a car?" Aggie had asked several times. "Or I could drop you off and pick you up."

"I've taken buses and trains my whole life," Beryl reminded her. "I don't mind. But thanks." She knew Aggie's offer was made only from a desire to be helpful, but Beryl found herself recoiling from anything that would tie her to someone else's schedule.

Once on the bus, she stared at the back of the seat in front of her, feeling confused by the jumble of emotions churning inside her. With Ridley, she had welcomed his nearness, his company – something she had never experienced with a man before. They had done nearly everything together in those weeks after she had left Claire, but now... She did little more than sleep at the mansion, often grabbing dinner out before she returned for the evening. Cory and Aggie welcomed her warmly whenever she got home, with no questions beyond whether she was hungry and how her day had been. They were perfectly fine with her hanging out with them or not.

207

"It's not them, it's you," said that voice in Beryl's head.

"That's stupid," she argued back. "I moved here to be with them."

"Yes, but," the voice returned, "you want to be with them so much, you won't let yourself be with them."

And she realized it was true. She was isolating herself deliberately. She felt like one of those fanatical monks or nuns who castigate themselves, punishing themselves to remove the desire, the temptation of precisely those things they most covet.

Her evening at the theatre with Aggie last week had felt like some kind of dream. Not sure whether Aggie was looking at the evening as a date or as some kind of obligation thrust upon her by her aunt, Beryl had dressed carefully, trying to make a good impression, *but don't overdo it,* she'd thought as she sorted through her limited choices. She was rewarded by the admiring look in Aggie's eyes when she came downstairs.

"Well, as Cory bought the theatre tickets, I insist on treating you to a birthday dinner," she'd said. "Except you'll have to pick the restaurant, and you'll have to drive..."

Aggie laughed animatedly and said, "Gladly."

The Ohio Theatre itself was beautiful, its ornate architecture and furnishings having been restored when the theatre was saved from demolition in the seventies. Sitting next to Aggie in the dark, Beryl caught whiffs of her perfume each time she leaned near to whisper something in Beryl's ear. Beryl didn't recall much of the show, but had a vivid recollection of the pressure of Aggie's knee against hers and the way she reached over for Beryl's hand when Maria sang "Somewhere." Looking over at her in the dark, she could see tears running down Aggie's face.

Lying in her room later that night, she had listened to the sound of Aggie's voice talking to Cory as she said good-night, the sound of her footsteps as she came upstairs and, more than anything, she had wanted to go to Aggie, hold her, kiss her, make love to her....

Beryl almost missed her stop as she let her mind explore that scenario. Jumping up, she ran to get off the bus. Hitching her backpack onto both shoulders, she walked through Bexley's streets, familiar now as twilight turned the sky to a Maxfield Parrish hue of rich indigos, the black silhouettes of the almost leafless trees standing out starkly against the saturated colors. She kicked through piles of crunchy leaves as she walked, enjoying the smells of autumn.

As she entered the kitchen door, she heard an unfamiliar voice. She peered into the study where Aggie and Cory were seated with another woman.

"Beryl!" Aggie jumped up as she saw her. "Come in. I want to introduce you to my mother, Debbie Warren. Mom, this is Dr. Beryl Gray."

Beryl came forward to shake hands with Debbie, who scrutinized her appearance. Embarrassed as she realized what she looked like in her sweats while Debbie smoothed her own meticulous – "and expensive," Aggie would have added – attire, Beryl was nevertheless surprised that Aggie's mother should be so... artificial, seemed the best word. "Hello, Ms. Warren."

"How do you do, Beryl," Debbie said, though her strangely puffed lips had difficulty forming a "b". "That's kind of an old-fashioned name, isn't it?"

"This from the woman who allowed me to be named Agatha?" Aggie scoffed in disbelief. "Like that didn't make my childhood difficult."

For some reason, Beryl found this hilarious, and had to turn away to hide her laughter.

"Well, anyway," Debbie said with a reproving glance at Aggie, "I'll leave you with those pamphlets. You think about it, all right?" She was still speaking with a bit of a speech impediment. "Oh, I just heard that David Fredericks, you remember him, the dermatologist, has separated from his wife," she said to Aggie as she picked up her purse. "You should call him."

She pressed her cheek to Aggie's with a weird attempt to pucker her lips, and left.

"She just had her lips injected," Aggie explained apologetically as they heard the kitchen door close.

"Oh."

Aggie shook her head. "Ever since Dad left her for a thirty-year-old, she's been trying to look younger. It's not pretty."

"Um, what about the dermatologist?" Beryl asked, still confused.

Aggie rolled her eyes with a heavy sigh. "She refuses to see the obvious. She keeps trying to set me up with rich men."

"Oh," Beryl repeated, her heart sinking to somewhere in the vicinity of her stomach. The fantasy she'd so recently been enjoying on the bus suddenly seemed very foolish.

"Sit down, Beryl," Cory smiled.

"What was that about pamphlets?" Beryl asked, hoping she didn't sound too nosy.

"Oh, she does this every month or so," Aggie said.

Winston, who had entered the room at the sound of Beryl's voice, yowled once before jumping up into her lap as she sat cross-legged in her chair. Percival trotted over, and politely sat in front of Beryl, waiting for an invitation to jump up, which he did as soon as she patted her thigh. Beryl rubbed both of them as she asked, "Does what?"

"Gives Aunt Cory information on various assisted-living facilities – places Mom insists she'll be happier," Aggie explained.

"I thought that was all settled when you moved in with her," Beryl said to Aggie, feeling very confused. "You're not going, are you?" she asked, turning to Cory.

"Of course not," Cory assured her. "But it doesn't stop the rest of the family from trying."

"Why are they so determined to get you to move out?" Beryl asked.

Aggie offered Cory an apologetic smile and said, "Because they are determined to sell the house. I think I told you, it's held in a trust that specifies that it is to remain Aunt Cory's home for as long as she lives or cares to stay here. And they can't break it. They've tried."

"It was the last thing my father did before he died," Cory said. "I know he did it because he wanted my brother to be taken care of, but... I don't know if he knew it would also become my jail."

*   *   *

"Peters," Helen finds the aged gardener working to cut back the pe-onies. "Have you seen Miss Corinne this afternoon?" she asks as she pushes a sweaty strand of hair off her forehead, the knees of her dungarees damp with mud.

"Yes, miss," he replies, doffing his cap respectfully and standing as straight as his arthritic spine will allow. "She came through here about an hour ago, headed toward the garden."

"Thank you."

Helen searches the garden, transformed under her guidance. "There's so much we could do," she had said to Corinne last fall when she arrived. "If your mother doesn't mind, I'd be glad to work with the gardeners."

"You can't be serious," Candace had complained when Corinne came to her mother with the idea. "How embarrassing, to have her grubbing about like some common laborer. We'll be the butt of eve-ryone's gossip."

"She only wants to do is make things grow, after all the death and destruction she saw during the war," Terrence had said to everyone's surprise as he looked up from his plate. Often it was impossible to tell whether he was aware of the conversations around him. "Why should that be embarrassing?"

With Mary's blessing, Helen had undertaken to create a few for-mal spaces by moving and replanting what the grounds already had. "Doing it this way, it didn't take any money," she'd explained as she proudly showed off the neatly-trimmed yew and boxwood hedges laid out in geometric precision.

"I feel like I'm in Europe," Corinne had said in wonder as she gaped.

"These are nice," Helen agreed proudly, "but my favorite space is back here," she said, leading Corinne back to a wilder, more serene part of the garden.

Here, hidden paths lead to small surprises – little benches and tables moved from other areas of the garden, some limestone or granite, others made from bent wood and logs, creating private re-treats where one could read or paint or just meditate.

Wandering now, Helen finally finds Corinne at the grotto, a steady stream of water issuing forth from Zeus's mouth into the limestone pool below. There, Corinne sits, sobbing as if her heart were breaking.

"What is it, my love?" Helen asks in alarm, wrapping an arm around Corinne's quaking shoulders. "What happened?"

Corinne wipes her eyes and looks up at Helen. "The entire board was there. They won't accept my resignation. They said if I resign, they'll vote to sell the bank."

"Would that be so horrible?" Helen asks with a sinking of her heart.

"Not in and of itself," Corinne sniffs, "but if they sell, any buyer will do a detailed audit. They'll discover what Father did. And what if I missed something? What if it's not all paid back? I can't. I just can't do that to Mother."

Helen stands, wrapping her arms around herself. "What about you? What about us? Are we never to be allowed to live our lives?" She doesn't mean to sound angry, but the injustice of the situation is tearing at her.

"We were to leave next month for the Hamptons with my par-ents," she reminds Corinne, "And from there we were scheduled to leave for Europe at last."

Corinne's eyes fill with tears again. "I know," she says bitterly. "But don't you see what this could do to my family? I can't –"

"What I see is that you weren't like this when we were in Wash-ington," Helen cuts in. "You enjoyed being free of them. You said so yourself. And now, you're letting them pull you – pull us – into this quagmire they've created."

Corinne's moist eyes blaze. "That's unfair," she protests. "No one planned –"

Helen kneels in front of Corinne, taking her by the shoulders. "Come with me," she pleads desperately. "We need to get away from here. Don't you see what it's doing to us? All you think about is that bank. We haven't made love..."

Corinne takes Helen's hands in hers – hands that have become callused and stained by her months of work outdoors. "Can't you be patient a little while longer? Another six months, and I should be able to –"

Helen pushes to her feet angrily. "I've been patient! It's always 'just six months more,' and in six months, something else will happen, Corinne! Another chain will be wrapped around you, keeping you tied to this place. I can't... I just can't," Helen says, her voice cracking.

She stumbles blindly down the path, dimly registering the sight of a skirt hem snagging on a rosebush deep within the garden as she storms away.

When Corinne returns to the house much later, the maid, in reply to her inquiry, tells her that she has not seen Helen. Wishing to be alone, she makes her way upstairs, where she encounters Candace in the hall.

"I'm glad to see that you're living up to your responsibilities at last," Candace says with a sanctimonious smile.

Pushed past enduring, Corinne whips around and says, "You have no idea what my responsibilities are! If I weren't living up to my responsibilities, you would have been out on the street long ago!"

*   *   *

"Do you really feel that way?" Aggie asked solemnly, leaning forward. "That this house became your jail?"

Cory's eyes slid out of focus as she looked back. "For a significant part of my life, it was. It wouldn't let me go." She blinked and looked around the study. "I love it dearly, but... my life is intertwined with the life of this house."

Beryl tilted her head. "Like Selina?" she asked, referring to the Godden book that had started her odyssey.

Cory smiled. "More like Rolls. Selina never left because she liked to think the house couldn't exist without her. Rolls got away for a while when he was young, but was pulled back by something he couldn't resist, the place he always came back to."

"I think I'd better read this book," Aggie muttered.

Chapter 32

Cory sat in her chair in the study, listening to the sounds of Aggie and Beryl moving about upstairs. Now that it was late October and the leaves had nearly all fallen from the trees, the morning sunshine came unimpeded through the leaded glass, softened further by the tiny bubbles and ripples in the hundred fifty-year-old windows. The golden light fell across an antique chess set, left in mid-game, sitting on the table between the wing chairs.

A few nights ago, Cory had been talking about the games they used to play to pass the evenings. "No one plays games anymore," she complained wistfully. "All people do is watch television." Aggie had brought a television to the upstairs sitting room, but it was rarely on.

"What would you like to play?" Beryl had asked, closing her book.

"How about whist?" Aggie had teased.

Cory turned to look at her sarcastically. "Even I'm not that old, Agatha smarty-pants. You read too much Jane Austen."

Beryl grinned, enjoying the loving banter that went on constantly between Cory and Aggie. *I can just imagine Marian's reaction if I teased her like that,* she thought as she watched Cory go to the book shelves, and pull out a tall, thick book. Percival dutifully followed her to the shelves and back, like an honor guard.

Bringing it to the table, she proceeded to unfold it. There, cleverly hinged together so that it could fold up compactly, was a full chess board, with tiny alcoves carved into its periphery to hold the chess pieces.

"This is exquisite," Beryl murmured, picking up one of the white knights. "Is this ivory?"

Cory nodded. "I'm ashamed to say it is, but back then, ivory wasn't considered to be the rare thing it is now."

"And the black pieces?"

"Ebony," Cory said. "All hand-carved. One of my uncles picked it up when he was in Africa. I've always loved this set." She set out the pieces. "So, who's up for a game?"

Aggie declined, preferring to watch with Winston curled up in her lap as Beryl, who hadn't played since she was a teen, was soundly beaten. "I can't believe I didn't see your rook waiting there," she moaned as Cory checkmated her. What she didn't mention was that the reason she hadn't noticed the rook was because she'd been so distracted by Aggie, who had positioned herself so that she could watch the game from behind Cory. Every time Beryl glanced up, Aggie was watching her.

"You have no idea," Aggie so wanted to say, "no idea what it means to me... I can't imagine Rachel being content to spend our evenings with my great-aunt. I love hearing Aunt Cory laugh... and I love you." She very nearly had to stuff her fist into her mouth to keep from saying it. But her eyes said all she couldn't say aloud, and Beryl, feeling her own face get hot, knew she was growing to feel the same way.

The games had become a nightly event since, though Beryl was getting better, and had won her first game last night. They had started a second game, but at last, needing to get some sleep, they had suspended the game, to be resumed this evening.

Cory heard noises in the kitchen. Veronica had been delighted when Aggie had moved in over the summer and had been very pleased to meet Beryl when she moved in as well. "It's nice to have young people in this house," she declared.

"Good morning, Miss Cory," Veronica said cheerfully as she entered the study. "I thought I'd find you up and about already." She rubbed her hands up and down her arms. "Brrrr, it's cold in here!"

Cory, wearing a heavy sweater with a wool throw over her lap, said, "We're trying to keep the heat costs down."

Aggie and Beryl had turned off the valves to all the radiators in the rooms they weren't using, diverting the steam from the ancient boiler in the cellar to the rooms they occupied, but it was still chilly. When the boiler kicked on, the house echoed with the clangs and bangs of the hot steam traveling through the pipes. "The house is talking," Cory laughed. "Well, I wish it had a little less to say," Aggie grumbled. Beryl still found herself jumping as the noises startled her.

"Come on, let's get some hot coffee inside you and warm up those old bones," Veronica said now.

"Who are you calling old?" Cory said, but Veronica just chuckled as she headed to the kitchen.

By the time coffee was on, Aggie and Beryl were downstairs getting their own breakfasts.

"What are you wearing?" Cory laughed as she saw Aggie wearing her most horrid orange Halloween sweater, bearing felted appliqués of jack-o-lanterns, black cats and witches.

"Every teacher has at least one of these," Aggie grinned. "Some have one for every season. Since Halloween is Saturday, we're dressing up today."

"Attractive," Beryl smirked.

"Watch it," Aggie threatened. "I've got another one upstairs that would fit you."

Beryl laughed. "What do you do for Halloween around here? Are we giving out candy?"

Aggie turned to Cory, eyebrows raised.

"I haven't had trick-or-treaters in ages," Cory said. "Would you like to?"

Aggie turned next to Beryl, who nodded. "It's tomorrow night. We could string some lights along our front walk to light the way to the house."

"This will be fun," Cory said excitedly.

By Saturday afternoon, the entrance to the house had been prepared, with cobwebs hung from the veranda pillars, pumpkin lights strung along each side of the walk and a large cauldron filled with candy sitting on the porch.

They ate an early dinner and then donned witches' hats and robes, and waited as darkness fell. Soon, costumed children and adults were wandering timidly up to the porch.

"We never got to come to this house before," said a diminutive Batman.

Cinderella, who seemed to be his little sister by the way she was clinging to his cape, said uncertainly, "We always heard it was haunted."

"Well, isn't that what you want at Halloween?" Aggie asked as she dropped candy into each of their bags. "A proper haunted house?"

"Thank you," they both squeaked before scurrying away down the walk.

Cory laughed heartily. "This will cement our reputation," she said happily.

For the next few hours, the three women greeted the trick-or-treaters brave enough to venture to the house, most of them accompanied by their parents. More than one comment of "I didn't think anyone still lived here" or "I've always wanted to see this place up close" could be heard.

At one point, Beryl and Aggie reached into the candy cauldron at the same time, their hands becoming tangled. Aggie smiled and gave her hand a squeeze before letting go. Though the night was becoming chilly enough for their breath to hang in frosty vapor, Beryl was warmed through and through by the look in Aggie's eyes.

By nine o'clock, the candy was nearly gone and the traffic had dwindled to an occasional teenager taking advantage of getting away with one more year of dressing up.

"Let's go in and warm up," Cory suggested, getting up stiffly.

Aggie made three cups of hot cocoa while Beryl laid out some oatmeal cookies.

"Oh, this feels good," Aggie murmured, cradling her cup in her hands to warm them. "Do you want me to make you a hot water bag for your bed?" she asked Cory.

"No," Cory smiled, "I'll be fine under my quilt."

Beryl yawned. "Well, I'm going up, then," she said, taking her cup to the sink. "Good night."

"Me, too," echoed Aggie. "Goodnight, Aunt Cory."

"Good night, girls."

Upstairs, Beryl and Aggie went to their separate bathrooms to wash up and brush their teeth. "Thank goodness my great-grandfather thought indoor plumbing was such a good thing and put so many bathrooms in this house when he had it built," Aggie had said when Beryl was first settling in upstairs.

They emerged from their bathrooms at the same time – "well, I was listening for you, waiting to come out at the same time," Aggie would admit coyly later.

"Tonight was fun," Beryl smiled, squinting a bit. Without her glasses, Aggie was a little blurry around the edges.

Aggie came to her. "Yes."

Beryl swallowed. "The trick-or-treaters, I mean."

"Mmm hmm," Aggie murmured, coming closer, clearly in focus now.

Beryl could smell her minty breath as she stepped closer still, while Beryl's breath seemed to be coming in shallow gasps. "I..." but whatever else she was going to mumble was lost as Aggie pressed her lips to Beryl's, not the soft, gentle kiss they had previously shared, but this time insistent, passionate. *Don't think*, Beryl thought, her hands coming up to caress Aggie's face as she returned the kiss, her mouth open, seeking, exploring.

They lost track of time as they stood there, kissing deeply, their bodies pressed together while their hands explored. At one point, Aggie pulled away long enough to ask, "Are you okay? Because I don't want to stop now."

Beryl ran her fingers through Aggie's silky blond hair and murmured, "Neither do I."

"Let's go to your room," Aggie whispered, her heart beating fast. "Percival's probably already on my bed."

"Winston can keep him company," Beryl smiled.

A long while later, or perhaps no time at all, Aggie and Beryl lay in a tangle of arms and legs, snuggled together under the covers.

"Are you all right?" Aggie whispered, her fingers playing with Beryl's soft hair.

"Yes. You?" Beryl murmured, her head resting on Aggie's shoulder.

"Better than all right," Aggie smiled in the dark. "I've wanted you for so long."

"I have, too," Beryl admitted. "I just didn't trust... us."

Aggie kissed her forehead tenderly. "I know. That part takes a long time." She lay quietly, feeling the beat of Beryl's heart against her ribs. "You told me the night we met that you needed to believe a relationship could last a lifetime and beyond. I didn't think I would ever again meet someone I would trust to be that for me, until I met you." She swallowed hard, waiting.

Beryl raised her head, placing a hand on Aggie's cheek. "A lifetime and beyond."

She pressed her mouth to Aggie's, sealing her promise with her kiss. Sighing, she laid her head back on Aggie's shoulder. A moment later, they heard the soft scuff of slippers out in the hall, followed by the click of dog nails and a little meow.

Aggie covered her mouth to muffle her giggle. Beryl, pressing her face into Aggie's shoulder in her embarrassment, could feel Aggie shaking with her suppressed laughter.

"You forgot to close your bedroom door, didn't you?" Beryl whispered.

Chapter 33

Monday morning, Aggie's first period was a planning period with no students. Shannon popped her head into Aggie's empty classroom.

"Hey, how was your weekend?" she asked.

"It was fine," Aggie said, though she could feel a slow blush creeping up her neck to her cheeks.

"Oh, my God."

Shannon quickly shut the classroom door and pulled a chair up to Aggie's desk.

"Tell me."

"What?"

"You did it. Didn't you?"

"I don't know what you mean," Aggie tried bluffing, but she knew it was no good. Shannon knew her too well.

Shannon ignored her protest. "How was it?"

Aggie's shoulders slumped. "All right. It happened, but please don't go shouting it all over," she begged. "You know I'm not out at work."

"The worst-kept secret in the entire school," Shannon said sarcastically.

"Shannon –"

"Who'm I going to tell?" Shannon asked indignantly. "But how was it?"

Aggie beamed. She couldn't help it. "It's... I don't know if I can describe it –"

"I don't need that much detail."

"No," Aggie grinned sheepishly. "It's not all fireworks and giddiness. It's... with Beryl, it feels steady and strong and... forever."

"Forever?" Shannon asked, her eyebrows raising in surprise.

Aggie sighed. "I know. I've only known her a few months, but... that's how it feels."

"But there were fireworks, right?" Shannon grinned wickedly.

Aggie laughed. "Yes," she admitted, blushing again. "There absolutely were fireworks."

Shannon laughed delightedly. "It's about damn time," she said happily. "Does Cory know?"

"Oh, Cory definitely knows," Aggie groaned, dropping her forehead into her hands.

Cory had already been up when Aggie came down Sunday morning. Beryl had insisted on their going down separately. Aggie considered telling her that the subterfuge was pointless, but decided that Beryl would discover the truth soon enough.

"Good morning," Cory said from the table where she was reading the newspaper as Aggie entered the kitchen.

"Good morning," Aggie returned cautiously.

"Coffee's already made," Cory offered innocently.

"Thank you," Aggie said, wondering how long this game would last.

When Beryl entered the kitchen a few minutes later, accompanied by the animals, Cory waited until she was seated at the table with her coffee before she smiled up from the paper and asked, "Did you girls sleep well last night?"

Beryl choked on her coffee. Abandoning all pretense, Aggie reached across the table for Beryl's hand and said, "You know perfectly well what happened last night, you wicked old woman. Don't give us a hard time."

Cory reached out, taking both their clasped hands in her old, arthritic ones and said, "I'm delighted for you. I love you both, and I was hoping for this."

"You were?" Beryl gasped, still gagging a bit on her inhaled coffee.

*　　　*　　　*

Terrence finds Corinne in the den at their father's desk, going over the household accounts, the ledger illuminated by a brilliantly-colored Tiffany lamp. Her brow is furrowed in worry. Every spare cent has gone to pay back what their father took, leaving Corinne to juggle the household bills, paying only those that are most overdue. In spite of her secrecy, the shopkeepers have started to whisper among themselves about the late accounts, and word has gotten out that the Bishops are in financial trouble.

"We are on solid ground," Corinne insists repeatedly to the bank's staff. "Please reassure our account holders that they have nothing to worry about."

"Here," Terrence says, holding out his hand and giving Corinne twenty-seven dollars and eighty-three cents.

Terrence, having somehow guessed at Corinne's worries, has taken employment at the local hardware store. Despite his war injuries, he has a knack for remembering every bolt, every washer, every tiny item stocked by the store. It has become a good-natured ritual for the men who frequent the store to place small wagers on how quickly Terrence can find obscure items on the miles of wooden shelves and bins. Every week, he turns his pay over to Corinne. Knowing how much he wants to help, she accepts without argument.

"It's embarrassing," Candace says scathingly. "He can barely remember where the kitchen is. He was to have been the bank president, and look at him, working with those low-lifes who have nothing better to do than hang about at that store."

"It's sweet of him to want to help," says Mary, who rarely chastises Candace. "You could do something more useful than complaining," she says pointedly.

Candace looks as if she has been slapped. "What do you want me to do?" she asks indignantly. "Take in washing? Clean houses?"

223

Mary looks up from her book and says quietly, "It would be sufficient if you would take on some of the cleaning here, since we have had to let some of the help go."

Candace's eyes narrow shrewdly. "And why did we have to let them go?" she asks. "No one ever did explain that satisfactorily."

"It is enough for you to know that it was necessary," Mary says. "Your sister has had to make economies of necessity."

"Oh, of course," Candace says bitterly. "Dear, perfect Corinne, who -"

Mary closes her book with a snap and stands abruptly. In the closest thing Candace has ever seen to her mother losing her temper, Mary says, "Your sister took on an enormous burden and has done the best she could with it. It is time you held your tongue."

"You should go to her," Terrence says now as he watches Corinne enter the amount in the household ledger.

Startled, Corinne looks up at him. "I can't go, just like that," she protests, wondering how much he knows of how and why Helen left. It has been two months, and there has been no word. She has cried herself to sleep nearly every night. Nothing, not even the war, felt as horrible as this angry, hurtful separation.

"Father has been dead for almost two years," Terrence reminds her. "Nothing they say or do can hurt him now. And we'll survive. You should go to her."

He leaves her staring out the window at the garden, a garden she can barely tolerate being in, the memories of Helen there are so strong. Terrence's words, so child-like in their simple insistence, seem wiser than he could possibly know, and yet....

She hears the bell for the afternoon post, and shortly after, there is a soft knock on the door. "Come," she says without turning from the window.

"I have your tea and the mail, Miss Corinne," says Frances, bearing a tray. "It looks like there's a letter from Miss Helen. Is she coming back soon?"

Corinne comes to the desk and inspects the envelope eagerly. "Why would you ask that?" Corinne asks.

"I just thought... what with her telephone calls," Frances said apologetically.

Corinne's head snaps up. "What telephone calls?" she asks.

Frances blinks at her and repeats, "Her telephone calls. At least five. Miss Candace took the messages from me each time and said she would give them to you..." Frances' hand flies to her mouth. "I'm so sorry, Miss Corinne. If I'd known –"

"It's all right, Frances," Corinne says, a cold fury filling her. "Do you know where Mrs. Bishop is?"

"She's in her study, miss."

Corinne nods vaguely as she pries open the envelope and pulls out a card which reads simply, "Sonnet XXIX. Please call me." Below is written a telephone number with a U.S. telephone exchange. Helen is still in the country.

Going to the bookshelves in the den, she finds a volume of Shakespeare and opens it to the sonnets. Whispering, she reads,

> "When, in disgrace with fortune and men's eyes,
> I all alone beweep my outcast state,
> And trouble deaf heaven with my bootless cries,
> And look upon myself, and curse my fate,
> Wishing me like to one more rich in hope,
> Featured like him, like him with friends possess'd,
> Desiring this man's art and that man's scope,
> With what I most enjoy contented least;
> Yet in these thoughts myself almost despising,
> Haply I think on thee, and then my state,
> Like to the lark at break of day arising
> From sullen earth, sings hymns at heaven's gate;
> For thy sweet love remember'd such wealth brings
> That then I scorn to change my state with kings."

Corinne's eyes fill with tears as the words blur. She leaves the office and encounters Candace descending the stairs as she enters the foyer. Corinne's anger is reflected in her eyes and Candace knows she knows.

Jutting her chin out mulishly, Candace sweeps past without uttering a word.

Corinne finds her mother doing needlepoint in the study and takes a seat next to her. "Mother, I'm taking a holiday."

Mary looks up and sees the tears still glistening on Corinne's cheeks. "For how long?"

Corinne shakes her head. "I don't know. Maybe forever. I don't know what they will decide to do at the bank, but I can't be tied here any longer." She reaches out for her mother's hand. "Do you think you can manage now?"

Mary's chin quivers the tiniest bit, but she says, "We'll manage."

*   *   *

"Why were you hoping for this?" Aggie asked, almost as surprised as Beryl.

"Not just me," Cory said, a twinkle in her eyes. "Ridley and I have both wondered if you would ever wise up."

"Ridley!" Beryl exclaimed, thinking he was going to have some explaining to do.

Aggie looked at Beryl, one eyebrow raised. "Gosh, maybe we should send out announcements."

Chapter 34

Beryl was working at her computer, humming to herself as she prepared a lecture course on rare book provenance as a proposed course to be taught at OSU, and possibly to be added to the University of Virginia's Rare Book School curriculum.

"This is right up your alley," Bart Hudspath had said to her when he heard an edited version of how she had tracked down Corinne Bishop.

She heard her cell phone buzz. Distractedly, she looked at the screen and saw that it was Ridley. "Hey there," she said warmly, intending to give him some grief about staying in contact with Cory behind her back.

"Beryl," he said, "listen to me –"

"Just a second," she interrupted, hearing another incoming call beeping on her phone. It was Claire. "Let me call you right back," she said.

"Beryl! No –"

She pushed the button to accept Claire's call and instantly regretted it.

"Hi," she said.

"Just when the hell were you going to tell me you aren't even living in fucking D.C. anymore?" came Claire's furious voice.

Beryl was so shocked, she didn't know what to say. Somehow, in all of her other farewells, it hadn't even occurred to her to tell Claire.

Her silence allowed Claire to gather steam as she continued, "I had to find out from that flaming asshole at the library when I came in there looking for you like some kind of idiot!"

Recovering enough to respond, Beryl said, "And just why is it any of your business where I'm living now?"

"Is Ohio where the bitch lives?" Claire continued as if Beryl hadn't spoken. "The one I saw you with?"

Taking a calming breath, Beryl said, "Ohio is where my job is."

"Job? What job?" Claire asked scathingly.

Wondering how much to say, Beryl answered, "Working in Ohio State's Rare Books Library."

Claire was silenced for a few seconds at this. "Ohio State?"

"Yes."

This time it was Claire's turn to be silent as this information sank in.

"What do you want?" Beryl asked before Claire could resume her attack.

"I... I wanted to talk to you," Claire said in a meeker voice.

"Then talk to me," Berly said coolly.

"No," Claire said. "I'd like to talk to you in person."

"You've sure got a funny way of asking."

Claire cleared her throat. "I know. I just... it caught me by surprise to go to Georgetown and find you don't even work there anymore."

Closing her eyes, Beryl repeated herself, saying, "It's really none of your business where I work anymore."

"I know," Claire acknowledged. "But... are you going to be back in D.C. anytime soon? Thanksgiving, maybe?"

With a shock, Beryl glanced at the calendar and realized Thanksgiving was only two and half weeks away. She hadn't even considered where she'd be spending it.

"Could we... could we get together, if you do? Please?" Claire asked.

Slumping back against her chair, Beryl said, "I'll call you."

Claire was quiet for a few seconds and Beryl knew she wasn't happy with that response, but she said, "Okay. Good. Good. I'll wait to hear from you, then."

Beryl hung up. Biting her lip, she dialed Ridley's cell phone.

"I tried to warn you," he said as he answered.

"Got that."

"Was it bad?"

"Let's just say, it's a good thing it wasn't on speaker," Beryl said wryly.

"Shit," he muttered. "I'm sorry. I know she thinks I enjoyed that..."

Beryl couldn't help chuckling. "Are you telling me you didn't?"

"I didn't say that," he answered and she laughed.

She shook her head, saying, "I just didn't even think about her when I was letting people know."

"You do know that's a good thing," he said.

"Yeah," she realized. "I suppose it is." Changing the subject, she said, "And what's up with you and Cory staying in touch?"

It was Ridley's turn to laugh. "She's great. And I understand congratulations are in order."

Beryl snorted. "Maybe Aggie's right, we should send out announcements," she said.

"Is this the real thing?" he asked.

Beryl smiled widely as she said, "It's absolutely the real thing."

Ridley laughed in her ear. "I'm happy for you, Beryl."

"How about you and George?" she asked.

She closed her eyes at the sudden silence on the other end of the phone. Ridley cleared his throat gruffly, and said after a moment, "Nope."

Beryl, knowing better than to be sympathetic, said, "Well... probably a good thing. More room for David." She could almost hear Ridley shaking his head. "What are you doing for Thanksgiving?" she asked.

*   *   *

"Are you sure we're welcome?" Aggie asked anxiously for about the fiftieth time.

229

Beryl gave a nervous hiccup of laughter as she drove her new Toyota Prius along I-66 as it transitioned to Constitution Avenue. "I told you, I'm not sure I'm welcome."

She glanced over and took Aggie's hand, lifting it to her lips to kiss it. "I also told you, they will absolutely love you. Not that being compared to Claire is a good thing, but by comparison, you are a God-send." She glanced into the back seat where Cory napped, wrapped in a wool throw, Percival curled up between her and Winston in his carrier. "And I have a feeling Cory will have them all off-balance anyhow."

"We'll be staying with Ridley," Beryl had told her mother pre-emptively when she had called to say she would be home for Thanksgiving. "So, if you can squeeze four of us in around the table..."

"We'll be your bodyguards," Ridley had joked.

But to Beryl, it wasn't a joke.

"I feel like such a different person than I was before," she'd confided to Aggie as they lay in bed.

"You are," Aggie agreed.

"But what if they won't let me be?"

Aggie turned to her. "It's not up to them," she said simply. "They can't beat you down if you don't allow it. And this time, you won't be alone. One signal from you, and we'll be right there with you. If worse comes to worse, we'll leave."

It sounded so simple when Aggie said it, Beryl thought as she wove through traffic, but she had thirty-six – almost thirty-seven the fourth of December, she realized – years of experience with her family dynamics and knew it wouldn't be quite that easy.

Ridley greeted them all delightedly. "God, I've missed you," he said, squeezing Beryl tightly before hugging Aggie and Cory as well. Winston meowed loudly, leading Percival in exploring the apartment as soon as his carrier door was opened.

For dinner, they went back to the Mexican place they had gone to previously as Cory decided she was in the mood for margaritas. "Maybe a few pitchers of these will make tomorrow easier," Beryl joked. They lingered over dinner, catching up with one another, but Beryl kept looking about, half-expecting to see Claire.

Ridley caught this and asked, "What are you going to do about her?"

Beryl glanced nervously at Aggie. "I don't know."

"If you feel comfortable, then meet her," Aggie advised, reaching over to give her hand a squeeze.

"But you set the time and place so you're in control," Ridley added.

If Aggie was uncomfortable in any way about Beryl seeing Claire again, she hid it well. Beryl wondered if she would handle it that well if Rachel were suddenly in the picture again.

Back at his apartment, Ridley gallantly tried to give Cory his bedroom, but she adamantly refused. "I'm the littlest one here. I can sleep on the sofa," she insisted.

Thursday dawned overcast with rain threatening. "I'll drive," Ridley offered. "Two legs today."

"Okay," Beryl agreed, "but let's not get there too early."

The four of them lingered over breakfast, watching some of the Macy's parade on television. They arrived at the Gray house at noon. Beryl made introductions.

"How are you going to introduce me?" Aggie had asked. "Just so I know what to expect."

"I honestly don't know," Beryl said. "It's been one of those unspoken things, but I've never said the words out loud to them."

Aggie gave a tight-lipped smile. "Thanksgiving might not be the best moment."

"Right."

Ridley, of course, charmed the women, especially when he asked what he could do to help in the kitchen.

Julie, waiting until Nick was seating himself at the table, said, "Beryl, you look wonderful. You've really gotten into shape."

"Uh, yeah," Nick agreed as his wife gave him an impatient nudge. "Yeah. You look good."

"Thanks," Beryl said dryly as Aggie pressed her knee against Beryl's under the table.

"So, Cory," Edith asked curiously as she passed the bread stuffing, "how exactly did you meet Beryl?"

Cory winked at Beryl. "Oh, we go way back. To 1945." At the puzzled expressions around the table, she recounted Beryl's search for the owner of the mystery book, tactfully omitting the details of the inscription, Beryl noticed. Together with Ridley, who filled in details Cory didn't know, they told how Beryl had found her.

"And now it's led to her doing an entire course on researching the provenance of rare books," Aggie said proudly.

"The what?" Marian asked.

"Tracing the history of prior ownership of old books," Beryl explained.

"Sounds pretty boring to me," Nick scoffed.

Beryl bit back a laugh as Julie said, "Yes, dear. Anything that doesn't involve a sports score or an alien attack is boring to you."

Just as Beryl was basking in the unfamiliar sensation of attention that wasn't driven by ridicule – *I should have known better*, she thought later – Marian said, "She's teaching a class. It's not like she's rewriting history."

"Actually," Aggie said, her cheeks flushing with what Cory recognized as anger, "rare book librarians just like Beryl discovered and proved, right here in D.C. at the Folger Shakespeare Library, that an incredibly rare Shakespeare folio someone was trying to sell was one that had been stolen from a British university. It was worth millions, but beyond price in its value to us culturally, so yes, in a way, she and others like her are re-writing history."

Marian opened her mouth, but before she could speak, Cory smiled sweetly and said, "I'm sure whatever you do is equally valuable to society, dear."

Nick snorted. "Yeah, right. Because we really need more accountants."

Edith, her instincts honed from years of heading off dinner-time explosions, picked up the bowl of mashed potatoes and shoved them into Marian's hands, saying, "Pass these around, please."

*　　　*　　　*

Back in Ridley's car a few hours later, Beryl breathed a sigh of relief. "I can't thank you all enough," she said sincerely.

Aggie shook her head. "I'm ashamed to say I thought you had exaggerated a bit before, but your family..."

"Not your parents," Ridley observed, "only your brother and sister. What is up with them?"

Beryl laughed uncomfortably, but Cory, turning in the passenger seat to look at her shrewdly, said, "No, your parents allow it to happen. They are part of it."

"What did Marian say to you when we were washing dishes?" Aggie asked.

Beryl's smile faded. Marian had cornered her in the pantry as she put away a roasting pan.

"You know, Mom is upset you brought strangers to dinner," Marian whispered. "Thanksgiving is supposed to be a holiday for family."

Beryl looked her sister in the eye, startled at first. Bracing herself, she replied, "If Mom was upset, it was her place to tell me, and she didn't say a word. As far as family goes," she paused, looking her sister up and down disdainfully, "they treat me more like family than you ever have."

Looking over at Aggie sitting next to her in the back seat now, Beryl reached for her hand and said, "It was nothing."

Chapter 35

Beryl sat on a Metro car Friday morning on her way to DuPont Circle.

"I can meet you at Kramer's at ten," she had told Claire over the phone last evening. To the others, she'd said, "I'm only going to give her this one option. How about you meet me for an early lunch and then we'll go to The Scriptorium? You just have to meet Mr. Herrmann – he was the start of everything."

"And this way, I have a definite stop to my time with Claire," but she didn't say that.

Nervously, she drummed her fingers on her backpack in her lap as she watched the underground pylons and lights flash by the train. Arriving about fifteen minutes early gave her the opportunity to get a table in the café that allowed her to keep her back to the wall and see the entire space. She smiled as she pictured Ridley saying, "Keep the tactical advantage."

When Claire arrived, Beryl's first thought was, *she's still beautiful.* Claire, though, glanced past Beryl at first, and did a double take in surprise.

"Hi," she said somewhat breathlessly as she came to the table. Beryl stood awkwardly. "I didn't want to hug her," she told Aggie later, "I wasn't sure how to greet her."

"Um, you want a coffee or tea?" Claire asked.

"I'm good," Beryl said, pointing to her mocha. "Go ahead and get something."

"Be right back," Claire said, flashing her brightest smile.

When Claire returned to the table, she looked at Beryl and said, "You look really good."

Beryl's guard immediately went up. "Thanks," she said cautiously as she sat with a rigidly upright posture. She quickly decided to take control. "What's up, Claire?"

Claire fiddled with the lid of her cappuccino. "Won't you come home?" she asked plaintively.

All control forgotten, Beryl slouched back against her chair, nearly laughing out loud. "Leslie's gone."

Claire's eyes filled as she nodded. "She... she decided she couldn't leave her husband..."

"I see. She's too good to be a dyke. She'll only fuck one." Beryl bit the words back just in time. Instead, she said, "And you're not content to continue having her on the side?"

Claire looked up at her, her beautiful dark eyes brimming with tears, and Beryl was reminded how, at one time, she couldn't have refused Claire anything.

"I want you back," Claire sniffed. "You're so much better than her. I was stupid. Temporarily insane. I was an idiot. Please forgive me."

A million thoughts ran through Beryl's head, all the myriad things she'd wanted to say to Claire over the past weeks – all the accusations and all the angry words rushed to the very tip of her tongue, but "I do forgive you," was what she heard herself say.

Claire's face lit up hopefully.

"I forgive you," Beryl repeated, "And I would have stayed with you forever, even if we weren't good together, but not now."

"But," Claire smiled tremulously, "we were good together. We had good times, lots of good times. Couldn't we be that way again?" She reached across the table and took Beryl's hand. "I love you."

Beryl stared at her, expecting to see some sign that Claire was kidding, but there was none. "I hated who I became with you!" Beryl wanted to cry, but "Claire, we weren't good together," she insisted calmly as she pulled her hand away. "I don't love you. I did, but not now. I don't even live here anymore."

As she looked into Claire's stunned face – *she honestly thought this was going to happen,* Beryl realized – she felt... pity. "Good-bye, Claire."

"It was the perfect opportunity to tell her what she did to you!" Ridley would say in disbelief a short while later when Beryl met him, Aggie and Cory for lunch and told them about her conversation with Claire.

"I know, but..."

As she felt Aggie reaching for her hand under the table, Beryl looked up. Her eyes locked with Aggie's and she saw the trust and the certainty and the love there. "I didn't need to say those things," she said simply.

*   *   *

The tinkling bell announced their arrival at the bookstore as they escaped from the hordes of Black Friday shoppers filling the sidewalks. Mr. Herrmann hurried out from the biography section, beaming when he saw it was Beryl.

"Oh, my dear!" he exclaimed, coming to hug her tightly. "It is so good to see you!"

"You, too," she laughed. "I've missed you and my favorite bookstore so much." She inhaled his cologne and rubbed his tweedy shoulders in delight.

She turned to make introductions, noticing that Ridley had faded into the history shelves.

"Miss Bishop's house," Beryl said, her arm wrapped around Cory's frail shoulders, "was the house those three boxes of auction books came from this summer."

Mr. Herrmann looked at them in surprise. "So, your detective work paid off? You returned the letter?"

There was a slight pause as Beryl tried to think. "Oh, yes," she said as she remembered she had told him she'd found a letter in one of the books.

Cory apparently caught on as well, for she said, "It was very dear to me, and I was so glad to get it back." Glancing around, she said, "I could get lost in here and never want to leave."

Mr. Herrmann beamed. "Just as my grandfather would have wished it. May I show you around?" he asked, offering Cory his arm.

George found Beryl where he would have predicted – in fiction. "Welcome home," he said shyly.

"George!" She gave him a tight hug. Releasing him, she looked up into his troubled eyes. "Can we talk?" she asked in a low voice.

He led her to the back room and closed the door.

"I'm sorry I have to be so blunt," she began immediately, "but we won't have much time. What is going on?"

George drew himself up a little. "Have you asked him?"

Beryl shook her head. "We haven't had any alone time for a talk like this."

George blinked rapidly, his jaw clenching.

"Do you love him?" she asked.

He met her eyes. "Yes. And he says he loves me, but..."

Beryl waited.

George's cheeks flushed. "We got to a certain point, physically, and he... I told him it was okay, and we could take it slow, but... he said it wasn't fair to me and he just..."

"He shut you out," Beryl finished for him. He nodded.

"I don't know how to get past the walls he's put up," George said. "I just don't know what else to do."

Beryl gave his hand a sympathetic squeeze. "I know. He can be tough to read. I will talk to him while we're here," she promised.

George removed his glasses and wiped his eyes. "Thanks."

It was a couple of hours before the four of them left the bookstore, weighed down with several books each, as Mr. Herrmann waved them off through the shop's window.

"Oh, I wish we had someplace like this in Columbus," Aggie said wistfully. "We have some used bookstores, but not like this."

"It's a good thing we don't," Cory laughed, "or we'd be poorer than we are now."

"It's not like you lack for reading material in that house," Beryl pointed out.

"I know," Aggie admitted, "but let's face it, old military histories and philosophy texts aren't exactly stimulating reading."

Ridley, who had barely spoken in the store, hopped beside Beryl, silent and brooding. The crowds of people shopping had thickened considerably and he was jostled by a group of women clutching large shopping bags, knocking him off-balance.

A small crowd gathered at the sound of Ridley's crutches clanging off a parking meter as he sprawled on the pavement. A couple of well-meaning people rushed to help him, but "Get off me!" he barked, red-faced and humiliated.

Beryl dropped her bag of books and threw herself between him and the passersby. "Stand down!" she hissed in his ear, grabbing him by the shoulders.

She could feel his tensed shoulders drop in response to her voice and she released him. Standing back, she held his crutches, giving him room to get himself upright again.

"We're fine, thanks," she smiled to the people who now stood back cautiously as Ridley got his crutches back in position.

Beryl retrieved her books from Aggie as they headed back to where Ridley had parked. The trip back to the apartment was a silent one.

When they got back to the apartment, Cory said, "I'm tired. I think a nap would be just the ticket."

"Me, too," Aggie said quickly. They disappeared into the second bedroom, the walls still lined with boxes of Beryl's books, and closed the door, leaving Beryl and Ridley sitting on the couch with Winston and Percival jockeying for some attention.

"You okay?" she asked after a moment as Winston hopped onto the back of the chair on the other side of the coffee table.

"I'm fine," Ridley said gruffly. "I suppose you talked to George."

"Yes," Beryl said truthfully.

Ridley said nothing more for long seconds.

"He loves you, you know."

"I know," he said, looking down at his hands.

"And you love him?" she prodded gently.

He closed his eyes. "It's not that simple."

She reached out and laid a hand on his arm, taking it as a good sign that he didn't jerk away. "Yes, it is. You are the bravest man I know, Ridley Wade. And believe me, I understand how utterly terrifying it is to put yourself, your heart, in someone else's hands. And, to a lesser degree than you, I understand how hard it is to... to bare yourself, literally, with someone when your body is less than perfect, but you don't have to be alone anymore. You told me so when you dropped me off in Ohio. What happened?"

Ridley expelled a pent-up breath and haltingly said, "When we... were making out, he was... responding, and I started to, but then, something happened, and..."

"Oh." Beryl sat, definitely out of her element. "Um, maybe, if you just focused on him initially... it might... and together you could find what works for you..." she said lamely.

Ridley watched as Percival deliberately walked under Winston's overhanging paw. Winston stretched just enough to drag a couple of toes over Percival's back, setting off a mad game of tag as the two animals bounced off the furniture like ping-pong balls.

With a small chuckle, Ridley said, "You're really not comfortable talking about cocks, are you?"

"Not so much."

Shaking his head, Ridley got up and went into the kitchen for a drink.

"I can hear you laughing, you know," Beryl said.

*   *   *

"Here you are," Helen says, finding Corinne standing at the rail near the bow of the ocean liner bearing them to Europe at last.

They are a week into their journey. They've barely emerged from their cabin. "We've barely gotten out of bed," Corinne would have corrected happily.

"Now that I've got you here, I don't want to share you with anyone," Helen had insisted, having noticed, even as they boarded, the admiring glances cast in Corinne's direction from many of the men.

Corinne, who cannot imagine Helen wearing a gown to the dining room or ball room, agreed gladly, and they have contentedly taken their meals in their cabin, emerging only for strolls around the deck, or to sit in the sun to read the travelogues Corinne has pored over so often that they are dog-eared. Helen laughs at her list of sites she wishes to see in England, Ireland, France, Austria, Italy. "It will take us years to get to all these," she says as they sit side by side on one of the beds and she glances down the list.

"I know," Corinne says happily, leaning against Helen, her head resting on her shoulder, breathing in her flowery scent.

Now, on the deck, Corinne smiles, closing her eyes and tasting the salt air. "I've changed my mind. I don't want to get there. I just want to stay out here on the ocean forever, where nothing can reach us, nothing can pull us back."

Helen lays her hand over Corinne's on the rail. Corinne smiles up at her, and self-consciously pulls her hand away, glancing around to see if anyone else is near.

"I was so afraid," Corinne confesses, "right up until we were underway, that somehow, something would happen."

"I know," Helen murmured, leaning close so Corinne can hear her. "I was, too. So many things have conspired to trap us, to keep us apart, but we are meant to be together. No matter what may separate us, we will always find one another."

*   *   *

When Aggie and Cory got up from their nap, if indeed they slept at all, Cory suggested staying in for dinner. She and Ridley went through his refrigerator and found enough in there to whip up a meal. As she stood at the stove, sautéing chicken breasts while he made a salad, Aggie and Beryl heard her say to him, "You're too young to understand , but... no matter what reasons you think there might be now not to act on the love you're feeling, I promise you, when you're old, you won't remember those reasons. You'll only remember the regret that you didn't do it."

Chapter 36

Beryl lay awake, listening to the clang of the mansion's pipes as the boiler kicked on and began sending steam coursing through them. She shivered as she crawled out of bed, trying not to drag the covers off of Aggie who was sound asleep. She slid her feet into waiting slippers as protection against the house's cold floors and scurried down the hall to the bathroom. While in there, she heard Cory's slippers scuffing by on her way down the hall. Aggie had warned her early on that she would most likely hear Cory up there occasionally. Beryl had never intruded on one of Cory's nighttime visits to her old room. As she left the bathroom, she hesitated outside the door to her bedroom where she could hear Aggie turning over, and continued to the end of the hall to find Cory sitting and rocking.

"Are you all right?" Beryl whispered as she entered.

"Oh, yes," Cory answered. "I just like to visit."

"Visit?" Beryl wondered.

"Come and join me," Cory invited.

Beryl sat cross-legged in the cushioned window seat, a light snow falling outside. It was chilly enclosed by the glass. There was a wool blanket lying there. She wrapped it around her shoulders.

There was enough moonlight to make out Cory's features as she asked, "Are you happy, Beryl?"

Caught off-guard by the question, Beryl answered, "Yes. Actually, I'm happier than I ever remember being."

Cory smiled and rocked. "I'm glad to hear that."

Beryl cocked her head, curious about some things, and now, while Cory was in a talkative mood, seemed like a good time to ask....

"How are you?"

Cory rocked for several seconds, watching Beryl who was only visible in silhouette before saying, "I'm waiting."

*   *   *

Helen laughs as she watches Corinne waving from the ramparts of Mont Saint-Michel. A short while later, Corinne runs to her, breathless, cheeks flushed with happiness.

"Oh, it's glorious!" she exclaims, hugging Helen impetuously.

"I know," Helen agrees, fighting the urge to kiss Corinne right there.

The past six weeks have been the happiest they have ever known. Touring Ireland and England, Corinne screamed as Helen maneuvered their tiny little automobile past lumbering lorries on the wrong side of the roads – "what roads?" Corinne had demanded indignantly. "These are cow lanes, and they think two vehicles are going to pass?" – but she had fallen in love with the English and Scottish countryside.

"Oh, I wish we could buy one of these little stone cottages and live here forever," she had sighed in Cornwall, and again in Yorkshire, and yet again near Oban.

"You think that now," Helen smiled indulgently, "until you haven't seen the sun for three months and you feel as if you'll never be warm or dry again."

"I wouldn't care," Corinne declared, smiling wickedly, "It's not as if we couldn't think of something to do with all those rainy days."

She was torn when it was time to cross the Channel to France. They had discussed going to Omaha Beach, but Helen didn't think she could bear to see that beach or the thousands of nearby white crosses....

Mont Saint-Michel is to be their only destination in Normandy before heading to "Paris!" Corinne exclaims in awe at her first view of the Champs-Élysées. Her open-mouthed delight as she hangs out the window of the taxi, trying to take in everything helps Helen put aside her resentment that London endured such devastation while Paris escaped, unscathed. She cannot help but laugh at Corinne's child-like amazement upon entering the lobby of the Ritz. Corinne's joy at every moment of this voyage has made her feel as if she is seeing everything through new eyes – eyes not yet jaded by years of being shunted from one boarding school to another by parents too rich and preoccupied with their own lives to want the burden of having a daughter about all the time, eyes that have never seen the things she saw during the war... and she loves Corinne more than she ever has.

"Are you sure about this? This must be terribly expensive," Corinne whispers as they approach the reception desk.

"We always stay here when we're in Paris," Helen assures her.

"Ah, bienvenue, Mademoiselle Abrams," says the registration clerk as Helen signs the register. "Et Mademoiselle Bishop?" he inquires, turning to Corinne. "J'ai un télégramme pour vous, mademoiselle," he adds, pulling a folded piece of paper from a small cubby behind him.

"For me?" Corinne's eyes are big and she can feel her heart pounding. She steps away from the desk and pries open the flap.

CANDACE ILL STOP DOCTOR SAYS STROKE STOP
PLEASE COME HOME STOP

Corinne's eyes fill with angry tears echoed by the pressure of Helen's fingers digging into her arms as she reads over Corinne's shoulder.

*　　*　　*

"Waiting? What for?" Beryl asked.

Cory rocked for a few seconds before saying, "Until I'm with Helen again."

245

Over her time since moving into the Bishop mansion, Beryl has gleaned bits and pieces of Cory's story - some from Aggie, some from Cory herself.

"When... when did she die?" Beryl asked softly. She has never felt she could broach this topic before.

Even in the moonlight, Beryl could see the sadness transform Cory's face and she instantly regretted asking. "I'm sorry," she murmured.

Cory shook her head. "I just try not to think about that part," she said. "It was 1963."

Beryl gasped in spite of herself. "So young? I... I just thought, from what Aggie said, that it was much later..."

"I think Agatha remembers my stories of her Aunt Helen from when she was a little girl," Cory said. "She has no direct memories of her... unless Helen has been visiting Agatha as a ghost."

"Was there never anyone else for you?" Beryl asked.

Cory smiled sweetly. "Never."

"1963? Really?" Aggie repeated in shock the next evening when Beryl had a chance to recount her conversation with Cory. They had finished dinner and were taking Percival for a walk along darkened sidewalks. Percival was enjoying this new routine of nightly walks, and had established a regular route of places to sniff and pee each evening.

Bundled up warmly against the December cold - "Thank you again for my new jacket," Beryl said appreciatively as she zipped up the down coat Aggie had given her for her birthday - their shoes crunched on a light dusting of snow as they walked and talked.

"All these years, she seemed so real to me, the way Aunt Cory talked about her..." She thought hard. "I can't have imagined it all. I know she used to talk as if Helen had been with her only a few years previously."

"Well," Beryl said uncomfortably, "by the time you were a little girl, wasn't Cory all alone in that house?"

Aggie frowned as she walked, trying to remember. "I think my great-grandmother died in 1973. Grandfather Terrence went soon after, in '75, just a few months after I was born I think. So she's been alone since then."

"By the time you were born," said Beryl, "maybe she talked about Helen the way she did to keep her real, keep her near."

Aggie tucked her arm through Beryl's, squeezing tightly. "How lonely she's been," she said sadly.

"And how faithful," Beryl said feelingly. "Do people love like that now?"

Aggie pulled her to a halt. "Yes," she said, kissing her in the shadows.

Beryl wrapped her arms around Aggie, holding her tightly. "I love you so very much."

They chuckled as Percival gave a soft woof, tugging on the leash.

When they got back to the house, Cory was waiting for them in the kitchen. "Beryl," she said worriedly, "I don't know what's going on, but your cell phone has been ringing almost non-stop since you left."

Beryl hurried to the oak sideboard where she and Aggie left keys and cell phones. She saw that there were three voicemails. She listened to the first one. "It's Mom. Dad's on his way to the hospital. They think it was a heart attack."

She tried calling her parents' house, but as expected, there was no answer. Next, she tried her brother and sister's cell numbers, but had to leave messages.

She sat heavily at the kitchen table while Aggie made cups of tea for all of them.

"What do you want to do?" Aggie asked. "Do you want to leave tonight?"

Beryl shook her head. "No." She pressed her fingers to her forehead, trying to think. "I need to plan. I don't even know what happened yet." She bit her lip. "I'll be gone probably for the rest of the week at least. I can't just leave. I need to go in tomorrow and make arrangements for the lectures I was to give, and there are a couple of other things I need to wrap up before I can go." She looked up at Aggie. "Do you think you could you get away, too? I really don't want to make that drive by myself."

Aggie reached for her hand. "Of course."

*　　　*　　　*

"What are you still doing here?" Shannon asked in surprise when she found Aggie at her desk during lunch the next day.

Aggie didn't look up from the papers she was grading. Shannon closed the classroom door, pulled a chair up to the desk and sat.

"I thought you would be on your way to D.C. by now," she said.

"So did I," Aggie said in clipped tones.

"What happened?"

Aggie's jaw worked back and forth a couple of times. "She got a call from her sister this morning saying she needed to be there for their mother and that she should have already been on her way. She left about ten."

"But," Shannon frowned, puzzled, "you were both making arrangements to have everything covered so you could leave by noon. I've got a bag all packed to go stay with Aunt Cory tonight."

"I know," Aggie said gratefully, glancing up at her.

"So why didn't she tell her sister she'd be leaving, with you, in a few hours?"

Aggie shook her head. "I don't blame her. How do you deal with that kind of guilt? If something horrible were to happen, and she hadn't even left yet..." Her expression hardened. "The part that makes me angry is I don't think they even considered the fact that she shouldn't be making that drive alone. She didn't sleep at all last night, and I could tell on the message she left me that she was crying. I was in class and couldn't answer, so I haven't talked to her."

Shannon sat there for a minute. "I heard Larry had Sharon Watson all lined up to sub for you."

"He did," Aggie acknowledged. "And then I had to go tell him, 'Nevermind. It was all a mistake.' And then there was the parent conference I cancelled for this afternoon. It's only taken two months to get these parents to schedule time off work to be here."

Shannon pursed her lips, biting back the things she longed to say. "So, do you know any more about how her father is?"

"Apparently, it was a heart attack. The last I heard after she spoke with her mother last night, no decision had been made about by-pass surgery," Aggie said. "I guess she'll call me with an update when she can."

"Well," said Shannon, getting to her feet. "Since I'm already packed for a sleep-over, how about I come anyhow?"

"Why not?" Aggie smiled. "Aunt Cory was looking forward to seeing you."

As Shannon reached for the doorknob, she paused, "You do realize how weird this is with you people..."

"What do you mean 'you people'?"

"Well, I know it's kind of early on, but you and Beryl have made a commitment to each other, which makes her father your father-in-law, only they don't see it that way because you're not married. If Beryl had a husband who needed to clear his work schedule so they could both go –"

"If I were Beryl's husband, her family would know about me," Aggie cut in bitterly. "I wouldn't be a secret."

"You're right," Shannon agreed, watching her friend sympathetically. "And I don't think that phone call would have happened. It's just weird," she said, shaking her head as she left.

Aggie sat there for a long time, staring into space and thinking about what Shannon had said.

Chapter 37

"You are welcome to stay here," Ridley said over the phone when Beryl called him en route to tell him what had happened. "You know that."

"Thanks," she said, "but I'd better stay with my mother this time. I can drive her back and forth from the hospital. He's at Georgetown, so I'll pop over to see you when I can."

"All right. Keep me posted."

Beryl tried to focus on the drive, and on the music playing on the car stereo. "Don't think about Dad," she told herself sternly. "Or Aggie." She recognized the sick feeling in the pit of her stomach – an all-too-familiar sensation. "It's called guilt." Why was that in Claire's voice?

After nine hours in the car - the last two spent crawling in rush hour traffic on the beltway as Beryl ground her teeth in frustration, muttering, "This wouldn't have happened if I'd left when I planned to!" - she finally arrived at the hospital. Her mother was alone in Gerald's room where he slept, a brightly-lit monitor graphing his vitals in the darkened room.

"Oh, Beryl, you're here!" Edith whispered, rising from her chair to hug her.

"Where is everyone?" Beryl asked, whispering also.

"They were here earlier, but Marian and Nick both had to go to work for a while." She glanced at her watch. "I guess they're home having dinner now."

Beryl pulled a chair up next to her mother and got an update on his condition. "They did the balloon procedure today and the doctor said he's going to be fine. He's very lucky."

"Have you eaten?" Beryl asked.

"Not since this morning," Edith admitted. "I didn't want to leave him."

"I'm so glad Nick and Marian were here for you," Beryl longed to say, but she wasn't sure her mother would get the point.

"Did Dad eat any dinner?"

"A little. He wasn't very hungry after the procedure," Edith said.

"He's sleeping. Why don't we go grab a bite?" Beryl suggested, her stomach growling hungrily as she also hadn't eaten since breakfast.

They informed his nurse where they would be in case anything happened and made their way to the hospital cafeteria. Occupied by scattered groupings of hospital staff and other family members of patients, the cafeteria atmosphere was hushed, conversations quiet. Filling a tray with sandwiches and drinks, Beryl and Edith found a corner table.

"Had Dad been feeling bad?" Beryl asked as she ate ravenously.

Edith shrugged as she nibbled disinterestedly on her sandwich. "You know him. He wouldn't say if he was." She frowned. "But he was up the past couple of nights, taking an antacid."

Beryl's eyebrows went up, but she tried to control her voice as she said, "And neither of you thought that was something to have checked out?"

Edith's face flushed a bit and she said a trifle sharply, "Well, now it seems obvious, but the thought of a ten-hour wait in an emergency room to check out what felt like indigestion didn't seem necessary."

"Sorry," Beryl mumbled. She rubbed her forehead, only now realizing what a horrendous headache she had. "I'm just tired. It's been a long day."

"I would have thought Aggie might have come with you," Edith said, a hint of disapproval in her voice.

Taking a deep breath before answering, Beryl said, "She was going to. But we needed time to arrange a substitute for her, and Marian called me this morning to tell me I needed to come now."

"I wonder why on earth she did that," Edith said.

"About now, I'm wondering the same thing," Beryl muttered.

When they got back upstairs, Beryl peeked in long enough to see that her father was still sleeping. "I need to make a phone call," she told her mother. "I'll be right back."

Down in the lobby once more, Beryl called Aggie.

"Hi," she said when Aggie picked up on the first ring.

"How are you? Are you okay?" Aggie asked immediately.

"I'm fine," Beryl said, rubbing her forehead again. "It was... I'm sorry I left the way I did. I didn't even get to say good-bye to you," she said, her throat tightening.

"I know," Aggie murmured. "How's your father?"

"They did an angioplasty earlier today and I guess it worked. My mother is here, but doesn't have a lot of information. I'd like to talk to the doctor myself."

"Your mother was there alone?" Aggie asked.

"Yeah."

There was a very pregnant pause, both sides of the connection bristling with things not said aloud.

"Were you able to get everything at work rearranged?" Aggie asked presently.

"Yes. Everything else I was working on can wait, but the lecture series will cause some other things to have to be rescheduled. It will impact about five other people, but they were very understanding," Beryl explained. "How about you?"

"It doesn't matter," Aggie said coolly.

"I'm sorry," Beryl said.

"I know."

"I'll call you tomorrow before school," Beryl said.

"Okay."

"Aggie?"

"Yes?"

"I love you."

"I love you, too."

*   *   *

Beryl spent a restless night in her old room, now redecorated in a garish floral pattern on the bedspread, with matching curtains and wallpaper border. Waking every couple of hours, she finally gave up and went down to the kitchen at five. She made coffee and sat with her mug cradled in one hand, her other propping up her pounding head. *I never get headaches like this,* she thought. She searched the medicine cupboard and found a bottle of ibuprofen. She took three and decided to try eating some toast. She felt moderately better by the time her mother came downstairs.

"I'd like to be at the hospital early to catch the doctor," Edith announced as she entered the kitchen.

"Fine," said Beryl. "I'll shower and be ready whenever you are."

She called Aggie briefly while upstairs, promising to call again later with an update, then hurried to shower and dress. Despite her mother's stated intention to get to the hospital early, it was nearly eight-thirty before she was ready to leave the house.

"Do you mind driving?" Edith asked. "It's so much more convenient to have a car there."

Beryl sighed, resigning herself to another crawl through traffic. She dropped her mother off at the entrance to the hospital and then spent nearly half an hour circling the parking lot, looking for an empty space, with the result that by the time she got up to her father's room, the doctor had come and gone.

"There you are," Marian said, gathering her purse. "I wondered where you got to. I have to go." She turned to Edith. "I'll be back later."

"Where are you going?" Beryl asked.

"I have an appointment with a client," Marian said.

"Then I guess it's a good thing your work isn't seven hours away," Beryl said coldly.

Did you say that out loud? Judging from Marian's double-take, she had.

She waited until Marian had left before asking her mother, "So what did the doctor say?"

"Oh, he said everything went well. Your father will be fine."

Beryl stared at her. "Mom, Dad is not fine. He must have said more than that."

Edith waved a hand dismissively. "Oh, the usual – no salt, lose weight, exercise. Doctors always say those things."

Beryl threw out both hands in exasperation. "They say those things because they mean those things! If Dad's angioplasty did go that well, he got lucky. And you both need to be making some changes."

Edith frowned up at her. "I don't need to be lectured by you, young lady."

With a renewed throb in her head, Beryl clamped her mouth shut and turned to the window.

Later that afternoon, Ridley came to her. Beryl met him in the lobby, and vented to him as they sat down in the cafeteria. "Dad hasn't said anything except he feels fine, and my mother acts like everything is normal now. My brother popped in once today for about thirty minutes, and my sister somehow manages to time her visits so she's always there for the doctor and acts like she's in charge of everything. And then she goes back to work."

"So in other words," Ridley grinned sympathetically, "nothing has changed."

Beryl stared at him and barked out a laugh. "You're right." She shook her head. "Nothing has changed."

She looked up at him shrewdly. "Or has it?"

Ridley flushed and a reluctant grin tugged at his mouth. "Yeah. It has."

Beryl grabbed his arm excitedly. "Really?"

He nodded. "It's still... we're working things out, but, thanks to you, we're together."

"Oh, Ridley, I am so happy for you. For both of you."

He held her hand tenderly. "I knew you would be." He looked down at her hand, so small against his palm. "I know the way you and I got to know one another was terrible, with David's death and all, but..." He looked up at her. "I can't tell you how glad I am to have you in my life."

Beryl bit her lip, trying to contain the impulse to fling her arms around him. Instead, she simply said, "Ooorah."

*   *   *

Gerald was kept in the hospital for two more days while they monitored his heart and put him through a nuclear stress test before pronouncing him fit to be sent home.

"You are a very lucky man," his cardiologist stressed the one time Beryl was able to be present. "As it is, you have lost about fifteen percent of your heart's output, so you will notice that you tire more easily. You are going to have to exercise and lose weight," he repeated for probably the fifth time. "And I want you to monitor your blood pressure daily. Bring the monitor with you for your follow-up with me in two weeks," he added as his assistant scheduled the appointment.

Friday evening, with Gerald settled in his den, Beryl told her mother she would be leaving in the morning.

Edith looked up sharply from the stove where she was heating up some soup. "I thought you would stay until Sunday at least."

"I've been here all week," Beryl pointed out. Taking a deep breath, she continued, "I live the farthest away now; once here, I can't run in to my work to take care of the things I left undone. Marian and Nick acted like I didn't care because I didn't drop everything and rush out here immediately. I don't have the luxury of panicking. If I'm to leave, I have to take the time to get things squared away so I can be gone for several days. Please keep that in mind in case something happens again."

"You really said all that?" Aggie asked later that evening when Beryl recounted the conversation.

"That's not all."

Pulling out a kitchen chair, Beryl had said, "Mom, we need to talk."

Once her mother was seated, Beryl took an adjacent chair and said, "There's something else I need to make absolutely clear." Her folded hands clenched tightly together, she took the leap she had never taken before. "Aggie is my partner. My spouse. I know you probably realized that with Claire, but we never talked about it. That... that situation was never a really good one, but things with Aggie are different. I'm different. So... any time I come home from now on, Aggie will be with me." Meeting her mother's eyes for the first time, she added, "I just wanted you to know."

Edith sat like a statue for several seconds. "Well..." She cleared her throat. "I don't think we should tell your father. At least not right now. I don't know if his heart could take this."

"She actually said that?" Aggie asked, chuckling when Beryl told her. "I'm sorry. I don't mean to laugh." But Beryl could still hear her giggling even with her hand covering the phone.

Chapter 38

Corinne and Helen arrive back at the Bishop house three weeks after receiving the telegram.

"You don't have to come," Corinne had said upstairs in their hotel room – the only night they would get to spend in Paris – when Helen announced her intention to accompany her.

Helen took her by the shoulders. "Of course, I'm coming with you. Going on without you now is unthinkable."

Corinne, who had contained her tears and her disappointment up to that point, broke down, sobbing as Helen held her.

When the tears subsided, Helen smiled at her and said, "Come on. Let's get dressed up and do the town. We've got one night."

"And what a glorious night it was," Corinne would recall later, not just on the voyage home, but for the remainder of her life.

Helen, looking resplendent in "a tuxedo!" Corinne had exclaimed, took her dining and dancing.

"We're in Paris," Helen said when Corinne held back. "The city of Renée Vivien and Natalie Barney. A city where no one will care that we are lovers."

Abandoning caution, Corinne let herself be swept away by Helen as they dined at an expensive restaurant, even taking the dance floor – "I didn't know you could dance," Corinne laughed – and strolled the streets during the early hours of the morning, reveling in the freedom to hold hands as they walked. They stopped for a late espresso at one of the cafés.

"No champagne," Corinne had declined. "I want to remember every second of this night with you."

They had stayed out all night – "time enough to sleep once we're on the boat," Helen had insisted – greeting the dawn from the Eiffel Tower as they kissed passionately, Corinne wishing the sun would never rise and the night would never end.

"Oh, thank goodness you're home!" Mary Bishop exclaims as Corinne and Helen are admitted to the foyer. She notices that Corinne makes no response as she returns her mother's embrace.

"Frances, could we have some tea, please?" Mary asks, ushering the girls into her study.

"Tell us what happened," Corinne requests as she sits wearily.

"Your sister had been complaining of headaches," Mary says, and Corinne understands the unspoken, "which we dismissed as another of her vague maladies."

She pauses as the tea tray is brought in. She prepares to pour for all three of them, continuing, "I was volunteering at the hospital and hadn't noticed that she hadn't come down. The servants thought she was with me, and so hadn't gone to check on her. When we found her on the floor of her room..." she pauses in her narrative, swallowing hard and trying to keep her composure. "The doctors say the stroke was very damaging. A bleed in the brain."

At this point, her hands are trembling so badly that she splashes tea over the edge of the cup. Helen kneels next to her and gently takes the teapot from her hands and pours. Mary sits back with a grateful smile.

"She has no speech, beyond unintelligible grunts," Mary says stoically. "She has no movement at all on her right side, and very little on the left. We cannot tell if she understands anything."

Corinne sits, stunned. She had known it must be bad for her mother to summon her home, but she'd had no inkling it would be this bad. "Will she be able to come home?" she asks.

Mary sips her tea before saying, "The doctors say we should put her in a care home."

Corinne slumps, and Helen quickly reaches out to brace her.

"The expense," Corinne says weakly. She sets her untouched tea cup down. "What is happening at the bank?"

"The board is actively looking for a buyer," Mary says. "But I think they may reconsider now you're home," she adds hopefully.

From the corner of her eye, Corinne sees Helen's hand tighten spasmodically on the arm of her chair, for they both know what this will mean.

*   *   *

"I have a Christmas card for you, Miss Bishop," Becka said sycophantically while the other students were still shuffling from the classroom.

"Thank you, Becka," Aggie said, opening the envelope and reading the card. "It's lovely," she said, as she propped the card up on her desk.

Becka beamed, wishing Aggie a Merry Christmas as Aggie quickly gathered up her bag and ushered her from the room before she could settle at a desk to talk.

"You, too," Aggie said, turning toward Shannon's classroom.

"Hey," she said, finding Shannon also gathering her things. "You all set?"

"Just a sec," Shannon said as she shut down her computer and locked her desk. "Oh, God, I can't wait to get to a warm, sunny beach."

Aggie smiled. Travelling at Christmas sounded anything but appealing to her. "Your flight stops in Atlanta?" she asked.

Shannon nodded. "And from there, direct to Cozumel."

Aggie tilted her head. She knew part of the reason Shannon travelled by herself was to avoid having to spend Christmas alone. She had no family she was close to, and now, since her divorce....

"You know you're always welcome at our house," she reminded her friend.

Shannon grinned. "I know." She faked a shudder. "But all that domestic bliss... bleah. Give me little umbrellas in tall drinks and men with big –"

"Stop!" Aggie held her hands up, eyes closed tightly as she tried to shut out the image.

Shannon laughed. "Just get me to the airport."

Half an hour later, with Shannon gleefully heading toward airport security, Aggie made her way home through rushhour traffic. "You have no idea what traffic is really like," Beryl often laughed. "This is nothing!" she would insist, and from what Aggie had seen of D.C. traffic, she couldn't argue. Nevertheless, the traffic this evening was testing her patience.

When at last she pulled into the driveway, she saw a black BMW 7-series parked there. "Oh shit," she muttered, hurrying into the house.

She had no trouble locating her father as his voice boomed from the study.

"I don't understand you!" he was shouting.

"What is the trouble?" Aggie asked, entering the study to find Aunt Cory sitting placidly in her chair while Edward paced agitatedly, his unbuttoned suit jacket flapping.

At the sound of her voice, Edward whipped around, pointing at Aggie. "Did you have anything to do with this?"

"With what?" Aggie asked, completely confused.

"You were supposed to be keeping an eye on her!" he yelled.

"Dad," Aggie said, holding up both hands. "Calm down and tell me what happened." She glanced over at Cory and saw a tiny satisfied smile on her face which worried her much more than her father's shouting.

Edward was pointing, almost incoherent in his anger. "She... she changed the terms of the trust!"

"What? I thought you can't change the terms of a trust." Aggie turned to Cory, her mouth agape. "When? How?"

"Do sit down, both of you," Cory invited calmly.

Ignoring her, Edward asked, "How did she get downtown to the lawyer's office? You were supposed to be keeping an eye on her," he bellowed again.

"Okay," Aggie said, getting angry herself now. "'Keeping an eye on her' means keeping her safe, not treating her like a prisoner in her own home."

"I will explain everything if you will only sit down," Cory repeated, gesturing to the two vacant chairs.

Clenching his jaw, Edward sat on the edge of Beryl's chair while Aggie took the other wing chair.

"First of all, Eddie –"

"Don't call me Eddie!" he exploded, getting very red in the face.

"First of all, Eddie," Cory repeated – Aggie smiled at her continued use of the diminutive, putting her father, Cory's nephew, in his place – "I don't need Agatha's permission or help to consult my attorney. James Hoffman's father drew up that trust. I've known him his entire life. He was more than happy to come to me."

Edward was finally listening, warily now, his nostrils distended as he continued huffing like an angry bull.

"One of –"

But Cory's explanation was interrupted by Beryl's sudden entrance.

"Sorry," she said uncertainly. "Am I interrupting something?"

"Who the hell are you?" Edward exploded again, jumping to his feet.

Rolling her eyes, Aggie got to her feet and went to Beryl. "Dad, this is Dr. Beryl Gray. Beryl, my father, Edward Bishop."

Recovering sufficiently to remember some manners, Edward reached out to shake Beryl's hand.

"Beryl lives here with us," Cory volunteered. "She's Aggie's partner," she added blithely. Beryl could hear a small groan escape from Aggie's throat.

Edward stared at each of them in turn, as the seconds stretched on. "Her..."

"Her partner," Cory repeated – "I seem to be doing a lot of that in this conversation," she could have said, "and we're not getting very far." – "They're not married yet, but I expect they'll be taking care of that detail soon."

"That bit was certainly helpful in easing the tension," Beryl would recall later with wry humor.

"Anyhow," Cory continued, "your arrival is most opportune, Beryl, as what I have to say concerns you also."

She stood, gesturing to the chairs. "I really would like all three of you to sit, please." She waited until they did as they were bidden, and then she continued. "As I was starting to say, one of the contingencies that we built into the original trust was a provision for me to pass the house on. Up until now, the assumption has been, since I have no children of my own, that upon my death or incapacitation, the house would be sold. But I have decided to name the next trustee."

"The next –" Edward said hollowly.

"Yes," Cory smiled. "The protections of the trust do not have to end with me. I can pass them on. And I have."

She beamed at Aggie. "Agatha, I have named you as my successor – as both trustee and beneficiary."

"What?" Edward exploded yet again, jumping to his feet.

"I don't mean to burden you with this house," Cory continued to Aggie as if Edward hadn't interrupted. "If you don't want to keep it, you may sell it when I am gone – and I assure you I will understand if you do. It's a huge responsibility. But if you decide you want it, you will set up your own trust and we will transfer the deed of the house to that trust."

Her words were followed by a silence so thick Beryl felt she was drowning in it.

At last, Edward recovered his voice enough to protest, "This is preposterous! You can't do this."

"I think you'll find I can, Eddie," Cory said sweetly. At his mutinous expression, her features sharpened. "And don't think I don't remember that you are the reason the house's possessions and furnishings had to be sold in the first place. If you hadn't mismanaged our investments –"

There was a vein throbbing alarmingly in Edward's forehead as he snarled, "I... you... that wasn't my fault!"

But Aggie was staring at her father as if she had never seen him clearly before. "You? You were in charge of the invested money?" she asked, and Beryl's heart broke at the disappointment and anguish she heard.

"No!" he protested furiously. "It wasn't like that –"

"Don't forget that I ran that bank for over thirty years," Cory was saying with a sympathetic glance toward Aggie. "I am not some dotty old imbecile. I understand the terms of that trust better than you do. I was there when my father had it drafted. You can't break it, if that's what you're thinking."

From the expression on his face, Beryl could tell that was exactly what he had been thinking. She looked at Cory with admiration for the way she was standing up to her bullying nephew and fought the urge to cheer out loud, quickly deciding that was not the best way to endear herself to Aggie's father – "my father-in-law," she realized with a nasty shock – another issue he had yet to come to terms with, she was sure.

"We'll see about that," Edward said mulishly as he got to his feet. Without another word, he stormed from the house.

Aggie sat, staring at the floor. "Why didn't you tell me?" she asked quietly.

Cory sat on the ottoman, resting a gnarled hand on Aggie's knee. "It was years ago," she said. "He begged me for the chance to manage the trust's assets. It was his biggest account up to that point." She paused for several seconds. "I have never known whether it was simply bad management on his part, or… if there was any malfeasance. It was partially my fault – I, of all people, should have kept better track of where the money was, what he was doing with it. By the time I realized…" She shrugged.

"I just feel horrible," Aggie muttered. "All your things…"

"Were just things," Cory said bracingly. "The auction brought enough to take care of me and the house. And it's all properly invested now."

She stood and went to the Christmas tree – "the first tree I've had in years!" she'd said in delight when Beryl and Aggie surprised her – and turned on the lights as the room was already darkening in the early dusk. "Anyway," she said philosophically, "there goes another surprise. Merry Christmas."

*　　*　　*

A couple of hours later, Aggie and Beryl sat snuggled together in the over-sized club chair, the room lit romantically by only the Christmas tree lights. Percival was snoring in his dog bed, having found a way of propping himself on his back with his short legs sticking up in the air while Winston was curled up in one of the wing chairs.

"What do you think?" Aggie asked worriedly.

Beryl didn't answer immediately. She knew the house meant a great deal to both Cory and Aggie, but....

"Buy a house together?" Claire had asked incredulously when Beryl suggested it. They had been together for about a year at that time, and were living together in their rowhouse by then. "Why would we do that?"

Beryl had bowed her head, allowing her hair to swing forward, shielding her hurt expression from Claire's probing eyes. "Don't you think it's part of making a commitment to each other?" she asked hesitantly.

"No," Claire scoffed. "I see my married friends go through this all the time – they divorce and suddenly have to deal with the legal hassles of deciding who's going to buy the house, or having a court order it to be sold. No way am I going through that."

In the immediate aftermath of her breakup with Claire, Beryl had recalled that conversation several times, feeling nothing but an immense sense of relief that there had been no legal ties to Claire – for she had a strong suspicion that Claire would not have capitulated or compromised on anything.

Now, the thought of Aggie owning not just a house, but this... this "dinosaur," she could hear Cory cackle sympathetically... it was a lot to grasp. Aggie seemed to sense the struggle taking place in Beryl's head.

"I know this is huge," Aggie said. "I mean, we're still so new –"

"No," Beryl cut in, turning to face her. "That's the one thing I'm not worried about." She took Aggie's hand. "I have no hesitation about us making such a big financial commitment together. It's more..." she looked around, "Can we afford the upkeep on this house and the grounds on our salaries? Will we ever be able to afford to go anywhere? Or will all our money be tied up here? Those are the things I'm thinking of." They sat silently for a few seconds. "What about you? Does this feel like a burden or a blessing to you?"

Aggie sighed. "I can't decide. Both, I guess. On the one hand, I love the history of this house, but, you're right. I've already got a taste of what the upkeep on this place is going to involve. I don't know if we'll ever be able to furnish it again – certainly not the way it was. Oh, I wish you could have seen it then," she said wistfully.

Beryl looked around the still mostly-empty study – the most furnished room on this level. "I'm kind of glad I didn't. It must make it harder to see it like it is now."

"Do we want to wander around a mostly empty house for the rest of our lives?" Aggie asked.

Beryl shrugged. "Maybe the only way to know is to go ahead with Cory's plan and see what happens. You can always sell later if you decide that's best."

Aggie raised Beryl's hand to her lips, kissing it tenderly. "If we decide, you mean."

Chapter 39

"You sure you'll be all right without me for a week?" Veronica asked anxiously.

"I'm sure," Cory laughed. "Agatha is off until after the New Year, and Beryl is taking the week off as well."

As if in response to their names, the two younger women entered the kitchen at that moment.

"Oh, Veronica, it smells wonderful!" Aggie exclaimed.

"My grandmother's pecan rolls," Veronica said proudly, checking on the tray baking in the oven. "My Christmas present to all of you."

After the rolls were done baking, she left, laden with wrapped Christmas presents from Cory and the girls.

Beryl's phone beeped. She looked and saw a text message from Ridley. "He and George just drove through Wheeling," she announced excitedly.

Edith Gray had not been happy that her younger daughter would not be home for Christmas.

"Mom, I was there for Thanksgiving, and then two weeks later I was back when Dad was in the hospital," Beryl reminded her mother. "I'm staying here for Christmas," she said firmly.

There was still a light dusting of snow on the ground, "just enough to make it white," Cory said happily. Beryl went out back and swept off the flagstones so they wouldn't be slippery for Ridley's crutches.

She and Aggie had already made up her bed with fresh sheets and laid out clean towels in the closest bathroom. She and Aggie and the animals would stay in Aggie's room while the guys were visiting.

The house, despite its continued emptiness, looked festive. Evergreen garlands wrapped the pillars on the front porch and adorned the fireplace mantels. In the kitchen, Cory and Veronica had made a project of stringing together an old-fashioned garland of apples and oranges studded with whole cloves and bits of cinnamon stick – "just like we used to do when I was a girl," Cory reminisced – and the kitchen smelled "like Christmas," Aggie declared as she and Beryl hung the garland around the island. The study, in addition to the tree, was now filled with wrapped packages and boxes.

Cory, rising before the sun was up to sit in her chair in the early mornings as was her habit, felt happier than she had in a very long time. And the house, *the house feels happy, too,* she thought contentedly, glancing at the mantel where the old photo of her and Helen stood in pride of place, next to a new photo of her sandwiched between Aggie and Beryl, taken that summer in D.C.

*   *   *

Corinne drives home from the bank. Parking in the carriage house, she sits for a long time in the car, tarrying as long as she can before going inside. It is spring, and it seems everything has popped into bloom at once. Helen is not home yet. At last, with a deep sigh, she gets out of the auto and enters the kitchen where Cook is busy preparing the evening's supper.

"Hello, Miss Corinne," says Frances, rushing over to take her coat for her. "I'll bring the tea to the study directly."

"Thank you," Corinne says wearily.

Going to her father's den, she hesitates, her hand on the knob, delaying the moment she must go in. Without warning, the door is opened from within and Corinne finds herself looking into her mother's worn face. Behind her, Candace lies in a bed placed where the desk used to be. A bathroom had been added – an expense that had been difficult to swallow – "but it will make taking care of Candace so much easier," Mary had reasoned.

"Oh, Corinne, dear," says Mary. "You're home." And Corinne can hear the relief in her mother's tired voice. "She's not having a good day," she whispers.

"Go rest," Corinne says. "Frances is bringing the tray to the study. I'll be in in a moment."

Adjusting the expression on her face, Corinne steps up to the bed. "Hello, Candace," she says cheerfully. "How has your day been?"

Only able to move one half of her face, Candace's right eye scrunches in a baleful scowl which Corinne ignores.

"Are you ready to exercise?" Corinne asks as a matter of habit, though she knows she is in for a fight. The physiotherapist at the hospital had shown them what exercises to do to move Candace's arms and legs and hands to prevent them from contorting into positions that would make it impossible to position her in bed or a wheelchair, and Corinne and Mary do them faithfully twice a day.

Leaning over the bed, Corinne goes through their routine of bending and straightening Candace's atrophied legs, a process Candace fights as much as she can. "Well, even that is exercise," Mary points out breathlessly on the days when Candace is particularly obstinate.

Moving to Candace's arms, Corinne looks into her sister's eyes. Despite Candace's lack of speech and facial expression, Corinne reads volumes in those eyes – the anger and the resentment there are unmistakable. "Hate me!" they say. "Curse at me, berate me for what I've done to you, to your life," Candace taunts daily.

But Corinne smiles, working as gently but as insistently as she can, talking to her sister about what is happening in the house and out in the garden, and when she is done, she rolls her to the side, propping her with pillows to give her backside some pressure relief. Smoothing Candace's hair, Corinne says, "We'll be in shortly with supper."

As she leaves, Candace's eyes fill with tears, hating her sister even more for refusing to be goaded.

By the time Corinne gets to the study, Helen is there. She has taken a position teaching French and German at Otterbein College in Westerville.

"Are you sure you want to do that?" Corinne had asked when Helen first came home and surprised her with the proposal.

Helen had grinned and said, "It's about time I grow up, don't you think?" At Corinne's somber expression, she had become more serious and said, "I know you worry that I'll feel trapped here, but the truth is that travelling without you is empty. I'm thinking we can settle into a life that will allow us both to have jobs to cover the expenses here, and maybe we can travel a bit each summer?"

Corinne's eyes had filled with tears as she wrapped her arms around Helen's neck and whispered, "I love you so much."

"How was your day?" Corinne asks now as Helen hands her a cup of tea.

"Très bien," Helen responds. "How about yours?"

"Oh, fine," Corinne sighs. "No bankruptcies or foreclosures or disasters of any kind."

"How boring," Helen grins. She shakes open the afternoon paper. "Oh, dear."

"What?" Mary and Corinne ask together as Terrence sidles into the room. Mary gestures him over for a cup of tea, but he shakes his head and takes a seat against the wall.

"Korea," says Helen, frowning. "The Soviets are getting more involved with the North. If we don't stop this, it will mean war," she predicts.

"Oh, not another war," Mary moans. "We're just getting over the last one."

Terrence leaves the room abruptly.

"I'll go to him," Helen says quietly, folding the paper and laying a restraining hand on Corinne's shoulder.

Mary watches her go. "I'm so glad you have Helen," she says, and Corinne, startled, looks at her mother, wondering how much she has guessed of their relationship.

"I worry about what will become of all of you when I am gone," Mary confesses.

"You're all right?" Corinne asks anxiously.

"Yes," Mary smiles. "But someday you'll be left to take care of everyone. I would like to think Helen will be there to take care of you."

*   *   *

Christmas Eve was a joyous affair at the Bishop home. Ridley and George had brought a case of wine, several bottles of which the five of them had consumed during and after dinner. Following supper, they retired to the study where a fire burned in the fireplace, highlighting the new sofa delivered that afternoon – a surprise from Beryl.

"Well," she had shrugged, "the house is filling up. We needed more seating anyway."

"It's lovely," Cory had exclaimed, her hands clasped over her heart.

She took a deep breath now as she looked at the room, filled with young people laughing and talking, the fire lending a cheerful glow to everything.

Late that night, Aggie had gone upstairs help George get settled as Cory also said goodnight, leaving Beryl and Ridley alone to talk for a bit as the fire burned itself out.

"Happy?" he asked, wrapping an affectionate arm around her shoulders as they sat side by side on the new couch.

"Yes," she smiled, settling against his shoulder. "You?"

"Mmm hmmm," he replied.

They watched the remains of the fire for long minutes, neither feeling the need to break the silence.

"It's hard to believe," Beryl mused.

"What?"

"How much has changed in six months."

"Wow," he said as he realized. "It has only been about six months, hasn't it?"

"When I think back, it all started with that book," Beryl said in wonder.

Ridley smiled and pressed his lips to her head. She could feel his struggle as he tried to choose his words. "I've been... not exactly bitter, but... angry – about what happened to me and my unit, the poor decisions that led to –" He paused and she waited as he swallowed the lump in his throat. "There didn't seem to be any kind of 'it all works out for the best' with this," he said, gesturing toward his legs with his free hand. "But... without this, I never would have gone into library work. I never would have met you. I never would have thought about a relationship with someone like George."

Beryl wrapped an arm around him and squeezed as he murmured, "Maybe things really do work out for the best."

*   *   *

The house was dark and all was quiet when Cory stole out of bed. The cold winter moon lit the foyer and staircase as she made her way to the upper floor. "Rest awhile," the house seemed to breathe to Cory as she paused at the window on the landing to look at the winter landscape outside. "I will keep you safe."

The animals, accustomed by now to her nocturnal visits, made no noise as she passed. In her room, she popped open the panel under the window seat and sat in her rocker.

"Oh, I wish you could be here to experience this," she whispered. "The house is awake and alive again."

She rocked, memories flooding in with the beams of moonlight.

Some time later, she blinked, disoriented. *Where am I?* she wondered, looking around in the darkness. *I must have dozed off.* Groggily, she tried to straighten up from where she had slumped a bit in her rocker. It was hard to move. *Oh, I'm so stiff,* she thought. Leaning forward, she reached out to push the panel shut, but found that her arm didn't want to move. *It must have fallen asleep.*

Shifting further out on the rocker, she leaned toward the window seat again. The last thing she remembered was falling forward into nothingness.

Chapter 40

Aggie paced agitatedly in the hallway of the ER at OSU's hospital, while Beryl leaned silently against the wall, staring at the floor. An intern emerged from the exam room.

"How is she?" Aggie asked immediately.

"She's stable," he said. "Do you have any idea how long she was unconscious before you found her?"

Aggie shook her head. "I didn't even know she was upstairs until my dog woke me." Guiltily, she remembered that Cory had stopped wearing her medical alert pendant back when Aggie moved into the mansion "and I thought it was okay, because I'd hear her if anything happened," she would lament to Beryl later.

"We're taking her for a CT of her head now," he explained. "We'll know more when we have those results, but it looks like it was a stroke."

At that moment, Cory was wheeled out of the exam room. She reached for Aggie's hand, trying to say something.

"What?" Aggie asked, leaning close.

Cory mumbled unintelligibly again. Aggie glanced questioningly toward Beryl, who shook her head.

"Don't worry," Aggie said soothingly. "We'll be here when you get back from your scan."

As they watched the gurney wheeling down the corridor, Beryl said, "She seems really agitated."

Aggie bit her lip. "The lawyer," she said. "I'll bet that's what she wants."

Beryl wrapped her arm around Aggie and said, "She's worried about what will happen with the house."

Aggie nodded. "I think so," she sniffed. "I hate to ask, but would you mind going home and trying to find his number?"

"Sure," Beryl said. "Do you want me to call anyone else?"

Aggie's face hardened. "No."

*   *   *

"It was a lovely ceremony," says a well-dressed woman in black crepe.

"Thank you," Corinne says automatically. *As I am expected to do,* she thinks as she turns to receive the next person in line who offers the same meaningless condolences.

What she longs to scream, but cannot say out loud to anyone, is what a relief it will be not to have to care for Candace any longer.

"I can't believe she's lived for over ten years," the doctor had said, listening to the fluid rattling in her chest. Candace was, by then, unconscious and the pneumonia was slowly filling her lungs. "She never would have lasted this long if you and your family hadn't taken such good care of her," he said kindly, meaning his words to be a comfort, but unaware of the irony Corinne finds in them.

"They all think I'm a wonderful sister and daughter," she cannot say, watching people mouth words that she doesn't even hear, standing beside Mary as they greet every last person. "But I know better. And Candace knew better. Though I tried never to show it, she knew how I resented my life. I could have taken lesser care of her and freed myself earlier..."

"But you didn't," Helen would have pointed out.

"I didn't do it out of love," Corinne argues – with whom? "I did it out of obligation, which isn't the same at all, is it?"

At last, they are home, changed out of the stiff black required for public mourning into casual clothes. Terrence, who could only tolerate the actual funeral service, had escaped home hours earlier. The staff, as a kindness to the family, have taken the bed upstairs and put the den back as it used to be. Staying out of sight in the kitchen, they have laid out tea and sandwiches in the dining room.

"Just ring if you need anything, anything at all, ma'am," Frances murmurs to Mrs. Bishop.

Seated quietly around the table, no one speaks for long minutes. The post is lying in a silver tray near Mary's place. She leafs through the missives.

"Here's a letter for you, Helen," she says, passing an envelope over.

"Thank you," Helen says, prying the flap open. "It's from my parents. They're hosting a fundraiser for John Kennedy's presidential campaign," she reads. "Next month, at their house in the Hamptons." She looks up hopefully. "We could all go for a week," she suggests. "It's beautiful there in September."

Corinne's eyes light up. "Oh, it would be wonderful to get away," she says. For all their wishes and intentions to spend their summers travelling, she and Helen have never again gotten farther away from Ohio than New York. "Mother?"

Mary also looks eager for a moment, but then her expression falls. "Terrence would never agree to travel," she realizes. "But you should go."

Corinne bites her lip. "If Helen and I go, then you must get away separately," she says to her mother. "Perhaps you and Aunt Eunice could take a trip to New York?"

Mary's face brightens. "It's been so long, what with Terrence, and your father's difficulties," – she still will not admit that he embezzled funds – "and then Candace's illness." She reaches for Corinne's hand. "Let's make our plans."

Helen's parents are welcoming in a detached, distracted kind of way. "Just make yourselves at home," they insist, as they busy themselves with the details of the upcoming gathering.

"They mean it," Helen says, taking Corinne's hand and leading her out the door toward the beach. "They don't want to be bothered taking care of us. So it leaves us free to do whatever we wish."

"Whatever we wish?" Corinne asks suggestively. She looks up at Helen, the streaks of grey beginning to show at her temples only serving to make her look more distinguished. It has been months since they have made love. They have both been so exhausted. This trip feels like an opportunity to turn back time.

Helen grins. "We can probably find a secluded dune," she says. "Come on." Taking Corinne by the hand, they jog along the beach. Before they have gone fifty yards, Helen slows, breathing raggedly.

"I hadn't realized I was that out of shape," she gasps. "Too much time behind a desk."

"Let's sit," Corinne says, pulling Helen over to a dune where they are sheltered a bit from the cool wind blowing off the water.

Looking around and seeing no one, Helen pulls Corinne to her for a kiss. The kiss grows stronger and more passionate as Corinne's hand slips under Helen's sweater and caresses her breast, kneading the pliant tissue. Helen suddenly gasps and pulls away.

"What?" Corinne asks, startled.

"It... it hurt," Helen says, reaching up and feeling the breast herself. Wincing, she sees the worry in Corinne's eyes and says, "It's nothing. I'll see someone when we get back to Ohio."

*   *   *

In a scene eerily reminiscent of her father's death, Cory lay in a bed in the neuro unit surrounded by her attorney, Agatha and Beryl, with Ridley and George as witnesses while the ownership of the house was transferred to Aggie's new trust. Cory's ability to communicate was hampered by her facial weakness, but, with difficulty, she could make herself understood enough to answer yes/no questions.

"Don't worry, Miss Cory" said Mr. Hoffman, who had insisted to his unhappy wife that he must respond to this summons, Christmas Day or no. "We'll get everything taken care of."

After he had left, Cory lay, plucking anxiously at her sheets with her good hand as the others kept vigil.

"It's all right now," Aggie said repeatedly. "Everything is taken care of."

But Cory shook her head in frustration, trying to mouth something that none of them could make out.

Eventually, Cory fell into a restless sort of sleep, continuing to moan every now and then. Beryl felt as if she were hypnotized, watching the monitor above the bed. *A life, a whole life,* she thought, *reduced to blips on a screen, little lines of color – how many blips does she have left? How do you measure that?*

Aggie must have felt her consternation and reached over for her hand. "Why don't you and the guys go back to the house?" she suggested. "It is Christmas Day."

A nurse came in at that point. "She's going to sleep now," she said sympathetically. She gestured at the monitor. "Everything looks stable. I can call you if anything changes."

"You need to eat," Ridley said gently. "Let us make dinner for you, and then we'll all come back later."

Reluctantly, Aggie agreed, leaving hers and Beryl's cell phone numbers with the nurse and eliciting one more promise to call if anything changed.

Back at the house, Ridley and George took charge in the kitchen, directing Aggie and Beryl who moved like automatons, doing as they were told. Before long, they were seated at the table with platters of ham, sweet potato casserole, sautéed green beans and steaming hot rolls.

"Aunt Cory was so looking forward to this," Aggie said, blinking back tears.

"Here," said Beryl, spooning a little of each dish onto Aggie's plate. "Try and eat a bit."

"Can you think of what she might have been so worried about?" Ridley asked.

Aggie shook her head. "I can't. We didn't have anything big pending around here that I know of. We got the legal stuff taken care of." She poked at her food worriedly.

"Maybe, you could take a look around her room and see if there's anything," George suggested.

"That's a good idea," Aggie said.

As soon as she was done eating what little she could, she went to Cory's room while Beryl and the guys cleaned up the kitchen. Beryl peeked in a short while later.

"Any luck?" she asked.

"No," said Aggie from where she was replacing Cory's clothes in a dresser drawer and sliding it back into position. "I've been through all the drawers. Nothing."

"How about under her mattress?"

"I haven't looked," Aggie said, brightening hopefully. "Help me?"

Together, they lifted Cory's mattress from different angles, feeling underneath for any papers, envelopes, books. There was nothing.

Beryl looked around. "There aren't any hidden safes or compartments in here, are there?"

Aggie frowned. "Not that I know of. But that would be just like Cory."

"This used to be her father's den, didn't it?"

"Yes," Aggie said thoughtfully, going to the dark paneled walls and running her hands over the wood, pressing here and there, while Beryl paid attention to the places where paintings used to hang, looking for any signs of secret doors or cubbies.

They both jumped as they heard laughter behind them. Ridley and George were standing there.

"What are you doing?" Ridley asked.

"Looking for hiding places," Beryl said. "Don't just stand there. Help."

So the men joined in, concentrating on the bookshelves.

"Hey!"

They all rushed over to where George had pulled some books down to reveal a sliding panel built into the back wall of the shelf. He stepped aside so Aggie could be the one to open it.

"There is something!" she said excitedly.

Pulling out some old papers, they hovered over her as she took them to the bedside lamp for better illumination.

"They're not Aunt Cory's," Aggie said, leafing through them.

"They're my great-grandfather's." She ran a finger down one of the pages. "It's a bunch of figures. Investments, from the descriptions."

She frowned. "But I can't see what this has to do with Cory."

"Maybe you should show them to her anyway," Beryl suggested with a shrug.

"All right," Aggie sighed. Glancing at her watch. "I want to get back over there." She turned to George and Ridley. "I'm sorry to leave you again. Please stay here and make yourselves at home. TV is upstairs. Why don't you stay, too?" she said to Beryl.

"I'm going with you," Beryl said firmly.

"We're going, too," Ridley insisted.

"We're family," George said with a shrug.

Chapter 41

Cory lay in a twilit place between sleep and wakefulness. She knew she was in a hospital and that she'd had a stroke.

"I would rather die," she'd said more than once to Helen when they were caring for Candace. "To be trapped in a body that won't obey commands... to know what has happened and that this is your fate, for as long as you last. I can't think of anything worse."

How ironic, she thought now. *Candace would find this fitting.* The thought brought laughter deep in her chest that caused her to choke and gag. A nurse came rushing in, turning her on her side until her weak cough cleared the obstruction, and giving her some oxygen until her breathing evened out.

"Better now?" the nurse asked kindly. Cory nodded as the nurse repositioned her comfortably.

Only then did Cory notice the nurse was wearing a Santa hat. *Is it still Christmas?* she wondered.

Everything seemed a blur as she floated in and out of her fog and her dreams.

*   *   *

Helen grips Corinne's hand tightly as they enter Sloan-Kettering's reception area.

"You simply must come here," Mrs. Abrams had insisted upon hearing of Helen's diagnosis. It was clear that she considered Columbus physicians little more than country doctors, but "We should go," Corinne had agreed. *Anything,* she thought. Anything but the dire prognosis they had been given.

"He'll have something to offer," Corinne insists as they ask for Dr. Heidelberg's office, but "I'm sorry," he says after reviewing Helen's test results and updates from the Columbus doctors. He looks at them both through his thick glasses, overhung by bushy grey eyebrows. "There have been some clinical successes with treating lymphoma and leukemia with drugs, but none in treating breast cancer." He glances back down at one report. "I see here that Dr. Westfall recommended a radical mastectomy. I'm afraid that would be my recommendation, also."

Numb at having this last hope dashed, they leave the hospital and stand on the crowded New York City sidewalk, still holding tightly to each other's hands as they are buffeted by passersby. "Let's go home," Helen says.

A couple of weeks later, Helen is back home at the Bishop house, recovering from a double mastectomy. Corinne has had a small bed from an unused staff bedroom on the third floor moved into her room so that she can be nearby without disturbing Helen's fitful sleep.

Helen, who has only cried a handful of times in all the years that Corinne has known her, cries now in pain as she tries to move her arms. When the bandages are changed, Corinne winces and nearly cries herself. There, where Helen's beautiful breasts used to be are angry red tracks, puckering and adhering as they begin to heal and scar. Just as she used to do with Candace, Corinne works at trying to move Helen's arms, stretching the taut skin as gently as she can until Helen cries out.

Frances and some of the others decorate a small Christmas tree and place it and a menorah in the room to add some holiday cheer.

"What do you want for Christmas?" Helen asks one day, trying not to wince as Corinne stretches her.

Corinne pauses, looking down at Helen's drawn face, still beautiful to her, and tries not to let her eyes well up. "I want Italy."

"Italy?" Helen asks, puzzled.

"You told me once you could smell the sun in Italy," Corinne reminds her.

Helen smiles. "That's right. I did promise you Italy, didn't I?"

Corinne leans over the bed and kisses Helen's lips tenderly. "You'd better keep your promise."

Helen reaches up, laying a hand lovingly on Corinne's cheek. "I'll try."

*　　*　　*

Cory blinked rapidly as tears leaked from the corners of her eyes.

"Hey," Aggie said softly, blotting the tears with a tissue. "I wish you could tell me what it is."

Cory looked at her, noticing how like her own Aggie's blue eyes were, and tried again to say what must be said. Somehow she had to tell them, make them understand... what if they never found it? What if Aggie sold the house and never knew? Why hadn't she shown her before now?

Shaking her head in frustration at Cory's guttural noises, Aggie said, "I'm sorry. I just don't know what you're trying to say." She felt a small push against her arm as Beryl held out the papers they had found. "Oh, yes," she said, taking the bundle. "We did find these hidden behind a secret panel in the den. Do you know anything about these?"

She elevated the head of Cory's bed a bit more and put the papers into her good left hand. Cory, who even at ninety-three had never needed reading glasses, squinted a bit as she tried to get her eyes to focus on the minuscule figures held in her tremulous grasp. For long seconds, she looked at the papers blankly as Aggie steadied her hand while Beryl, Ridley and George watched hopefully.

"Anything?" Beryl whispered.

"I can't tell," Aggie murmured, watching Cory's face closely.

Cory laid her head back, closing her eyes as she let the hand holding the papers fall to the bed. Though she couldn't express it, she had realized what she was looking at – *the hours and hours I spent trying to quantify exactly how much Father had taken and from which accounts, and here, hidden in the den all these years, was everything. That's what he tried to tell me and now I can't tell them.*

"Was this what you were trying to tell us about?" Aggie asked, not really expecting to receive affirmation from Cory.

Cory shook her head.

"Could you write it for us?" Beryl suggested.

Cory's left eye opened a bit wider, which Aggie took as an affirmative. Scrabbling through her bag, she found an envelope and pen. She tried to place the pen in Cory's right hand, but it fell from the limp fingers which had no grip. Trying her left hand, Cory was at least able to close her fingers around the instrument. Aggie placed the envelope on top of a magazine and tried to hold it at an angle that would permit Cory to write.

Laboriously, the pen scratched, making worm-like squiggles as Cory's unsteady hand moved over the paper. After working agonizingly for a long time, Cory frowned and dropped her hand, exhausted.

Together, Beryl and Aggie examined the envelope, trying to decipher the squiggly lines there.

"H?" Aggie made out

Beryl nodded. "H... e... Helen?" she guessed.

Cory nodded.

"But I can't tell what the next word is," Aggie muttered.

"Neither can I," echoed the guys, looking over her shoulder.

They were interrupted by the doctor coming in with a nurse to check on Cory.

"We'll go wait outside," Beryl volunteered.

Ridley and George followed her down the hall to the small waiting room for the neuro unit. The flat grey twilight coming in through the windows as evening fell did nothing to soften the harsh glare of the fluorescents above. Mutely, they sat, each automatically reaching for a magazine which they stared at, rather than reading, as they flipped through the pages.

*　　　*　　　*

How many days has it been now? Beryl wondered as she stared at the same magazine covers scattered about on the little tables between chairs.

Ridley and George had left – when? Yesterday? Maybe. The days were all melding together, no one any different from the others, punctuated only by a few hours of sleep here and there. "Call me every day, or if anything happens," Ridley had insisted. Aggie's parents and brothers had had to be told, and they had descended – "like vultures," Aggie had told Beryl disgustedly. "They don't care that she gets well. They just want whatever they can get from her. They think they're owed something just because their name is Bishop."

Beryl had stayed out of the way as much as possible, alternating her time between the dismal waiting room and the cafeteria, only coming in to be with Cory when it was just her and Aggie.

In the waiting room now, she nodded to a middle-aged couple who had been there all day as well. His father had suffered a brain aneurysm and was having surgery.

"We're still waiting," said the wife with a tired smile, a mangled tissue clenched in her hand.

How strange it is, Beryl thought, taking one of the hard plastic chairs, her elbows on her knees, forehead resting on her hands. *We don't even know one another's names, but we learn these intimate details about each other – matters, literally, of life and death, simply because we're thrown in here together and we feel this strange need to explain why we're here, almost like we're embarrassed about being caught here, all raw and emotional.*

Objectively, she knew and had repeatedly told herself, at Cory's age, something had been bound to happen at some point, but it was so hard to see her this incapacitated and distressed over her inability to communicate. Why couldn't she have died in her beloved garden, or just gone to sleep and not awakened? *Damn, I hate hospitals,* she thought, getting up and pacing restlessly.

She heard sudden cries and moans behind her, and turned to see the middle-aged couple clinging to one another as a white-coated man sat uncomfortably beside them. With an awkward pat on a shoulder, the doctor left them to deal with their grief. Feeling like a voyeur, Beryl sidled away down the corridor, fighting the urge to run as fast as she could.

Down the hall, she saw Aggie's mother, Debbie, emerge from Cory's room, saying loudly, "I'll see you tomorrow, Aunt Cory." She gestured Aggie from the room and, together, they had a whispered conversation in the hall before Debbie walked away toward the elevator.

Aggie saw Beryl and waited for her.

"What was that about?" Beryl asked.

"Oh," Aggie sighed tiredly. "She's after me to start looking at nursing homes, and reminding me how expensive they are."

Just then, a pair of young women entered the room, saying hello to Cory and Aggie.

"It's the therapists," Aggie explained. "They come a couple of times a day."

"Let's go eat something, then," Beryl suggested. She wasn't really any hungrier than Aggie, but someone had to make them eat, rest, do a few normal things – *what's normal now?* she wondered. *Normal has changed.*

Chapter 42

Everyone in America is glued to televisions and radios. They will all remember where they were on November 22nd, 1963. Corinne, as she sits at Helen's bedside, is vaguely aware that some tragic event has occurred elsewhere, but her world is here – in this room. Helen's brave fight against her cancer is ending, and Corinne has insisted on taking care of her at home.

"Why?" she asked when the doctor suggested she go to the hospital. "You can't make her better. Can't we just keep her comfortable here?"

"This seems to be your lot in life," the doctor sighs with a mix of admiration and sympathy. Corinne is still pretty, but her eyes have lost some of their light and her face is worn and fatigued. He arranges for a nurse to come to the home to assist Corinne and Mary.

Terrence, who rarely came in to see Candace after her stroke, comes to visit with Helen daily when he gets home from the hardware store. And Mary, who has come to see Helen as another daughter, has been an invaluable help to Corinne in caring for her.

Helen's parents came to Columbus the past summer as Helen became too weak to travel. They were clearly uncomfortable being around their daughter.

"It is a terrible thing to have your child go before you," Mary said to them sympathetically, but Helen laughed and said to Corinne later, "I'm not sure what shocked them more – the realization that I would go before them, or the reminder that they're mortal as well."

Until recently, Helen was up, often sitting in her garden, her frail body wrapped in sweaters and heavy coats against fall's chill. Peters, the gardener, doffing his cap respectfully, would still consult with her about the garden's upkeep and future projects.

Corinne has stood, watching from the back patio as they plan, *as if there are going to be future projects*, she thinks angrily.

Helen, as if she can feel Corinne's anger, turns to her as Peters totters off, gesturing her over. Reluctantly, Corinne obeys, sitting stiffly next to Helen on the bench.

"Don't hate it," Helen says, taking her hand.

"What?"

"The garden. Don't hate it because it reminds you of me." She turns to face Corinne. Her features are skeletal, she has lost so much weight, but to Corinne, she is still the handsome, cocky woman she first met twenty-three years ago. "Love it," Helen says. "Care for it as you have cared for me."

"It's so unfair," Corinne says, her voice cracking. "Doesn't it make you angry?"

Helen holds her hand more tightly. "It is unfair," she concedes. "But... the things we've seen in our lifetime..." She shakes her head. "We may not have had as much time as we would have wished, but the love we squeezed into those years is more than most people get in a lifetime."

Corinne reminds herself of that conversation as she sits and listens to Helen's breaths becoming shallower... *I should call someone*, but she doesn't want to leave for even a second....

And then, the breaths are no more.

*　　*　　*

Beryl sat bolt upright in bed. Aggie, startled from a restless sleep, sat up beside her.

"What is it?" she asked groggily.

"We are such idiots!" Beryl exclaimed, jumping out of bed.

"What?"

"Where did she always visit? Where did we find her that morning? Come on!"

Aggie slid out of bed and followed Beryl down the hall to Cory's room, Percival and Winston trailing, snuffling their displeasure at being awakened so rudely.

Beryl was already on her knees in front of the window seat, prodding and pressing the base. "Turn on the light, will you?"

Aggie flipped the switch just as Beryl depressed a panel that opened with a soft click.

In unison, they gasped as the panel swung open on hidden hinges to reveal – "a shrine," Aggie whispered.

There, laid out lovingly, were small sprigs of holly leaves and berries, arranged around a handsome earthenware urn.

Off to one side was a stack of books. Aggie pulled the top one off and opened it. "A journal," she murmured in wonder. "Aunt Cory's journals."

Next to the journals was a bundle of letters and old postcards, tied with a faded ribbon. "I've seen her reading these recently," Aggie said. "And here's your book," she said, picking up the Rumer Godden book which had led Beryl to the Bishops in the first place.

"Look at this," Beryl said, reaching in and retrieving a hand-calligraphied scroll sitting on the other side of the urn.

Aggie leaned close as Beryl unrolled the parchment and read:

"Surprised by joy – impatient as the Wind
I turned to share the transport – Oh! with whom
But thee, deep buried in the silent tomb,
That spot which no vicissitude can find?
Love, faithful love, recalled thee to my mind –
But how could I forget thee? Through what power,
Even for the least division of an hour,
Have I been so beguiled as to be blind
To my most grievous loss! – That thought's return

Was the worst pang that sorrow ever bore,
Save one, one only, when I stood forlorn,
Knowing my heart's best treasure was no more;
That neither present time, nor years unborn
Could to my sight that heavenly face restore."

They sat, tears streaming down their cheeks as they read the lines of the poem over and over.

"Who –?"

"Wordsworth," Aggie murmured. "Oh, Beryl," she whispered, as she pressed her fingers to the calligraphied page, "This is what she wanted to tell us."

Beryl wrapped an arm around Aggie's shoulders. "It must have been breaking her heart to think this might never have been found. Or that the house might have been sold with all of this still here."

They sat for long minutes, staring at Cory's shrine to Helen, to their love.

"I know it's the middle of the night," Beryl said, "but I feel like we shouldn't wait to tell her we found these."

Aggie looked at her in alarm, but didn't question. "Let's get dressed."

*   *   *

"Who called you?" Cory's nurse asked in bewilderment as they encountered her in the corridor.

"No one," said Aggie. "We just... we had a feeling we should come. Why? What's the matter?"

The nurse's face fell. "She had another stroke. A massive one. I was just going to call you to tell you to get here right away. You should go in."

Aggie and Beryl hurried to Cory's bedside. The nurse followed them in. A doctor they didn't recognize was standing next to the bed.

"These are her nieces," the nurse said by way of introduction.

"Her systems are shutting down," he said clinically. "We can put her on a ventilator, and for nutrition, we can insert a feeding tube."

"Don't!" Beryl nearly blurted. She clamped her mouth shut, waiting, hoping Aggie would be strong enough, now that it was time to make the hard choices....

"You said she didn't want any resuscitation," the nurse reminded them.

Beryl held her breath. She loved Cory dearly, but this was Aggie's decision.

Aggie nodded tearfully. "That's right. She was adamant that she didn't want to get to ninety-four unless she could walk to the party."

Beryl smiled through her own relieved tears.

"We'll leave you then," the nurse said respectfully. The doctor followed her out of the room.

"You should tell her," Beryl prompted.

Aggie nodded again. Going to the bed, she leaned close and said, "Aunt Cory, we found it. We found all the things you had collected under your window seat. They're safe now. We'll take care of them. We'll take care of both of you. We'll take care of everything."

There was no indication that Cory heard or understood. Her face was slack, her eyes closed, her breathing labored.

"Just keep talking to her," Beryl said, positioning a chair near the bed for Aggie. "I know she can hear you."

*   *   *

Beryl waited until a decent hour to call Ridley.

"She never woke up?" he asked.

"No," Beryl said, sniffling. "They said this last stroke was massive. I'm glad she went. She wouldn't have wanted to be here if it meant being a vegetable."

"How's Aggie?"

Beryl shrugged. "She's lying down right now. We've been up since about one. I think she's okay. She knows it was Cory's wish not to have any kind of machinery hooked up. It's just hard to be the one who says 'no'."

"Better than being the one who has to eventually step up and say 'turn it off'," Ridley pointed out. Beryl could hear the hard edge to his voice, the one he usually had when he was reliving something related to the ambush, and she wondered – though she had never asked – whether any of the members of his unit had survived on machines for a while.

"Is there going to be a funeral?" he asked.

"I don't know yet," Beryl said. "We found her journals and papers." She explained the cache hidden away in Cory's room. "There may be instructions in there for what she wanted done."

"Well, let me know," he said. "I want to be there. She was really special."

"Yeah, she was. I will let you know as soon as plans are made."

"Take care – of you and Aggie."

"I will."

Beryl peeked into the bedroom, thinking she might also lie down for a while, but the rumpled bed was empty. Going down the hall, she found Aggie sitting in Cory's rocker, leafing through some papers.

Aggie looked up as Beryl entered the room. "Look at this," she said, holding out a handwritten page.

It was Cory's request to have her ashes blended with Helen's and have them both scattered together.

"Where?" Beryl asked.

Aggie shrugged. "She doesn't say. Maybe it didn't matter as long as they were together."

Beryl sat down on the floor and pulled out one of Cory's journals. "Do you mind?" she asked before she opened it.

"Of course not," Aggie said. After a moment, Aggie pulled out another. Mesmerized, they read, occasionally reading passages out loud to one another, saying "did you know this?" or "listen to this."

"I had no idea," Aggie said a few hours later, her eyes moist with tears. "No idea she gave up so much of her life to take care of everyone else. Terrence, then Candace, then Helen. And finally her mother. And the time she and Helen lost..."

"I know," Beryl murmured, her finger marking a passage. "But listen to this."

Chapter 43

The cherry trees in D.C. were in full bloom as Beryl, Aggie and Ridley made their way to the Lincoln Memorial. A gentle breeze blew from the south, bringing the promise of warmer weather to follow, swirling the pink blossoms on the ground into small eddies of color and texture.

Ridley, wheeling himself along the pavement, said, "I wonder if this is legal?"

Beryl laughed. "That's why we're not asking."

Aggie laughed also. "Somehow, I think Aunt Cory and Helen would like it better if it isn't legal."

At the base of the steps, Ridley parked his chair and stood with his crutches. "Do we go up, or stay down below?"

"I think we'll be less noticeable down here," Aggie said.

They walked around the base of the memorial until they came to a relatively unpopulated area where the wind was blowing toward the river. Aggie reached into her bag and pulled out a small wooden box, inlaid with an intricate design of ebony and mother of pearl.

"Twenty-some years is a lot to some people," Aggie said, "but I imagine to Cory and Helen it felt not nearly long enough. Now, they're together for eternity. Nothing else will ever separate them again. No more loss, no more sorrow."

"I envy them that," Ridley said.

"A love that lasted a lifetime and beyond," said Beryl, smiling at Aggie whose eyes were bright with tears.

Aggie met her eyes, blinking rapidly and nodding as she slid open the top of the box and tipped out the ashes within. The three of them watched the grey flecks swirl and scatter on the breeze, landing on the surface of the Potomac and gradually floating away on the current.

"What are you going to do with the rest of the ashes?" Ridley asked.

"We've interred some in the garden," Beryl said. "We had a plaque made and tucked it back near the grotto."

"And the rest?"

Aggie took a deep breath and said, "Italy. Helen promised Cory they would get to Italy, but they never made it." She reached for Beryl's hand and kissed it. "So we're going to fulfill that promise."

*   *   *

Corinne wanders the house, and though she encounters no people, it doesn't feel empty. The house feels alive - filled with art and furniture and books and - *life,* Corinne thinks. The others are there: Father in his den, Mother in her study, Terrence working on airplane models in his room, Candace at the piano. She feels them, just out of sight, but there nevertheless. Corinne is in no hurry to get - there. She doesn't know exactly where there is, but she is confident she will know when she arrives. Light comes through every window, so that she cannot tell what time of day it is. As she passes a mirror, she catches a glimpse of her reflection and is not surprised to see her blond curls and her large blue eyes looking back from a young face.

In time, though she has no idea how much time, she leaves the house to enter the garden. The air is filled with scent, and she cannot tell whether it is the irises and lilies and roses or... Helen stands at the grotto, young and whole and beautiful, her face wearing a jaunty grin.

"I've been waiting for you," she says.

"I know," Corinne breathes, unable to tear her eyes from Helen's face. "I came as soon as I could. It was... I missed you so terribly."

"I know," Helen says, caressing her face with warm hands.

Corinne reaches up, pressing Helen's hands more closely to her cheeks, kissing her palms. "Sometimes, it felt as if I were in hell, having to go on without you."

"No more," Helen smiles. "Nothing will pull us apart ever again."

Together, they walk, their arms wrapped around each other as they take in the familiar sights in the garden.

"Do you want to stay here?" Helen asks.

"Can we?" Corinne asks curiously, looking around.

Helen laughs. "We can be wherever we want to be. I know how important the house was to you."

They are emerging from the garden. Corinne looks up at the beloved edifice.

"No," she says. "I'm ready to move on. The house is in good hands. It's Agatha's now, to do with as she wishes."

Helen smiles and her face is radiant. Corinne takes her arm as Helen leads them away.

"Where are we going?" Corinne asks.

Helen leans close and her breath tickles Corinne's cheek as she whispers, "You'll see."

THE END

About the Author

Caren was raised in Ohio, the oldest of four children. Much of her childhood was spent reading Nancy Drew and Black Stallion books, and crafting her own stories. She completed a degree in foreign languages and later another degree in physical therapy where for many years, her only writing was research-based, including a therapeutic exercise textbook. She has lived in Virginia for over twenty years where she practices physical therapy, teaches anatomy and lives with her partner and their canine fur-children. She began writing creatively again several years ago. Her first novel, *Looking Through Windows*, won a Golden Crown Literary Society Award for debut author. Her second, *Miserere*, was released in December 2012, followed by *In This Small Spot* in May 2013. *Neither Present Time* is her fourth novel.

Made in the USA
Monee, IL
21 March 2023

30257679R00174